THE MOVERS SERIES:

THE ASTRIDIANS

Written by

ERICA WALSH

Writer Chick Press Publishing

The Movers Series:
The Astridians

By Erica Walsh

First Edition
Copyright © 2019 Erica Walsh
All rights reserved.
Published by Writer Chick Press
ISBN: 978-0-578-89797-4
Cover Illustration by Nick Kia Alimohammadi

Dedication

Dedicated to my dear family and friends, you all have played a role, big or small, in the creation of my novel. Also dedicated to women writers throughout history, named or unnamed. May I carry your voices within me so they may always be heard.

Part I

Chapter 1

Astrid

Alessaria, New York
April 14th
1835

The only woman from the battle stood next to a tree holding a magnificent Damascus steel sword. She watched beads of fresh blood drip off the curved blade onto the snow-covered ground. The ivory grip had spiral groves filled with twisted brass wire. It was inlaid with roses made of precious jewels which gave it beauty and great value. Attached to the hilt, a lock of braided red hair. Slowly opening her hand she let the sword fall. Blood had oozed in little rivulets down her milky face from a hairline gash. Her sapphire-blue eyes were glossy with tears. Her long wavy black hair fluttered about in the wind adhering to her damp cheeks. She looked down and saw her favorite blue dress ripped and sliced in various places.

Men's bodies littered the unseasonably frozen landscape and the stench of gunpowder clung to the air. The survivors divided the bodies into two piles; one for burial of their fellow townsmen and the enemy bodies would meet with a bonfire. As they worked, their breath hung in the air like small patches of fog in the cold air. Many hunched in mourning over fallen friends and family. Even the trees seemed to be in mourning bent over from the harsh winds. There were men of all paths of life and class lying on the tainted soil.

To her left was the body of a decapitated man and several yards away rested the head. Next to the body was his sword, decorated with bloodstones; a green stone with specks of red. With clenched teeth she looked down and spat on the body. Turning, she saw across the clearing the body of a friend slumped over by a tree. She limped over and looked down at him. She dropped to her knees and winced in pain as she moved. Turning his face towards her, she looked into his gray-blue eyes and saw no life. She caressed his thick and curly strawberry-blonde hair. Slowly she closed his eyelids and sat on the cold ground cradling his head in her arms. Then she repeated the horrific phrase The Cleaver said before she took his head.

"Blood of the martyr is the seed of the church."

She saw something in the snow and picked it up. It was a piece of bloodstone from his sword. As she held the stone, tears rolled down her cheeks quick and hard. She closed her eyes and fainted.

Chapter 2

A Comforting Lie

A spindly middle-aged maid stood in the kitchen watching a floating kettle pouring boiling water into a porcelain teapot. After it stopped pouring, the teapot lid settled back into its nook and floated over to a tray. She walked down the hallway towards the two-story foyer and went up the west staircase to a door. She willed open the office door with her mind and walked in. By the fireplace were two chairs, filled with piles of papers stacked haphazardly. The maid placed the tray on a table between the chairs. She had the teapot dip its spout and fill the cup. She walked over to the desk and gently placed it on the corner.

"Here is your tea, ma'am."

Astrid pensively watched the pen write furiously. Many would say she had the appearance of a woman ten years her junior, but her posture over the desk told another story.

"Thank you, stoke the fire, please," Astrid pointed towards the fireplace.

The maid turned and Astrid pulled out a laudanum bottle from a drawer. She poured some into the teacup and placed it back into the drawer. With her mind, she stirred the cup and then took a long sip. The maid watched as the embers glowed brighter as she stoked fire by pointing at the

8

fire. Then the maid stepped towards the desk and crossed her arms behind her back.

"Will that be all, ma'am?" the maid asked.

"What is the date today?"

"October the eleventh. The morning does have a chill to it, doesn't it?"

"Yes, autumn is upon us."

"Must be why Miss Audrey has taken ill this morning."

Astrid stood up, "Audrey is ill? Why wasn't I informed?"

"I don't know, ma'am. I thought you knew. Your daughter was in with her a little while ago…"

Astrid went down the hallway into Audrey's bedroom. It was dark from the heavy drapes. As she looked at them they opened letting in the morning sunlight. Astrid rushed to the bed and sat down, taking the girl's hand in hers. She then tucked a piece of hair behind the girl's ear.

"Audrey, how are you feeling, my darling?" Astrid asked in a soothing voice.

The girl stayed silent. Astrid moved her hand around in circular motions over the girl's chest and with a sigh put her hand on her hip. She then discovered several dolls in the bed and the lamp next to the bed was still warm.

"Darling, there is nothing wrong with you. Now listen, why does the maid think you are ill?" Astrid inquired and Audrey bit her lip. "Don't worry, I will not be mad. Please tell me."

"I told mother I was feeling ill and could not work with the teacher today," she said as she sat up.

"Why did you feign illness? You always love your studies. Did something happen with one of the other children?"

"No, nothing happened with them. I heard something."

"What did you hear?"

"I don't want to tell you," Audrey said and shifted her weight.

"Why do you not want to tell me? I won't be angry."

"Because it's about you and I don't want to worry you."

"I am strong, you know that. I can handle anything you tell me."

Audrey sighed, "I heard mother and father talking about you. They said that there are revolutionaries in the town who want to kill you. I thought if I didn't go to school I could stay and protect you."

Astrid smiled, "Now that is just nonsense. No one will kill me, you hear?"

"I don't want you to die."

She lunged forward and grabbed Astrid around the waist. She patted Audrey on the head and felt the little girl's body heave with sobs.

"Darling, don't cry. Remember when your cat died, what I said at the little funeral?" Audrey looked up with tears in her eyes.

"That if nothing died, nothing would be born," Audrey said.

"That's right. Remember after that the dog had puppies."

"In the kitchen," she said, smiling through her tears.

"Yes, in the kitchen. Remember how happy you were to see them born," Audrey nodded in response. "They never would have been born if your cat hadn't died."

"Why?"

"Well Audrey, the world seems big, but in fact it is awfully small. God knows this and makes a deal. We are allowed to stay here and live, only if we eventually give up our spot. Do you understand now?"

"Yes, but I have a question. Is it true that you were touched by God?"

"Where did you hear such a thing?" Astrid said with a chuckle.

"The teacher said so."

"I don't know why I'm special," Astrid smiled. "But that will be our secret," she stood up. "Now, I won't tell your parents you're feigning illness. It couldn't hurt to have you as an extra guard, just in case."

"Okay," Audrey said and pulled the blankets over herself. Astrid looked at the drapes and they closed.

Astrid's daughter and Godson were down in the breakfast nook. Nadine's hair was elaborately pinned up with an ivory hairpin her mother gave her for her thirtieth birthday. Flynn wore a custom fitted black suit with a blue silk vest. The door creaked open and they saw Astrid enter. She had changed out of her housedress into her favorite blue day dress. She sat down at the table, took a piece of toast, and placed a napkin in her lap.

"Mother, what a pleasant surprise," Nadine said excitedly. "You never dine with us, what a treat this is."

"I figured I would have to come out of my office eventually," Astrid said with a chuckle as she buttered her toast.

"You look stunning today, I love you in that dress," Nadine said with enthusiasm.

"You're not wearing a corset, which is highly inappropriate," Flynn said, disapprovingly.

"Thank you, Nadine, you look lovely as well," she said and took a bite of her toast. She looked over at Flynn, "Did you remember that today you are to pick up the writer?"

"I don't see why I must go. Why can't you send one of your underlings?" he said with a scowl.

"Do not take that tone with me. I need you there because you will make a better impression than some random employee. I would send Nadine, but you full well know it would not be entirely appropriate to send your sister."

"Ah yes, because she's your actual daughter and I'm some supposed adopted urchin. Careful calling her my sister, we don't want your followers finding out about the bastard,

11

do we? I have five beautiful children, do you even know their names? No one would even believe I'm part of this insane family anyway. Why would I want to publically be known as relation to you people?"

"What does that imply?" Nadine said pointing at him with her fork.

"I was simply correcting her. Hell, we don't even look alike," he said pointing at Nadine with his fork. Turning to Astrid he said, "She has brown hair and brown eyes and I have blue eyes and blonde hair. Must have been a relief I came out looking unlike you lot. Sells the story better does it not?"

"You look like your father," Nadine interjected.

Flynn shot Nadine a perturbed look and she averted her attention to her plate.

"I know that bothers you, Mother, that I look like my father."

"Don't be so sour," Astrid said and took a bite of toast. "I love you for who you are, not taking any likeness to your father's image into account at all. I do love you, even if you are most disagreeable at times."

"I can be however I please, I am not one of your followers. I neither fear you nor revere you."

"I just finished showing my true affections and you lash out. Why are you being so contemptuous?" she paused and set down her toast. "Is it my will that has you throwing jabs?" Flynn looked shocked as Astrid spoke, throwing his napkin on the table. "Don't act surprised. Did you really think I wouldn't know you read my will?"

"One day I will expose your little spies and gouge out their little spying eyes."

"That was too harsh," Astrid said and pointed at him with her toast. "Have you been drinking this morning?"

"That is laughable coming from you. How much laudanum have you had today, Mother?"

12

"Bite your tongue," she snarled. "Anyway, I don't see why you are so upset about the will. It is only a draft, nothing final. But I'm leaving you valuable real estate and a tidy trust fund. I think that is quite generous," she said with a mouth of toast.

"You are going to leave everything to her," he pointed at Nadine, "Leaving me with nothing. She gets this house, the title of being your heir, and everything else."

"You know it would not be right for appearances for me to give you the title or the house. It is purely political."

"Appearances and political? With such words it seems all I am to you is your secret bastard of a son."

"Shut your mouth," Nadine said in a hushed voice.

"It's true. No one treats me with respect, even you. I don't see why I have to be punished because my mother was a whore who couldn't keep her legs closed."

Nadine gasped and placed her hand over her mouth.

"Are you finished?" Astrid asked and put her hands in her lap. Nadine looked down and saw Astrid's clenched hands were violently shaking.

"Yes, I'm finished," he sneered.

"Will you be picking up the writer at the train or should I make other arrangements?" she asked and he shifted his weight.

"Why are you even bringing a writer here in the first place?"

"You know I need a professional to help me with my memoirs. They must be finished."

"Right, the impending death causes immediacy to write the great story of your life."

"You are allowed an opinion. That opinion is allowed to differ from mine. However, I expect you to be loyal to me and my cause," she paused, "Will you or will you not be picking him up?"

He took a swallow of wine from a mug and stood, "I do so only because I'm your loyal hound."

"Sit down; I am not finished with you," she said sternly. He grunted as he sat and crossed his arms. "I would appreciate it if you didn't discuss my mortality in front of the children. It upsets them. Don't try to deny it. I realize the current political climate seems stormy, but you should keep your opinions to yourself when you are around the children."

"Your arrogance astounds me. The revolutionaries want you dead and they will murder you if you give them the slightest opportunity," as he spoke, he violently pointed to the window.

"Those people you speak of are not revolutionaries, just squeaky wheels. They will not be successful in any attempts they may make."

"You cannot be so certain. Besides, which child said I spoke about such things?"

"They are innocent, thankfully I calmed them down," she said and took a bite of toast.

"What did you say? Not the truth, I hope."

"No, of course I didn't tell them the truth," she said and rolled her eyes.

"So, you lied to them, how befitting," he crossed his arms and scoffed.

"I gave an answer to a question to which there is no answer. If that is lying, then so be it. A comforting lie is better than the terrifying truth to a child," she said as she buttered another piece of toast. "Moreover, you say you don't fear me. You should, as should those so-called revolutionaries," she said as she pointed at him with the butter knife.

Flynn stormed out of the room in a huff almost toppling his chair.

"I wonder how long this bad mood will last," Nadine asked and took a sip of tea.

"He has been in this mood since infancy, so I'm not hopeful for an improvement anytime soon. You spoke to Audrey earlier, did you properly inspect her?"

14

"It never ceases to amaze me how you discover my comings and goings with such seeming ease," Nadine put her tea cup down and shook her head in dismay.

"You know I have my ways," Astrid said with a sly smile.

"When I checked her I came to the conclusion that nothing was physically wrong with her. Although, I knew something was troubling her emotionally, but I could not decode her. My gift is not nearly as strong as yours, Mother."

"Only time will tell with that child. Hopefully, in the long run, she does not adopt her father's grumpy disposition."

"I pray he will be kindly to the writer," Nadine said as she clasped her hands.

"Dear Nadine, I expect him to be completely in usual character."

"The poor writer fellow," she said wincing.

"Indeed," Astrid said and took a long sip of tea.

Chapter 3

The Writer

New Alessaria, California
October 11th
1869

A young man on the cusp of turning twenty-five looked out of the train window watching the Northern California landscape fly by. The thick forest of redwood trees was a constant viewing pleasure. A thin layer of fog eerily hugged the base of the trees. He had never been on a train before so he was excited and nervous. His mother's words of warning that the train would crash ran through his head. He took off his hat and nervously combed his fingers through his wavy light-brown hair.

He was in his best business attire. His well-worn Wellington boots were scuffed, despite the fact he gave them a shine the night before. The only new piece of clothing he had was a cravat he bought especially for this trip. He drummed his fingers on a brief case in his lap. The man in the seat across from him looked at him with squinted eyes and a clenched jaw. He continued to look up at the young man and then back to the offending fingers. The young man noticed this attention and stopped. He looked at the man sitting in front of him. He was dressed in a gray tweed suit, matching hat, and a narrow black short bowtie.

The young man reached into his suitcase and pulled out a letter:

Dear Mr. Connor,

I am sincerely looking forward to working with you. A driver is going to meet you at the train station and will bring you to New Alessaria. My trusted Godson, Flynn Patrick, will accompany you to our home. You may lodge with us as long as necessary. Have a safe journey.

    Sincerely,

      Astrid Borrows

The young man looked ahead to the man across from him, "Sir, do you know when the train is to arrive?"

The man delved into his pocket and pulled out his gold timepiece. The young man noticed it had a grand eagle engraved on the cover. He looked down at the man's front-laced boots and they looked worn for wear.

The man said in a leisurely Southern accent, "Well, we are to arrive any minute, if the train is on time of course." He put the watch back into his breast pocket. "Is this your first time on a train, Son?"

"Yes, sir."

"I might 'ave guessed, you being all twitchy and such. What's your business in this North end of California?"

"I'm heading to New Alessaria."

The man moved his nose back and forth, wiggling his wide gray mustache.

"You one of those Mover freaks?" The young man was startled and did not know how to answer. "I did not mean that in an offending way. My daughter in-law is one of you and she's a mighty fine young lady. My minister says y'all are from hell, but I don't believe it. This same man told us not to eat meat on a Friday. I personally don't think the Lord cares one inch what a man eats on Friday. What do you think?"

"Yes," the young man said quickly.

"Yes to what, Son?"

"Yes, I'm a Mover and I don't think the Lord cares what a man eats on Friday."

The man leaned forward and looked about.

"What can you do? I mean those tricks you people can do." The young man looked around. "Don't you worry about them, they won't notice anything."

The young man took one more look around and then looked back at the man. The man watched as his pocket watch wiggled out from his breast pocket and floated into the young man's outstretched hand.

"That was amazing. Now give it back." The watch quickly floated back to the man. "Woo-eee son. That's all I have to say. What is your name?"

"Alan, sir."

"Pleased to meet you, Alan. Everyone calls me Uncle Bob."

"What are you doing all the way in California?"

"Gold, son, gold. I may be late to the party, but hopefully they left a nugget or two out there with Uncle Bob's name on it. It took me four years to gather enough money for this trip. General Sherman made sure I was broke as a dog come the end of the war." The train car lurched forward and the sound of a whistle blared. "Looks like we're here."

Alan looked out the window and saw a crowd of people on a train platform.

"It was a pleasure meetin' you, Alan." He started to walk off the train car and turned. "I hope you get what you came for."

Looking out the window Alan surveyed the platform and then stood up. He gathered his black scarf his mother knitted for him, his black frock overcoat, and put them both on. As he walked off the train onto the platform, he saw a man holding a sign with his name."

"That's me," Alan said pointing to the sign the man was holding.

"Allow me take your luggage, Sir."

Alan handed over his luggage and followed the man around the corner of the station building to a line of coaches and buggies.

"Which one is yours?"

"Just follow the stench of money. This way, Mr. Patrick is expecting you."

The driver stopped at an elegant coach painted with a rose wrapped around a sword, with an overlaid 'A' initial. Alan saw Flynn sitting in the front-facing seat and sat in the coach across from him. He was much more muscular than Alan, which was intimidating. The fact that he wore a frown was even more intimidating.

"Shakespeare, I presume. What is your name again?"

"My name? Oh, yes, of course. Alan. My name is Alan, well Alan Connor."

"My name is Flynn, well Flynn Patrick," he said in a mocking tone. "My, that is an ancient suit, must be at least a decade since you bought that thing."

"More like nine years," Alan said meekly as he perspired.

"Have my mother buy you a few new suits. I insist, for the integrity of all involved."

Alan looked at Flynn in his silk vest and got a whiff of his expensive cologne. As he breathed in the scent, he realized what the driver meant by the stench of money. He felt like a pauper in his old suit.

"Thank you for meeting me at the train, I realize you must have more pressing things to do."

"That I do, I'm a very busy man after all. However, you are an important fellow to the lady of the house, so I was tasked with fetching you."

"I wouldn't say I'm important."

"For me to take time out of my day to pick a man up at the train, he must be important."

Alan nodded and looked out the window. There was silence for the rest of the ride. The coach suddenly stopped and Alan realized he had dosed off. Flynn had a smirk on his face.

"Wake up, Rip Van Winkle. We have arrived." After Alan left the coach, Flynn turned to him, "Now if you will excuse me, I am off to town to do some real business."

Alan watched the coach drive off down the driveway towards town. He looked around and saw that this was not a mere house; it was a mansion. It was perched on the highest hilltop with a view of the entire valley. He turned and saw a butler with his luggage standing next to the spindly maid.

"Welcome to Borrows Manor," she said with a dry smile.

As Alan followed them up the entry staircase he felt a pit in his stomach. He could not decide if it was excitement, nerves, or both. After entering, he was amazed at the glimmering décor. Mirrors adorned the walls of the foyer. He was faced with his reflection from various angles. Both, he decided. Definitely both.

Chapter 4

Take the Gun

Astrid sat at her vanity vacantly staring into the mirror. She closed her eyes as a wave of nausea washed over her. With her hand on her belly she smiled a knowing smile, thinking that she would tell him about the pending child that night. She breathed deeply as the sickness passed. There came a playful knock at the door.

A man with a thick Irish accent called out, "May I enter?"

"You may," she declared.

In the doorway stood a dashing man in a new outfit. He was tall, with curly strawberry-blonde hair and gray-blue eyes.

"What do you think?" he asked as he slowly turned around.

"What do I think of what?" she said with a coy smile.

"The clothes, what do you think of the new clothes?"

"It is a handsome outfit for a handsome man."

He grinned and tossed his hat to her. She giggled and put it on.

"Have you thought about what we discussed?" he said as he walked towards her.

She removed the hat and looked at it in her hands, "I have."

"And…" §

She let the silence drip in the air.

"If you are referring to your marriage proposal, the answer is…" she paused.

"Is what?" he said impatiently.

"Of course I will marry you." He lifted her into his arms kissing her deeply while twirling around. "I am so happy, my darling, I love you and count the hours till I'm your wife."

He looked into her eyes and smiled, "I notice when you are happy that little glint of gold in your eye shines brighter."

She smiled and touched his strawberry-blonde hair, "You need to get a haircut, my dear."

"Oh, you don't find my flowing locks appealing?"

"You know what I would find most appealing?"

"What would that be?"

"You, shed of all articles of clothing."

She reached up and brought his head down to kiss her. As he undressed, he put his clothing neatly on a chair.

"Do you have to be so tidy in a moment of passion?"

"I do, it's a new outfit after all. I paid a pretty set of coin for this."

She slipped out of her dressing gown and lay on the bed. She curled a finger beckoning him to come to her.

"I will be in control much better if I straddle you," she said firmly.

"Do what you like to me, my Astrid. I serve your every want and need," he said while she switched positions to be on top.

She bathed after their afternoon lovemaking and put on her favorite pale blue dress, of which Seamus was especially fond. She sat in front of the vanity fixing her hair into a bun. As she stared at her reflection, she smiled.

"I will soon be Mrs. Seamus Flynn Patrick," she whispered.

She descended the staircase, seeing Seamus reading on the sofa.

"I thought you Irish are all illiterate," she said with an impish lilt in her voice.

She snatched the book from his hands and skipped to the other end of the sofa. She cleared her throat and read aloud, "'With this night's revels and empire the term of a despised life, clos'd in my breast, by some Vile forfeit of untimely death.' I do love *Romeo and Juliet*," she said with a sigh.

"I thought everyone knows the fairer sex are a bunch of dullards. It must be a miracle one can read the likes of Shakespeare."

He took the book back playfully and they laughed together. He pulled her next to him and gave her a gentle kiss. As he stared into her eyes, she started to twirl his hair.

"You really do need to get a haircut."

"Alright, I'll go tomorrow."

"Do you know how much I want to be your wife?"

"I have no earthly idea. I think you should show some proof."

As she leaned in and gave him a deep kiss, the town warning bells chimed.

"Was there going to be a test of the bells today?" he asked.

"I would have known about something like that," she said with great concern.

They went to the front door and saw utter chaos outside. Men with weapons were running down the street toward the East end of town. She saw the town butcher with a large knife and ax running in his bloodstained apron. Astrid flagged him down.

"They're here attackin' the outskirts, we're goin' to head 'em off," he cried out.

"Who's attacking?" Seamus asked, but the butcher ran off without an answer or goodbye. "What the bloody hell is going on?" Seamus cried out in frustration.

Astrid did not answer him and she sprinted to the library. He followed her and watched her take the gun and its bag off the wall. She opened the glass case that held a bejeweled sword. She was about to run out the door when Seamus grabbed her by the shoulders.

"Where do you think you're going?" Seamus demanded.

"There's a battle and I need to go help protect the town. The people need me."

"Who's out there?"

"The P.G.I., along with The Cleaver would be my guess."

"Jesus, Mary, and Joseph," he said and his face filled with terror.

"Get out of my way," Astrid yelled as she started to walk to the door.

"I'm the man. So, I'm going and you're not," he said firmly as he tried to grab the gun from her.

"I have more power than the men, including you. Let go of me."

There was a pause. He lunged forward and kissed her passionately.

"Okay, but you are the most stubborn woman I have ever known."

"Here, you take the gun," she said as she handed it to him.

The warning bells were still violently tolling as they left for battle.

Chapter 5

The Famous Astrid Borrows

New Alessaria, California
October 11th
1869

A tear fell down Astrid's cheek as she listened to the last chime of the walnut longcase grandfather clock. A loud knock at the door startled her.

"What is it?" Astrid snapped.

The spindly maid announced, "The writer is here, ma'am. Should I have him come up to your office or stay in the parlor?"

"Thank you, the parlor is fine. Make sure his belongings are taken to his guest room."

"Yes, ma'am."

After the maid left, Astrid went to her bedroom. At her vanity she let her hair down and brushed it. She put it up in a tight bun with a sapphire and emerald butterfly comb pin. After she was satisfied with her hair, she put on some light rouge, dabbed French perfume, and applied lipstick. Picking through her jewelry cabinet, she decided on her pearls. After one final look in the mirror, she wrung her hands as she took a few deep breaths.

Meanwhile in the parlor, Alan looked up and smiled as he saw Nadine enter.

"Why hello there," he said in an uneven burst and quickly bounded up to greet her.

"You must be the writer," Nadine offered her hand and he gently kissed it.

"Yes, the writer. That is, well, yes I'm a writer. Newspaper man, really."

"Pleasure to meet you. My name is Nadine, I'm Astrid's daughter."

"I know who you are, Nadine. You're the young heir to the Astridians."

"Heavens, I'm hardly young anymore. After a husband and three girls you are no longer young. Let's sit, shall we?"

He sat down in a chair and she on the couch.

"I did not mean to offend."

"No offence was taken. What is your name? I did not seem to catch it."

"Alan Connor."

"Mr. Connor, I do hope you will find your time here pleasant as well as productive. Was Flynn kind to you on your journey here?"

"He seemed preoccupied, but I didn't take his demeanor personal."

"That is good to hear. I assure you, mother will be coming down shortly."

"I cannot believe I am about to meet *the* Astrid Borrows."

"Are you a follower?"

"I wouldn't say that I'm a follower exactly. My mother believes Astrid is the devil come to life. But I don't agree with that, of course."

"What type of faith do you subscribe to? If you don't mind me asking, of course."

"Truth be told, I haven't made up my mind on the subject. I'm not even sure what it means when someone is a follower. Of her I mean. A follower of her, Astrid is her, of course. That sounded a bit strange. Never mind that spell of awkwardness; I guess I am quite excited to meet her. She is famous after all."

26

"That she is."

"Is it true she bested over fifty men in battle?" he blurted out.

Nadine chuckled, "You should ask her. I honestly do not know the exact figures and details. Some say twenty, others swear it to be in the hundreds. To hear some people talk about her, you would think she was Christ reborn."

"What are your thoughts? About your mother, I mean."

Nadine clasped her hands together and looked out the window.

"What do *I* think? I don't know how to fully explain my mother, or how to define her special qualities. But, she has gifts never seen in another, and I'm not alone in that observation. She is simply a miracle. I believe if there is some cosmic plan, or fate, she will be important. She already is," she paused and looked to Alan with an arched eyebrow, "Are you interviewing me?"

"I apologize, I wasn't meaning to pry, my curiosity getting the better of me."

"Your questions are fine. Off the record, of course."

"Of course, it was not intended to be an interview. If you do not mind me asking one more, do you possess any of her exceptional gifts? In addition to the normal abilities we all have."

"I don't know if being able to move things with our minds can be called a 'normal ability.' I'm nit-picking, I'm sorry. To answer your question, yes. I do not compare to her power, not even close, but I can do certain, parlor tricks."

She paused and looked him up and down. She put out her hand and waved it over his body, "You have an ulcer."

"How do you know that?" He looked at her with a gaping mouth and she just smiled back.

"I also know you have great strength. More than even me. You must learn your own power to control and harness it. You should find your true potential."

The door opened and Astrid stood in the doorway. Alan found her to be the most beautiful woman he had ever seen. The light behind her gave a soft heavenly glow. Even though he assumed her to be in her mid-forties, she appeared to be ten years younger. She had a confident and graceful presence. Her pale skin glowed against her black hair and sapphire eyes. He felt as if she was an enchantress hypnotizing him. Her royal blue dress shimmered as she walked. She extended her hand to him and he shook it. Mid-shake he bent down and kissed her hand.

"Alan Connor, I presume," she purred, maintaining steady eye contact. "Please sit and relax after your long travels. You must be quite tired."

He sat down immediately, almost missing the chair. She motioned to Nadine to leave the room. She gave a quick bow of her head and closed the door behind her.

"It is such an honor to meet you Mrs. Borrows. I feel privileged for your generous invitation."

"You can call me Astrid. Have you been to our New Alessaria before?"

"No, but I always wanted to. Thank you for allowing me lodging in your beautiful home. It is quite impressive."

"It is my duty to take care of all I employ. About your job description, I realize my letters were vague in nature. I will inform you of the particulars, if you decide to take the job of course." She cleared her throat. "I want to write my memoirs as quickly as possible. I found it prudent to employ a professional to help me speed along the process and add a few polishing touches. I heard you are well respected at the newspaper."

"I'm glad to hear I have a good reputation. I would be beyond honored to be in your employ."

"Good, then it's settled. I think we could wait to discuss your salary at a different juncture, if you agree. But don't worry, I can assure you the pay will be more than fair compensation. I will also set up credit at several businesses around town, just give your name. I assume you are a person who would not take advantage of such a generous situation."

"I would never think to exploit your kindness. Thank you."

Rapid knocking at the parlor door startled them and a man rushed in. Road dust floated around him from riding horseback. His appearance reminded Alan of the gold panners and cow wranglers he would sometimes see in San Francisco. The gruff man bent down and whispered in Astrid's ear. Alan noticed a pistol in a hip gun sling.

Astrid quickly stood up, "Alan, I must go. You can accompany us, but we must make haste."

She retrieved her shawl from the foyer closet, "Come along, quickly now."

The coach driver sprinted down the steps after them and flung himself into the seat. They sped down the road.

"May I ask where we're going in such a panic? Is something wrong?" Alan asked, gripping the widow edge.

"There is an injured boy and he needs my medical attention."

"Don't you have any qualified physicians?"

"They have me and I'm better than ten doctors." As she boasted he felt her bewitching confidence turn into appalling arrogance. "Oh, my apologies, I forgot proper introductions. This is Edward Delving, my personal guard. This is Alan, the writer."

"Pleased to make your acquaintance," Alan said and extended his hand.

Edward grunted, and Alan put his hand away. The remaining ride was in silence, Alan held on as the coach abruptly lurched. They stopped in front of a working class home. Astrid knocked and a young man opened the door half covered in blood. He gave her a quick hug, taking care to avoid getting blood on her dress.

With a posh English accent the young man said, "Thank you for coming, this was beyond my skill to fix."

"Of course I came, Benjamin," she said as they walked into the house.

"Who's he?" he pointed at Alan.

"Ignore him. Which O'Brian boy was hurt?"

"The youngest, he's in the kitchen, it does not look promising, but I have complete faith in your skill."

As they walked down the hallway, they could hear unnerving screams.

"Can you stand the sight of blood, Alan?" she asked without slowing pace.

"I think so. I've never actually seen much blood."

"Brace yourself, there will be plenty to see."

He looked ahead seeing smudged bloody handprints on a swinging door. As they went in, he immediately saw the boy on a large table, blood oozing onto the floor in a growing puddle. His pallor was ghostly and, without the boy's screams, Alan would have thought him dead. He noticed white on his arm and in horror realized it to be a protruding bone. The frantic mother held a bloodied rag around her son's shoulder and praying to the Virgin Mary. Two older brothers and a sister were huddled in the corner with the father. Astrid took off her shawl and put on an apron.

"When was the accident?" she asked as she approached the table.

The mother talked incoherently as she fiercely wept. She turned and latched onto Alan wailing into his chest. The father pried his wife off Alan and he scurried to another corner of the kitchen. Astrid removed the rag and saw the extensive damage.

She put her hand on the boy's forehead, "Can you hear me, darling?"

"Yes," the boy said with a weak croak.

She motioned for the brothers, "Listen now, your brothers are going to hold you down. Try your hardest not to fight them. Hand me a clean rag," she instructed and the sister handed one over. "I'm going to fix this. I know you are such a strong boy and you can handle the truth. This is going to hurt very much. But you have to be strong like I know you are. Just bite down on this rag. I know you are going to do great. Open your mouth," she said before putting in the rag. "Where is your favorite place to go in the world?"

"Creek," he whispered.

"He loves fishing," the father said and bit his finger to keep his tears at bay.

"Okay, close your eyes and imagine fishing at the creek. Can you do that for me?"

The boy nodded and closed his eyes. After a deep breath, she looked around, "He will most likely involuntarily move things. Hold on to something and don't be alarmed."

Astrid placed the rag in his mouth and waved both her hands just above the wound. After closing her eyes, she took deep slow controlled breaths. The air buzzed with an electric quality. The boy bit down and balled his fists. Tears flowed from his tightly closed eyes. A pot on the stove rattled around. Then an increasing number of things around the room shook. The brothers held him in place as much as they could as the boy lurched. He cried out muffled screams through the rag.

Soon, the boy's screams faded and he lost consciousness. From Alan's vantage point he only saw the boy's face and feet. He heard a strange sizzling sound and a smell he could not identify. It felt like hours until Astrid dropped her hands to her sides and sighed deeply. She took the rag from the boy's mouth and dipped it in a bowl of water. As the family moved around, Alan saw Astrid wipe the blood from the boy's chest. The wound appeared to be melted shut. The mother wept as she rushed to the table. She looked at her son and grasped Astrid's hand.

"You are an angel," she said with tears of joy. "We thank you. Bless you, Astrid."

"Glad I could help. Thank you for calling me instead of that quack doctor in town." Astrid removed the apron. "He might have a slight fever for a day or so. If it becomes worrisome or his condition does not improve contact me." She put the apron on the counter and took her shawl off the hook. "Please keep me updated on his condition. Good-bye," she said as she left the kitchen with Edward shortly behind.

"Come along," Edward barked at Alan.

The ride up to the house was quiet. Alan had so many questions but could not find a way to speak. As Astrid gazed out the window, he studied her. He cursed himself for thinking she was arrogant. In his eyes, her talent was nothing short of miraculous.

"The boy, will he be alright?" Alan asked at last.

"I believe so," she said without looking away from the window.

"How did you do that? Heal him with your gift, I mean. I've never seen such a thing or knew it could be a possibility."

"It does not matter how I can do the things I can do. What does matter, in my opinion, is when and why I use my power. Power is a tricky force to reckon with. It can both save and destroy. If you are not careful, it destroys things you love. This is why powerful people cannot afford to love. To do so is dangerous; the price is much too high." She continued to look out the window. Alan saw something in her face he did not expect, sadness.

The following morning, Alan walked down the staircase and stretched. He stopped in the middle of the foyer and realized he had no idea which way to go. As he stood wondering why they did not hand out maps, a maid walked past him.

"Excuse me miss," he called out.

"Go into the hall between the staircases and go to the right," the maid said.

"Excuse me?"

"The breakfast nook is down the hall between the staircases and to the right."

"How did you know what I was going to ask? Is everyone clairvoyant in this household?"

"Sir, not to patronize, but it is breakfast time. Also, you looked lost, happens frequently around here. If you will excuse me, I have a house to clean. Unless you want to gawk at my mopping as well?" she countered and walked away.

Alan shook his head and followed her instructions. He opened the door and saw a lovely breakfast nook filled with soft morning sun. The table was set with blue and white Wedgewood china with a fine white linen tablecloth. He thought it strange no one was eating. He shrugged and sat down. There was a basket of fresh bread in the middle of the table and a plate with butter. As the door opened he looked up from buttering his toast and there was a different maid. She had a tray with coffee, plus a plate of eggs and bacon.

"Morning, Sir," she said as she set the plate and coffee next to his bread plate.

"Amazing," he said with astonishment.

"Didn't quite get that, Sir?"

"It's just that everyone seems to know my every want and need in this house. How did you know I was to sit down at this moment and wanted breakfast?"

The maid scoffed, "Sir, the upstairs maid sent word to us in the kitchen that you were awake and taking a bath. If you didn't come downstairs, we would have taken it to you."

"That's remarkably efficient."

"It's our job, Sir," the maid said and crossed her arms behind her back. "If you ever need anything let one of us know. Happy to help."

"Well, thank you. You can call me Alan, no need for formality," she nodded in response and left.

After he took a bite, Nadine came into the room. He quickly stood up and she sat down across from him. She was wearing a fashionable pink and brown bustle dress.

"I apologize for beginning without you, I thought I was going to be alone," he said as he sat back down.

"We keep odd hours at this house, you'll get used to it. I heard you had quite an eventful day yesterday," she said as she placed a napkin in her lap.

"Calling it eventful is an understatement. I mean, I had heard the stories that she had the power to heal. I never believed it, until now of course." He paused, "Do you know when Astrid, I mean your mother, will be coming down for breakfast? I want to know when I'm to start the interview."

"Mother almost always takes her meals in private. She is not one beholden to ceremony, so you can approach her at your convenience."

"I think I will stay and eat some of those biscuits, if you don't mind. I just noticed them."

She smiled, "It's nice to have company. Usually, I eat with Flynn and our spouses. It is refreshing to have someone new in the house."

"I have yet to meet everyone. Who all currently resides here?" he asked and took a bite.

"My husband Eddie is out of town on business for the month. The children run about the house, when they are not with the teacher of course. I have three girls, the apples of my eye, and Flynn has five lovely children. It's a shock he is their father, it really is astonishing how lovely they all are. I give full credit to Anne, Flynn's wife, a saint of the first order. How he captured such a good woman we'll never know," she chuckled.

"You don't think much of him, do you?"

"Did you care for him?" she smiled coyly and took a sip of tea.

"Good point," he said with a nod.

After breakfast Alan stood in front of Astrid's office door with his notebook. He heard a man's voice bellow from inside the office. The door flung open, startling him. A disheveled Edward stood before him.

"Mr. Delving, good morning."

"Stalking the door, eh kid?" he asked gruffly.

"I just wanted to…"

"Go in, she's expecting you," he shouted as he walked away.

Alan peered inside the room and Astrid stood gazing into the fire with her hands on her hips. The firelight shone onto her cornflower blue house dress.

"Come in," she said softly as she sat in the chair.

Alan walked in and closed the door behind him. She motioned for him to sit across from her. He sat down and opened his notebook awkwardly on his lap. He then retrieved his pen and ink well with the awareness she was watching his every move.

"Do you want anything? Something to drink, perhaps before we start?" she asked.

"No, I'm quite fine. Just had a lovely breakfast. I was thinking we can begin with a question and answer format."

"Very well, start with the questioning."

"To start, start from the beginning. How about you tell me a bit about your parents?"

"John and Rose Cooper. My father's family had roots going back to just after the Mayflower. Proud to fight for the revolution and much of his extended family died in battle against the red coats. My father fell in love with my mother on sight. It was all terribly romantic. But, my paternal grandmother did not approve. My mother was a Mover, but more importantly British and the war was still fresh for many. The nuptials continued, without my grandmother's blessing. She passed away shortly before the wedding and father always held guilt for his mother's sudden death. After my parents married, they discovered a fast growing Mover settlement in upstate New York. My father was not a Mover, so it was considered a mixed marriage. The townspeople were never really accepting of him, but he insisted they were happy there. Then I was born, November 20, 1815. Another birthday rounding the corner."

Alan wrote down the date and then paused while calculating her age, "You're fifty-four?"

"Not until next month, it's rude to round up," she took a sip of tea.

"I cannot believe that. You look at the most forty. I never would have guessed that," he said and stared dumbfounded.

"I will take that as a compliment. While I'm flattered, shall we move on to a more important topic?"

"Oh, yes, right. What about your childhood?"

"Tragically, my mother died in childbirth, so I never met her. I was raised by my father, it was only he and I for many years."

"I'm sorry, that must have been difficult."

"Yes and no. As I said, I never met her, so I never knew what I lost because I never had it to begin with. My father went out of his way to keep her memory alive. He had a flame of love that never faded. He never remarried. Every night, he would tell me the story of the sword," she pointed to a sword encased in glass on the mantel, "It's a 1796 light cavalry sword. Quite rare and expensive with the embellishments such as an ivory grip and gems. He said it was a wedding present from my mother. The inscription says 'sword from your Rose. When she died, he cut a braid of her red hair and attached it to the hilt. As a child I would call it the Sword of Rose. When I was old enough, my father taught me how to use it. My father was always a bit of an odd duck, according to the townsfolk. He was a reasonably respected and skilled doctor. But in their eyes, he was not one of them, an outsider and I was his mixed breed tomboy. The other children would call me names, like half-breed, and say things like I was a boy in a dress. I guess it is slightly better than being called a Satan's Plague Witch."

"Didn't quite catch that. Did you say Satan's Plague Witch?"

"Oh, you have a lot to learn. It is a slur against us Movers. It's quite self-explanatory, don't you think?" she gave a short disdainful snort. "Next question?"

"It's safe to say you are quite powerful, when did you realize your exceptionality? Was it always apparent that you were special?"

"My peers could move and manipulate things, as we all can. But only to a certain extent of course. I was simply the best. It started as simple as heating a cold cup of coffee for my father and progressed to floating large objects such as a cart with ease. I could also determine the sex of an unborn child and how many weeks the mother was into the pregnancy. That, among other things, is why my father wanted to take me on in his practice. However, the town would not have stood for something as radical as a woman doctor. Thus he hired a young apprentice named Nathaniel."

"Was that your husband, Nathaniel Borrows?"

"Safe assumption, but to answer the question, yes. My father decided Nathaniel would eventually take over the practice. That we should be married for the good of the family. It was good sense and the advantage that Nathaniel was a Mover."

"Did you ever love him?"

"You still have that idealism of youth. I envy that so. No, we did not love each other. We cared for each other, but I never loved him. Soon after we were married I was pregnant with Nadine," her voice trailed off and she gazed into the fire.

"Everything okay, do you wish to take a break?" asked Alan.

"I'm simply not accustomed to revisiting the past. Some memories are a heavy burden and are hard to pick up once put away. Before Nadine was born, father and Nathanial were to go to a nearby town to get medical supplies. They promised me some fine clothing and such. I was excited for their return, mostly because of those indulgences. Silly priorities really, looking back on it." Her eyes welled up, "They were attacked. It was never investigated fully to see if they were robbed or targeted for being Movers," she dabbed her tears with a handkerchief.

She looked at the clock and sighed, "Would you like to go to the park with me?"

"The park? What about the interview?"

"I have an appointment to see to. You may join me, if you wish."

"What kind of business would you be seeing to in a park?"

"I do not like to discuss it. Come or don't, it is up to you."

"Yes, I will accompany you. Some fresh air will do us both some good."

As they left the office, the upstairs maid was watching a rag wipe down the railing. At the front of the foyer a maid held their coats.

As they walked towards the coach, Edward bellowed from behind, "Where are you going without me?"

"To the park, of course," Astrid said as she got into the coach.

"You know better, we have talked about this," he scolded. "It's my job after all."

"A job I gave you, remember?" she said as the coach sped down the driveway. She turned to Alan, "Ed is the head of The Chosen," Astrid said.

"What is that? I'm not familiar."

"Should you be telling him any of this?" Edward said in a hushed tone.

"The Chosen is common knowledge and you know it, Ed."

"He doesn't know about it, so not common enough," Edward grumbled.

"I apologize for all that, Alan. The Chosen are very protective of me and loyal."

"Like mercenaries?"

"More like faithful bodyguards," she said and smiled at Edward.

"There is so much I don't know about this world."

"Can I ask you a personal question, Alan?" she asked.

"Of course," he said quickly.

"Was your mother or father the Mover?"

"My father was a Mover, my mother is a Non-Mover. Why?"

"A half-breed, like me. I suspected, I just wanted confirmation. Let me guess, your father died when you were young and your mother did not know he was a Mover."

"How can you possibly know that?"

"I have my ways. I too often come across Movers who were and are in your situation, brought up to hate the very essence of who they are and not knowing their history. Not knowing who they are. You should come live here. It is where you belong, to be with your own kind. You have so much power and if you knew how to harness it, you could do great things."

"Was I employed just so you could try to convert me?"

"No, you misunderstand. I was only trying to help. You came here under your own free will and are always free to leave."

They arrived at the park and Alan saw a beautifully kept rose garden, a grass field and knoll. As they walked towards the knoll, he noticed a small platform towards the center with a crowd of people forming.

"Are we heading over there? Looks like an event of some sort."

"It's an execution," Edward said matter-of-fact.

"An execution?" Alan exclaimed, "Why are you going to an execution? Seems like an odd thing to go to."

"You ask too many questions," Edward snarled.

"I have an appointment to perform the execution," she said.

"Why wouldn't that be done at a prison? We are not barbarians," he said while shaking his head with a tone of condemnation.

"Most of the time prisons can't hold or execute our people. We have to do it ourselves, like everything else. Now, excuse me a moment," she said as she walked ahead towards the platform.

Edward forcefully put his hand on Alan's shoulder and pointed at the crowd.

"That is where we are going," he said forcefully.

Astrid stepped up onto the platform and two men were brought up without handcuffs by a pack of guards.

"Do you have any last words before your people, myself, and God?" she asked the first man.

"I'm sorry for what I done. So, sorry. Oh, God, I'm so sorry. That there woman didn't deserve what I done to her. I was drunk, but that's no defense. I pray for God's forgiveness," the prisoner said breaking down sobbing.

"Do you have any last words before your people, myself, and God?" she asked the second prisoner.

"Fuck you, Astridian whore," his voice thundered as he crossed his arms defiantly.

Astrid nodded and as she grounded her energy she lifted her arms.

A guard shouted, "Take your positions, gents. May God have mercy on your wretched souls."

"We are to be silent from now until the end, kid. Get it?" Edward whispered.

Alan nodded. The audience was hushed.

The guard yelled out, "1…2…3…"

Astrid cocked her head to the left and the two men's necks snapped. Alan flinched at the sound. The bodies fell to the ground with an ominous thud.

The audience responded in unison, "Amen."

Four guards carried away the bodies of the prisoners and tossed them in a push cart. The crowd dispersed as Astrid descended the platform.

"I think I understand what she meant now," Alan said as he watched her.

"What nonsense are you spewing?" Edward growled.

"The day I arrived, remember what she said in the coach? After she healed the boy?" Ed shook his head no. "'Power is a tricky thing. It can save and also destroy.'"

"You hang on every word that woman says, don't you?" Alan scoffed as Edward glared at him with a cocked eyebrow. "I can tell, so don't bullshit me. Just remember one thing when you have that pen in your hand. Although she may think otherwise, she is no deity. She is flesh and blood. She's only a woman and not to be worshiped. Save the worshipping for God. It's a sin after all to worship anyone else. I think it may be one of those commandments; one of the top ten at least."

Astrid took Edward's arm and looked over to Alan, "Would you join us tonight for my granddaughter Vera's small recital? Nothing formal. You can meet the family."

"I would love to go," Alan said and tipped his hat.

Edward gave a quiet chuckle and Alan shot him a glaring look as they entered the carriage.

Chapter 6

Mandrake by Moonlight

New Alessaria, California
October 11th
1869

That evening Alan walked into the parlor and was overwhelmed with the amount of new faces. Alan sighed in relief as he noticed Nadine conversing with Flynn and his wife Anne in the corner.

She noticed him enter and waved him over, "I am so pleased to see you have joined us,"

Astrid approached them with a young adolescent girl, "Alan, this is my granddaughter, Vera. She is Nadine's eldest and we expect great things from her."

"Pleased to make your acquaintance," Vera said and curtsied.

"Why, aren't you a proper young lady?" Alan said and gave a half bow.

"Run along to the piano," Astrid said and patted Vera on her hand. "You are in for such a treat, Alan. She is quite talented."

The family sat around the piano and watched as Vera played Beethoven's *Moonlight Sonata*. As the haunting melody poured from the piano, Alan noticed Nadine wiping a tear from his eye and smiling proudly. Alan noticed Astrid watching him instead of the performance. He brushed it off as being paranoid. There was a nagging question that tickled the back of his mind. Why would she be watching him?

Later that evening, Alan was in his sleeping gown and robe reading when a playful knock got his attention. He opened the door and saw Astrid in her sleeping gown and holding a lamp. He quickly closed his robe and tied it nervously, fumbling here and there. Her hair was in a long braid tied with a light blue ribbon. The light from the flickering flame showed a glint in her eyes and a mischievous smile. While he knew it was Astrid before him, she seemed to be a different person. Her air of formality disappeared, even her posture was relaxed and flirtatious.

"Mrs. Borrows, quite a surprise. Is something the matter?"

"Remember, I told you to call me Astrid. I was wondering, would you fancy a swim? There is a private lake less than a mile away," she leaned against the door frame and fiddled with her braid bow.

"It's well after midnight, you mustn't be serious."

"Alan, where is your sense of adventure?" she said and led him by the hand down the hallway.

He was surprised with every step that he simply followed her lead. It was nearly a mile before they reached the small lake and the moon gave the world a silver glow. The forest was full of sounds of the night, putting him on edge. He shivered as thought it foolish to go swimming at this hour. When they reached the water's edge, he watched as she knelt down and placed her hand over the water lapping on the shore.

"Ready to dip in?" she said as she slipped off her sleeping gown and he quickly averted his eyes. "Alan, decency will spoil the fun. It's only the female form. Many of the best works of art were created to honor the beauty of womanly curves."

43

He reluctantly turned and watched her enter the water without hesitation.

"Isn't the water freezing?" he exclaimed, holding himself to keep from trembling.

"Only one way to find out," she said impishly and curled her finger for him to come closer. "Trust me," she purred and swam out into the deeper water.

He grumbled sounds of protest under his breath as he removed his robe and sleeping gown. He stood in his long underwear and walked towards the water.

She laughed, "Don't be such a prude, a man's body is no mystery to me."

He turned away and shook his head. After a deep breath, he grimaced as he removed his underwear. He cupped his privates and dipped his foot into the edge of the water. To his surprise, the water was comfortably warm.

"How can this be?" he asked, astonished. "Does it not kill the fish and such?"

"I warmed the water for us and there are no fish in this lake, it's man-made. Now, stop dilly-dallying and swim."

He entered the water continuing to conceal his privates. Astrid was gleefully bobbing around. In the moon light he could see her large grin.

"Isn't this divine? I come here when I'm under great stress."

"It actually is quite pleasant," he said conceding.

She swam up to him and tussled his hair. She leaned in to kiss him and he dodged her.

"I apologize, I can't. I'm flattered, but I'm not...I mean...I'm not a man who...I..." Alan sputtered.

"Do you not find me desirable?"

"You misunderstand, you are of course, I mean, and I think you are beautiful. Actually, you are the most beautiful woman I have ever seen. I'm not a man with any romantic inclinations. A man who does desire love would desire a woman like you. A lucky man that would be."

For a moment she looked away at the moon light shimmering on the water. She gently held her hand to his chest. He felt a strange intense vibrating sensation flow through his body.

She smiled and put her hand on his cheek, "I understand your predicament. You are simply a mandrake. Don't worry, your secret is safe with me."

"Why would you say I'm a mandrake?" he whispered.

"In your youth you loved a young man, Timothy. He was quite dashing. Regretfully it did not work out for you."

"How do you know that? I do not want to reject your advances. I've tried to force away these abnormal thoughts, I just…" he looked away.

She turned his face to her, "I do not judge your inclinations, nor should you. I believe love is pure. I will keep your secret, but never feel the need to hide from me. I accept you as you are. When I met you, I knew you were my soul mate. I still believe that," she said and swam deeper into the lake. "We are to be best of friends you and I. You'll see," she called back to him.

For the first time someone, other than Timothy, knew Alan's secret. He felt her acceptance and he felt a release that could only be defined as freedom. Smiling, he gazed up at the stars and cried. He looked out at Astrid swimming and decided he wanted to know everything about this mysterious creature in the lake.

Chapter 7

Thirty-Three

New Alessaria, California
October 13th
1869

Alan sat in his chair with his notebook open in his lap. Vera was at the piano down in the parlor and the jovial tune *Camptown Races* floated in through the open door. He flicked his pen to the melody. Astrid sipped her tea across the room looking out the window. She was dressed down in a soft pale blue housedress with little pink flowers. She poured herself into her chair and swung her legs over the armrest. She bounced her toes to the music.

"Shall we begin?" Alan said gesturing to her with his pen.

"Where did we leave off last time?" she asked.

Alan looked down at his notes, "Your father and Mr. Borrows tragically passed away and…"

"That's right, I remember. After they were killed was a hard time, obviously. I inherited my father's estate and Nathaniel had a large amount of assets as well. I didn't have to worry about such things as money and such in my time of grief."

"Good thing you got the money then."

"Good thing, is that what you said? I would give back every cent to have my father again."

"I apologize, that was insensitive. I didn't mean to imply it was all about the money."

"Forget it," she paused. "I remember being at their graves one afternoon, I don't remember exactly when, maybe a month after they passed on. I was cursing the world for leaving me alone. I was lost. Adrift. Until my Seamus."

"Seamus?"

"Seamus is the love of my life. I remember the first time I met him, it was a cool day in September. I was practicing with my sword in a clearing in the early morning. There was still dew on the blades of grass. I was wearing my father's hooded black coat and trousers. Seamus walked along thinking I was a man. I can understand why. He walked towards me and was about to speak when I heard his footsteps. I stopped just short of cutting his throat, a mean trick really. It frightened him half to death. Then when he saw I was a woman, he was dumbfounded," she chuckled.

"After the initial shock of it all I invited him in for tea. The first thing he said, in his beautiful Irish accent, was 'Will it be Irish tea? Just a wee bit of whiskey will do me." She smiled. "I said that is the only way I take my tea," she laughed. She gently touched her lips as if to touch the words from the memory.

"So, it was love at first sight?"

"Absolutely, I had never met anyone like him. First, I had never met an Irishman before. Where I came from, they were always talked about as if the whole country was poor and ignorant. Seamus was smart, funny, and handsome. He had this head of thick, curly, strawberry-blonde hair, and he was tall with a strong build. His eyes, oh, his eyes were a soulful gray-blue," she sighed. "Yes, it was love at first sight."

"Forgive me for prying, but was he Flynn's father? Does that mean you are Flynn's mother?"

"Sharp as a tack you are. Yes, he was Flynn's father. We were to be married."

"What happened? Why did you never marry?"

She looked into her tea, "He died at Bleeding Valley."

"Oh, forgive my blunder. I'm curious, why was it called the Bleeding Valley massacre?"

"The valley where it happened was called Bleeding Valley by the savages who had lived there. Alessaria is nestled in a valley in upstate New York, somewhat near the falls. The valley was littered with waterfalls and sometimes the waterfalls turned red from a trick of light. It looked like the valley itself was bleeding. I assume you have never watched a man die."

"The execution was the only time. I do not plan to do it again."

"I have too many times watched a man take his last breath. That day, the day The Cleaver attacked us, such violence changes you. Such loss. Although, there is something worse than watching a man die."

"What could be worse?"

"Watching a man die because you killed him. I took men's lives that day and remember every single one. Thirty-Three men died because of me. The Cleaver brought them there, but it was my choice. I chose my life over theirs and had the skill to do it."

"Who was this Cleaver you talk about?"

"Which one would you like to hear about, the real man or the legend?"

"Both."

"The legend is mostly about his sword and savagery. His sword was adorned accordingly with bloodstones. The legend of the bloodstone is that it was stained by the blood of The Christ. Highly symbolic. The Cleaver's name was Brother John, although he was not an official member of the church. He belonged to The Protectors of God and Innocence, the P.G.I., or as we affectionately call them, 'Piggies," Alan laughed.

"It's not a funny matter. That man and his henchmen murdered my people. Our people. They still do. We won the battle, but they survive and thrive. She cried anger-tinged tears, "Before I took his head, he told me, 'The blood of the martyr is the seed of the church.' I will never forget that. I can't forget. I held my dear Seamus, but never got to say goodbye. He was just gone." She dabbed her eyes with a handkerchief, "I defeated the Cleaver and took his bloodstone for my own. I had it fashioned into a ring," she held up her hand. "It holds a shard I broke off in the battle. Now it's mine," he looked at Astrid and no longer saw the beauty in blue, but a powerful woman with a broken heart.

Alan sat across from British Benjamin at The Drunken Fish bar. They were sitting in a private room away from the raucous crowd. Alan had recognized him from Astrid's fateful visit to heal the O'Brien boy. Up until that point they had engaged in meaningless small talk and had come to an awkward silence.
"What do you know about the massacre?" Alan blurted out.
Benjamin looked down at his ale; a thoughtful expression frozen on his face. He slowly and rhythmically tapped on his mug. Alan watched him leisurely take a sip. He slowly put the mug down and sighed.
"Are you wanting an interview? Is that what this is?" Benjamin asked and stifled a belch.
"Oh, I wasn't intending to interview you, I was just asking…" Alan said, flustered.
"You're a newsman. I'm Astrid's friend and you are writing about her. Thus, I infer that you want to know about her, not me. If not, you would be a lousy newsman."
Alan quickly pulled out his notebook, his pen and inkwell at the ready, "What can you tell me about her?"
"Ever since she was a little girl, she was extraordinary. People can be cruel when plagued by jealousy. When her

father and husband died, many people were critical when she took over her father's medical practice. The competing doctor in town said she'd never make it. She always loves to prove people wrong."

"You seem younger than me. How do you know all this?"

Benjamin grinned, "I hear things."

"She did well I assume, at doctoring?" Alan asked.

"Well? Everyone figured out she was ten times a better doctor. She almost ran him out of business. There were the few who still saw him, who believed a woman couldn't and shouldn't be a doctor," he shook his head then took a sip. "I will always be grateful to Astrid."

"For anything in particular?"

"She saved my life. I was a broken man when I met her. She gave me a reason to live. Well, you know all about that. You're a follower of her."

"Not to be rude, but not every Mover is a follower."

"I realize that, but whether you realize it or not, you're hooked. Besides, this is Mover history, follower of Astrid or not."

They both took a swig of ale and stared at each other for a minute.

"What do you believe? I don't understand this religion," Alan asked staring into his ale.

"It depends. Do you mean you in the collective sense or you in a 'me' sense?"

"Both, I guess."

"That massacre was the day Astrid became a hero. Larger than life. Outnumbered three to one, with her help, we won an un-winnable fight. She took out thirty-two all by herself."

"Thirty-three," Alan corrected.

"Pardon?"

"She told me thirty-three," Alan repeated and Benjamin looked deep into the bottom of his mug.

"She said that? Interesting. Whatever the number, it was a large share of the heavy lifting. A couple years after she moved out here, two-thirds of Alessaria followed her to this valley. You know, Astrid was one smart little bird. She bought up massive amounts of land and put Flynn in charge of selling and managing. Say what you will about his lack of politeness, he's good at what he does. He was the one who named the town New Alessaria. Although, Astrid is the real star. Not only is she our leader, but the mayor. Although, some disagree with that arrangement."

"What do you mean?"

"People, some people, believe she is in violation of the separation of church and state. These same people also do not like that she is spending town tax money for the massacre monument in the town square park. Ed has been telling her to be careful. She has a habit of not backing down."

"What do you mean by careful?"

"There have been previous assassination plots and those are just the ones we knew about. She says she knows the day she will die, so she isn't worried. Always with a flair for the dramatic, she put the date of her death in a sealed box. Upon that death the town is to open that box to find out a secret prophecy. Like I said, flair for the dramatic."

"Do you know what's in the box?"

"Let's just say you'd better finish those memoirs soon," he said and winked.

Chapter 8

Day of Remembrance

New Alessaria, California
April 14th
1870

The afternoon sun shone down through the clouds on to the river, making it glisten. Astrid's white lace dress and blue silk sash were luminescent from the light of her office window. Sipping at whiskey from a tea cup she listened to Vera playing Beethoven's *Moonlight Sonata* downstairs. The maid knocked on the open door.

"I was told you asked for me," the maid said hesitantly.

"Yes, I want you to gather the grandchildren and keep them entertained in the playroom for the remainder of the afternoon," Astrid instructed without turning from the window.

"Are they not going to the ceremony?" the maid asked with surprise.

"They are to stay here," Astrid said sternly.

"But it would be such a good experience for them, I know Miss Audrey was looking forward to it."

"You will do as I say or you will be fired. Is that clear?"

"Yes, ma'am, of course. I'll keep them in the playroom."

"Good," Astrid looked over her shoulder and saw Ed in the doorway. "You are dismissed," the maid nodded and quickly left the room. "Will there be enough guards here at the house? You don't have all your men posted at the ceremony, do you? We need some here as well, the grandchildren will be here."

"Good-afternoon to you as well," Ed chided.

"Do not sass me, not today. What about the crowd overflow?"

"My men have this covered. It has been planned and will go smoothly. You still do want to go to the ceremony, right?"

"Today we unveil the monument. How could I miss it?" Astrid looked over, worried. "My life is in your hands you know," a lump formed in her throat, making her voice waiver.

"Everything will go as planned, don't you worry," he turned to leave and then turned around. "I'll see you at the ceremony."

Astrid walked into the sitting room and saw Flynn pacing and Nadine knitting in a chair. Flynn fumed and glared at Astrid. Nadine looked up from her knitting and watched her mother and brother share an intense stare.

"Did you tell the maid to keep our children here in the house during the dedication?" he asked with clenched fists at his sides.

"I did."

"You have no right, they're our children."

"What is this about?" she asked. "I was just being cautious, I want them to be safe. Truthfully, I'm nervous about you and Nadine coming."

"We wouldn't think of missing it, would we, Flynn?" Nadine interjected.

He let out a deep sigh, "Please don't go out there today," he said choking back tears.

She was surprised that Flynn was showing his vulnerability, but she had made up her mind.

"I have an obligation to our people. I will not be a coward."

"There are people who want to murder you. You have an obligation to your family not to die."

"If it is my time, so be it. I will go out there because I do not live in fear. I love my family, never question that. It's ultimately my life and I will always live it the way I intend." Astrid started to walk away and turned back, "I hope your bitterness fades, or else you will live with a heart full of darkness. That is not a life at all. Just know that I do love you, no matter what you may think. Excuse me."

She went up to her office and closed the door. She let out a hushed moan as she slid down to the floor. She wept deep, hard tears. Her entire body heaved and she made stifled gut-wrenching wails. After what seemed like only a moment, a knock came. Astrid looked up at the walnut longcase grandfather clock and saw that she had been crying for nearly an hour.

"Ma'am, the dedication is underway and you are being called upon," the maid said through the closed door.

Astrid wiped her tears with the back of her hand and whispered, "Showtime."

Alan sat in the parlor in a spiffy new suit. He drummed his fingers excitedly on a book in his lap. The door opened and Astrid stopped in the doorway. There was no evidence of her earlier crying spell. He bounded up to greet her.

"Alan, so good to see you," she said as she kissed both his cheeks.

"I must say you look amazing. You always look amazing."

"Thank you, and you are always too kind." She saw the book in his hand, "Is that what I think it is?" she asked and he handed it to her. *"The Story of Astrid, An*

Autobiography," her eyes teared up, but she did not cry again. "Thank you, for this, I couldn't have done it without you," she said.

The maid entered the room with Astrid's shawl and gloves. She also had Alan's coat and hat.

"Ma'am, you are late and will miss it if you do not leave this instant."

"Nadine and Flynn, are they here?"

"They've already left," the maid said as she draped the shawl around Astrid's shoulders.

"Is the carriage ready?" Astrid asked as she put on her gloves.

"Yes, of course."

"What of the grandchildren?" "They're in the playroom, as requested."

"Thank you," Astrid hugged her.

"I will see you later, ma'am," the maid said looking at Astrid awkwardly.

"Alan, are you coming to the dedication ceremony?"

"I wouldn't miss it for the world."

"Then let us be off."

In the carriage, Astrid looked out the window in silence. She remembered snatching the book from Seamus and reading the passage from *Romeo and Juliet*.

She whispered under her breath, "'With this night's revels; and empire the term of a despised life, clos'd in my breast, by some vile forfeit of untimely death.'"

The carriage came to a stop, "Alan, I had a seat set aside for you next to Flynn and Nadine. We must part ways, for now."

She kissed his cheek and leapt from the carriage.

A member of The Chosen, approached her, "You arrived just in time, Mrs. Borrows, come this way," he said and pointed toward the stage.

In the center of Town Square Park was a large monument covered in a tarp. Next to the monument was a stage where Nadine and Flynn and town dignitaries sat. New Alessaria's newly retired sheriff was winding up his account of Bleeding Valley. The audience applauded after he introduced Astrid to the stage. The Chosen guard helped her up the steps. As she walked across the stage it seemed all the sounds around her muted and only Vera's rendition of *Moonlight Sonata* played in her head. She looked out over the crowd and waited for them to settle.

"Today is a day of remembrance and celebration. We are not commemorating death, but celebrating life. All pass on from this world, but few live fully and with honor. Celebrating those who lost their lives with purpose helps remind us to live our own with meaning. On this occasion, my words to you are to live life to the brim and hold back nothing. Those who are great never truly die if we always remember those who are gone. With that, I will be brief as this is about remembering the fallen, not about me. I dedicate this park, Remembrance Park, the focal point being this beautiful monument."

That was the cue for the men to pull down the tarp revealing the massive monument. As the audience cheered, Alan barely heard the loud pop and Astrid suddenly lurched. She placed her hand on her chest and he watched in horror as she lifted a bloody hand. She cascaded down onto the stage with a thud. Alan rushed to her side and saw blood pour from her chest. Her big blue eyes looked up at him and she grabbed his hand. Nadine screamed as she rushed over and Flynn stood shaking, as gray as the monument.

"Mother, are you okay?" Nadine screamed.

She placed her hand on the wound then looked at her bloodied hand. She let out a scream and laid herself over Astrid. The audience cried out in anger and scrambled about. Two guards pulled Nadine away and Alan saw Astrid close her eyes. He sobbed as her hand went limp in his. He kissed her hand and wailed. On a nearby rooftop, Edward Delving put down the smoking gun and cried as he lit a cigarette. He pulled a letter out of his pocket.

My Dearest Ed,

Our affair has been the best thing to happen in my life since I cannot remember when. I know this deed I ask of you is a lot to shoulder. But, know that I will always be with you and will forever care for you. You did right by our people. I thank you for your loyalty and service.

Until we meet again,

Astrid

He hid behind a chimney and put the letter to the end of his lit cigarette. He watched the flames consume it as he blocked out the screams of terror from below.

Chapter 9

The Battle of Bleeding Valley

Alessaria, New York
April 14th
1835

Astrid held her sword up as they heard the commotion of battle in a clearing in the woods just outside of town. It was an unseasonal snow storm, a seemingly bad omen. As they approached the clearing, Seamus made the sign of the cross and charged past the tree line. Astrid soon followed with trepidation. She saw men from the town fighting off the members of the Protectors of God and Innocence. The members took the moniker brothers because of their traditional garments, a brown monk-like robe. Their numbers were overwhelming the Movers. Three P.G.I. for every Mover funneled into the valley. Even with the Mover's varying abilities, it was no match for the deadly force that crashed down upon the men in the clearing.

Astrid felt paralyzed as snow fell. A brother swung a sword and gashed her hip. She put aside her fear and grounded her energy. She snapped his neck as two more came at her. She broke their necks and they fell in unison. She looked across the field and saw the leader. Anyone who knew his legend shuddered at his name: The Cleaver.

She saw Seamus run out of bullets and begin to use the gun as a blunt weapon. She watched The Cleaver come up behind him. She cried out for Seamus to turn around, but the wind took away her words of warning. She watched as The Cleaver's sword swung. Seamus staggered for a moment. Someone came at Astrid from the side with a sword. She dodged the swing, but it still sliced her shoulder. She felt too weak to snap his neck. She fought back, sword to sword and pushed him to the ground. After slicing his throat, she looked over but could no longer see Seamus.

She looked around the clearing in a panic but saw no trace. The snow kept falling and the biting wind blew harder. She fought her way across the clearing. Benjamin fell backward as he fought The Cleaver. Standing over Benjamin, The Cleaver brought down his sword to strike, but she blocked it.

He turned and sneered, "You must be the Satan's Plague Witch we heard about," he bellowed over the wind.

"I'm no one," she yelled with a touch of fear in her voice. "We are good people, why are you doing this to us?"

"We all know what you things really are. I will take great joy in destroying you, the Star Woman."

"I don't understand. Please, leave and stop this bloodshed," she pled.

He swung and she met his sword. She was exhausted and her powers were limited at best.

"A woman killed most of my best men. If I did not find your kind repulsive abominations, I would admire your effort."

"I will stop you," she roared and swung her sword.

He dodged her swing and let out an unsettling laugh.

"I wish you would. Killing me would make me a martyr for my brethren. Blood of the martyr is the seed of the church."

She swung, nicking his arm. He held his wound and laughed again.

"Either way, I win."

As he prepared to swing again, he stumbled and fell to his knees. She gathered all her strength and took off his head.

She limped over to the severed head and whimpered in relief. As she looked around, all of the P.G.I. were either dead or held prisoner. Her fellow Alessarians were all occupied and the wind too high to call out to them. She looked up at the tree line which were bent from the cold gusting wind.

"Why did you do this to us?" she whispered gazing up at the sky. "Why did you make me have to deal so much death? I never wanted this. Why did you turn your back on us?"

She felt ill and gently rubbed her stomach. As she looked around, she saw Seamus and staggered to him. Wincing from the several gashes as she knelt down, she touched his face but saw no life in his eyes.

"No. God, please, don't let him be dead," she whispered. "I can't live without him."

She kissed his cold lips and still no life. She tried to gather energy and sent a shock into his heart. She took his limp body in her arms and kissed him on the cheek. Her tears fell onto his face as she bent over him. She looked at her hands covered in his blood.

"No, God no," she cried out as she wiped the blood on her dress.

She rocked him back and forth and stared into his clear blue eyes. Someone draped a coat over her shoulders. She turned and saw Benjamin.

He knelt next to her, "Seamus was a good man. The Lord takes him kindly to the kingdom of heaven."

"I don't care, I want him here, why did this have to happen?" she asked quietly as she put her fingers into Seamus' curly strawberry blonde hair.

Benjamin teared up, "God only knows why a good man such as he died and we live to see another day." She wept as he took her in his arms, "We should leave this town. It's not safe anymore. I know you are in mourning, but listen to me now. You need to be a leader; you are the best of us. You can change the world."

60

"His death is on my head, Benjamin. All I can think is that I want to follow him into oblivion."

"What about your young daughter? Nadine needs her mother."

"I wish none of this happened. We lost everything."

"No, this is the day we won the battle of Bleeding Valley," he said with confidence.

"But look around. So many died needlessly, how is that victory?"

"Always know, history is what you want it to be. It's not *the* story, it's *a* story. How we all came together and fought the common enemy. We came out the victors and survived to live another day. We will write the history, that is what matters. You get to choose the story the world hears."

"But what happens now? What could the future possibly bring after so much wreckage and death? I cannot help but despair."

"You know what I always like to say is there are two rules I live by. One, I always protect the people I love. Two, I only take life an hour at a time. For this hour, we rest."

As she rested her head on his chest, she looked into the clearing and saw the gunfire smoke that had settled as a fog was starting to clear.

Part II

Chapter 10

Moonlight Sonata

New Alessaria, California
April 14th
1958

Dusk gave the road a gray hue and redwood trees lining the road seemed ominous. A couple in their early twenties in a Belfast-green Pontiac Chieftain zipped down the winding road. The trees reminded her of the tree scene from *The Wizard of Oz*. Her hands clutched onto her large protruding stomach. She was in an off-the-shoulder emerald-green cocktail dress that still felt more like maternity wear than glamor. Her eyes were wide and her heart sped along with the car. She looked over at her husband at the wheel, a stump of a cigarette hung limply from his lips.

"Damn it, slow down," she cried out.

The man slowly let his foot off the gas. He took the cigarette out of his mouth and extinguished it in the ashtray. He cleared his throat and gave her a quick sly glance.

"Quite the mouth you've got there, sweetheart. You shouldn't use such profanity around the kid, for Christ's sake," he noticed the drumming of her fingers on the car door. "Are you nervous, Evie?"

She stopped and placed her hands back on her stomach, "Of course I'm nervous. I haven't seen my family since the wedding. That's over six months ago. You know how they get under my skin."

"Honey, don't get so upset, it's not good for the baby."

"Thank you, Doctor Spock," she said and rolled her eyes.

"Would you grab me another smoke?"

She floated the pack of cigarettes up and it hovered as she willed one out of the pack. Then she floated it to a hovering lighter. She took a drag and then gave it to him. As she floated the pack and lighter back to their home, she noticed something peculiar about the lighter. She floated it back. It appeared to be an antique and of great value.

"Hon, what a neat lighter."

"Yep."

"I've never seen this lighter before, why is that?"

"My mom gave that to me last night while you were at the baby shower. It's a family heirloom. It belonged to my grandfather or great-grandfather, I don't remember which. Whoever he was, he brought it from Russia during the revolution or something. She said since it's just her and I family wise I should have the heirloom. It's sweet that she did give it to me. It breaks my heart, I know she doesn't have much longer. I wish she could have come tonight," he paused. "Although, it's not as valuable as your little future heirloom. You know, a certain bloodstone ring. Do you think Astrid found it in a Cracker Jack box and didn't tell anyone?"

"Don't mock me. Who I am, or should I say whom I'm related to, is very important to me."

"Sorry, I'm a little nervous about tonight, too. You know, seeing your entire family in one evening."

"You should do..." her voice trailed off.

There was a long pause, "What? You should do...what?"

"Never mind."

"I don't like it when you start to say something and then stop. Besides, I think it's ridiculous that we're going to this thing anyway. You are very pregnant, should you be going to whatever kind of party this is. What is it called again? Day of Remembrance, right? Of all days, too. I looked it up and today Abraham Lincoln was shot and the Titanic sank. Then the beloved Astrid was martyred. I mean who has a party for a person's death anyway?" he said, gesturing with his cigarette.

"I know you're Jewish, but have you ever heard of Easter," she retorted.

"Easter is the resurrection, so that doesn't count. I do know some things."

"Astrid died proudly leading our people. We're celebrating her life, the sacrifice she made, and the prophecy."

"This all seems strange to me. What kind of religion is this anyway?"

"Just because you're not an Astridian doesn't mean that you have the right to pass judgment. Also, it's not a religion, but more a community and a culture. There are so many out there who hate Movers. Astridian or non-Astridian, we shouldn't squabble amongst ourselves."

"Sometimes I hate being born a Mover. The gift as we call it is a God damn burden I would rather not bare. What's the big deal about being able to move things with your mind?" his voice raised in volume.

"I'm not going to discuss these things with you when you're in this mood. Also, don't take the lord's name in vain."

"I'm not in a 'mood' as you call it."

"I don't want to get into a theological debate with you."

"I thought you said Astridianism is not a religion and theology is about religion."

"Don't be a smart ass, you know what I meant. Besides what I believe in is my business."

"Don't tell me you believe? Even in that prophecy?"

"I certainly do," Evie said with confidence.

"Let me get this straight, you believe that Astrid will be reborn in your bloodline to save the world?"

"Don't mock me."

"You have red hair and isn't that the sign? Does that make you the reincarnation of Astrid?"

"I have auburn hair, you should know this. Besides, that isn't the only criteria."

"Tell me," he demanded.

"You don't care, you're just mocking me."

"Seriously, tell me, I want to know. What if our kid is the reincarnated Astrid? Shouldn't the father know such things?"

"Alright, the prophecy says that the reincarnation of Astrid will have red hair, a pyramid birthmark, and the strength of Thirty-three men. In the meantime, my mother is the current Keeper, the designated leader of our people. When mother passes on, I am first in line to be the next Keeper. So on and so forth until Astrid returns."

"Isn't it a lot of pressure? I know if I was destined to be the leader of a religion, I mean community, just by being born, I would crack up."

"I was meant to be born into my family, it's my destiny. I know that when I become Keeper there will be a time of adjustment. But, that isn't going to happen for a long time so why think about it. You should have known this, the prophecy is part of the fundamentals of Astridianism."

"You know how I was raised. My parents thought Astridians were a cult. How ironic, I'm married to the future leader of a group my parents despised. Wait, is that irony?"

"I don't want to talk about this anymore," she said. There was a long pause, "Hershel?"

"What?"

"Do you think this is a bad idea?"

He lifted one eyebrow, "Can you narrow that down?"

"Moving in with my parents. Do you think it's a bad idea?"

"It was your idea," he pointed out.

"I know it was my idea. But now I'm not so sure."

"Remember why we decided to move in with them in the first place?"

"For the baby. We couldn't afford to live on what you make. I know all that. But they don't like you."

"They have to like me, I'm a likeable guy."

"Be serious."

"I am serious, I'm quite the charmer," he grinned with the cigarette between his teeth.

"They only see you as the boy who got me 'in trouble.'"

"We were engaged for Christ's sake. Hop and a skip from the wedding. We just got a head start. Besides, your dad knocked up your mom with you when she was fifteen. Also, if they hate me so much, why did they buy us this car for our wedding?"

"They still don't like you."

"Because I'm not rich and a non-Astridian, right? That's so pretentious. Look, I can use big words, I can even spell it. P-R-E-T-E-N-T-I-O-U-S. Damn elitists."

"That reminds me, don't curse around my family. I want you to make a good impression."

He snapped his fingers, "Damn it," he said and she glared at him. "What? I'm getting it out of my system."

"The good part is that it does show promise that they're letting us live with them. They could learn to love you, like I did. Besides, it's a big house."

"That's no house," he pointed up to the Borrows manor on the hill.

"It's home to me. Remember no cursing or sass tonight."

"Women sass, men kid."

They pulled into the first driveway. A short older man was in a guard station.

She rolled down her window, "Working hard or hardly working?" she said and the guard laughed and tipped his cap.

"You kids enjoy the party tonight. Nice to see you Miss Evie," the guard said and opened the massive gates.

They drove up the long winding main driveway of the estate. At the top of the driveway he pulled into the garage next to five other cars, one of which was a Rolls-Royce. He jogged around the car and opened the door for his wife. With a loud grunt he helped her out of the car.

"Jeez, you're heavy."

"I'm almost nine months pregnant, you'd be heavy, too," she scolded. She looked at the other cars, "We're way too early."

"You said you wanted to come early so you could lie down before the party."

"I know what I said. I was hoping there was going to be someone here to take the heat off us. No offense to my mother, but she can be a little on the stiff side," she sighed. "Lying down does sound good."

He helped put on her black dress coat. She gathered up her long auburn hair to avoid getting it caught. After her coat was on she let her hair cascade down. The beautiful little moment made him smile.

"There are five cars here," he pointed out.

"Those are my parents' cars. Now remember, I'm seventh generation blood relation to Astrid. My mother is the 6th Keeper, the first was Astrid's daughter, Nadine. People will tell you if they are from Astrid's bloodline, they like to flaunt it. If not, all of us of the bloodline will be wearing a red rose. Oh and never, never take Astrid's name in vain or mock our community around anyone here tonight. This is a very important night. Mother invited the Flynn Patrick descendants tonight. You know, Flynn Patrick was Astrid's Godson?"

"That was a lot of information. I can't remember all that."

"I have faith in you. Oh and honey…you need to shave."

"Nag, nag, nag," he said with a playful smile.

After a walk from the garage to the front door Evie was already exhausted. Hershel rang the doorbell with trepidation.

A silver-haired maid answered the door, "Miss Evie," the maid squealed and hugged her enthusiastically.

"This is my husband, Hershel."

"I know this is Hershel, child. Y'all had a party here after the weddin', remember? Come on in out of the cold, Miss Evie. Hershel, too."

The maid whisked way both their coats as Hershel stood in amazement at how dazzling the manor was, even just the foyer. He went over to a row of framed photos.

"Was this Astrid?" he asked, pointing to a sepia toned photograph.

"Seriously?" she said with a look of derision.

"There's only the one photo of her and it's not even a good photo. Excuse me for showing an interest."

"Sorry, I'm extra cranky. Yes that's Astrid. It's a copy, the original is in storage. I've thought about establishing a library or local museum. We have a beautiful portrait she had commissioned in her youth. I feel all that stuff should be out where people can see it."

"The rest of the photos are all women?" he gestured to the 5 other photos, then pointed to the last, "That's your mom."

"Yes these are all the Astridian Keepers. Nadine, Vera..."

The maid burst in, "Your mother has been asking after you. I'll take you on in to her, you know how she gets."

"Here we go," he said under his breath.

They looked into the large ballroom busy with people. Staff were moving tables and organizing elaborate place settings. Beethoven's *Moonlight Sonata* played in the background in contrast to the high energy organized chaos. A graceful woman vibrantly dressed in red stood in the middle calling out orders like a symphony conductor. She turned and gave a forced but polite smile. He noticed the bloodstone ring for the first time, as she only wore it on special Astridian occasions. He was surprised by its large size.

"Hello, my darling," she said as she hugged Evie. She touched his shoulder, "Hello, Hershel," she said while continuing to smile politely.

"Mother, we are going to go up to our room, if you don't mind? Hershel needs to shave and I want to rest up before the party. Did our things arrive okay?"

"I had it taken care of. Don't tell me that you have been dressed up since this morning?"

"No, Mother. We changed just before coming, the clothes we we're wearing and other things are in the car."

"Let me have the boy fetch all that," she snapped her fingers at a young man moving chairs.

Before he rolled down his sleeves Evie saw a glimpse of a tattoo on his left arm of a red rose wrapped around Astrid's sword and her first initial.

"Bring in my daughter's things from the car."

"Yes, Mrs. Goldbarry," he said as he rushed out the door.

"Skittish little fellow," she said and shook her head.

"We're going to go upstairs now, Mother," Evie said as she gave Hershel's arm a little tug.

"That's fine. I cannot chit-chat, I just do not have the time. I put your things in your old room, since we are still fixing up your permanent room next to the nursery."

"Thank you," she said and her mother resumed calling out orders.

Hershel helped her navigate up the East staircase. Halfway up, the young man with their suitcases bounded up the stairs.

"Hey you," Evie said in a hushed tone. The young man heard and turned is head. She motioned with her finger for him to come closer.

"Yes, Miss?"

"Don't let my mother see that tattoo on your arm or she'll fire you so quick your head will spin clear off," she said. The young man nodded. "You can finish what you were doing now," she said and he bolted up the stairs.

"What was that about?" Hershel asked as he helped her up the rest of the staircase.

"I'll tell you in the room."

Upon entering the room, it was disturbing how it was exactly the same as the day she left.

"Where are the boxes?" he asked. She pointed to the dressers and opened the second drawer to the top, "My socks," he exclaimed. "They put away all of our belongings?"

"What do you expect? Today my parents have more people working here than the Titanic. Are you surprised they had someone unpack for us?"

He retrieved his shaving kit from his suitcase, "I'm going to shave now, just following orders."

"Hush up, you. Remember, no sass tonight," she called out. "Take off your jacket, you don't want to get shaving cream on it," a tuxedo jacket flew at her. "And unbutton your shirt; you don't want it to get wet."

"Yes, dear. What did you tell that guy?"

She folded his jacket over a chair, "I told him to cover his tattoo around my mother," she said as she sat on the bed and took off her shoes.

"What's the big deal with a tattoo? Would your mom completely flip her Tupperware lid over a tattoo?"

She heard the sound of water splashing, "When did you become such a rebel? Don't get your shirt wet."

"I just believe that it's their body and they can do whatever they want to it."

When he came out cleanly shaven, he sported a large grin as he buttoned his shirt.

"Did you clean up in there? You know how I despise whiskers in the sink."

"Nag, nag, nag. Tell me more about this tattoo, you have me curious now."

"You know about The Chosen?"

"They're the guys who guarded Astrid, right? Now they're a version of the mob or something."

"He had a tattoo that means he is in The Chosen. My parents are strictly against being associated with them."

"What does it look like? So I'll be able to recognize it."

"Shouldn't you know this?"

"I'm not an Astridian, remember?"

"Of course I remember. That's one reason my parents don't like you."

"What's this tattoo look like anyhow?"

"It's a rose wrapped around Astrid's sword and her initial."

"Nifty. Are you against those fellas, too?"

"I don't think they're all bad. They do a lot for the community. You better let me rest before the party starts."

"When does the party start again?"

"It is supposed to start at eight. But won't start until at least nine and dinner will be at ten."

"That sure is late."

"Don't be a fuddy-duddy. You'd better get used to it."

"All the other parties I've been to here were not that late."

She rubbed her eyes, "Hershel, I mean what I'm about to say with love. Shut up and let me nap."

"Alright, I'll read my book."

"Don't sit up here reading that science fiction junk. Go down and mingle with my family."

He put on his tuxedo jacket and wiggled his bowtie.

"How do I look?"

"Amazing, dahling," she said like Tallulah Bankhead.

"Hon, can I ask you something?"

72

"Alright," she said impatiently.

"It's just that…I don't see why my mother couldn't be invited to this thing. After all, she's now technically family."

"Can we not get into this right now?"

"Come on."

"Okay, according to my parents unless, you are a blood relation to Astrid or are married to blood, you're not invited. Besides, why would she care? She's not Astridian. Oh and if you forgot she called me your Astridian tramp."

"That was once. It doesn't seem in the spirit of family to hold a grudge."

"Even if she wasn't a bigot, it's the rules baby. Blood is blood. Go downstairs, and don't forget to come get me when everyone arrives."

"I won't forget."

"Now get out of here."

"I love you, too. Don't let the bed bugs bite."

A loud bang woke Evie from her deep sleep. It was dark, except for a stream of light coming in from under the door. She sat up and listened to more bangs and screaming. Her stomach sank and she was afraid to move for a moment. Grunting, she got up and sped as fast as she could to the door. With a deep breath, she opened it. The bangs and screaming were deafening in the hallway. She quickly waddled over to the railing and looked down at the foyer below with trepidation.

She saw her little cousin running across the foyer and a man with a gun chasing him. He fired and the boy fell to the ground. She screamed, and the gunman saw her standing at the rail. As she turned she felt her body lurch as if someone pushed her. She stumbled back into the room and locked herself in the bathroom. She placed her hand on her shoulder and to her horror her hand was covered in blood. She started to hyperventilate. Shaking her head, she told herself to calm down.

In a panic, she looked around the bathroom. Tears flowed down her face and her chest heaved with sobs. On the counter she saw the straight-edged razor Hershel used to shave. She picked it up and held it tightly. She heard someone breaking down the door to the bedroom and with her mind she turned the light off. She stepped into the bathtub and pulled the curtain shut. She tried to quiet her breathing. Through a gap in the curtain she saw boots blocking the light from under the door. She floated the razor in front of her.

"God forgive me," she whispered.

A man kicked in the bathroom door and opened the curtain. Laughing, he pointed the gun at her. The razor flew piercing the man's neck and sending out a spray of blood. After a long unsettling gurgling sound his body fell to the ground with a thud. Slowly and awkwardly, she picked up the gun. She shook uncontrollably, holding the gun against her chest. Police sirens graced her ears and she sighed in relief.

"God, let me be saved."

She felt a creeping wet sensation between her legs. She lifted her dress and saw fluid in the bathtub. Touching it, she realized her water broke.

"Police, stop," she heard a man yell and shots fired.

After some time passed, she heard "All clear on the first floor."

"Go check the second level," another yelled.

She closed her eyes and whispered, "Thank you, God."

A shadow came into the room, "Police, anyone in here?"

"Help," she said meekly. The policeman stepped over the body and turned on the light. He gasped at seeing the blood sprayed all about the room. Pulling back the shower curtain, he saw her sitting in the tub quivering violently.

"Are you hurt?" she could not speak, but nodded. "I'm going to leave you for a moment to get help, hold on." He left the room, and yelled over the rail, "I found Evelyn Rose,

74

she needs a doctor," then came back into the room. He knelt down, "Can you walk?" she nodded, nearly blinded by tears. He helped her to the stairs, "I need you to close your eyes and I'll help you down the steps," he said and she nodded. At the bottom of the staircase he had her sit, "Keep your eyes shut, I'll be right back."

She heard his footsteps leave. She knew she should not open her eyes, but she did. Across from her against the wall was Hershel. A bullet hole in his forehead and a river of blood glistened on his face. His eyes were wide open and his mouth contorted. She did not realize she was screaming until after the officer grabbed hold of her. The record player was still playing, Beethoven's *Moonlight Sonata,* the soundtrack to the repeated scenes of horror around her. She vomited to the side and stumbled. Upon trying to stand up she had her first contraction.

The medic brought over a gurney, "Mrs. Rose, we need to take you to the hospital."

"I can't have my baby, not like this," she said to the officer holding her up.

The officer looked into her eyes, "Is there anyone we can call?"

"I want my mother," she cried out. The officers shared a knowing look

"Is there a friend we can call?" another officer asked.

"Mother didn't make it, did she?" she asked and the officer looked away. "I'll take anyone. What about my Aunt..." she looked around at the officer's faces and felt faint. She gritted her teeth, "Who's left? My family, who's left?"

The officer took his cap off and tears welled up in his eyes, "Just you, Mrs. Rose."

Her legs buckled and the first officer caught her. He carried her to the gurney and started to walk away.

She grabbed his hand, "Don't leave me, please. I don't want to be alone."

"I will stay by your side for as long as you need, Mrs. Rose."

At the hospital the officer came into the maternity room and saw her holding her baby boy. She looked up and smiled.

"Beautiful, isn't he?" she asked and he nodded as he removed his cap. "Officer...I never asked your name, but thank you," she looked down at her son. Tearing up she said, "We thank you. What is your name?"

"Billy Gondory."

"Go by William, it is a more distinguished name."

"Speaking of names, what are you going to name him?"

"We were going to name him Morris after Hershel's grandfather. But now it feels like there's only one name that will do. William, meet Hershel Rose."

"A fitting tribute."

She looked down at her son, "I just know he will do grand things."

"I'm sure you're right."

"Of course I'm right. Just you watch, my boy will save us all."

Chapter 11

The Three Faces of Astrid

Flynn, Kansas
April 15th
1958

Astrid opened the front door with hesitation. She wore a pale blue silk robe and held a tumbler of whisky. Ben stood on her doorstep holding up the morning paper. The news of the Borrows Manor Massacre was splashed across the front page. She threw back the whisky as she opened the door wide. With a nod, she walked back into the house and Ben followed. He watched as she poured herself another drink.

"Day drinking?" he said as he sat down in the living room.

"Are you judging me?" she asked, pointing the bottle at him.

"I learned a long time ago that in life, hard situations require prayer or drinking."

She sat her glass and the bottle on the coffee table. She curled under a white knitted wool blanket as she looked out the window at the flat Kansas field.

"What does having all but one of my bloodline murdered by the P.G.I. via your mother's orders require? Drink or Prayer?"

"Both, excessively. I'm far too sober for the conversation we need to have," he floated a glass over from the kitchen.

"I wish I could reach out to Evelyn, she must be feeling so alone right now. But I am technically dead to the world. It would be jarring for Evie to meet her never-aged long lost ancestor."

"She's your great-great granddaughter?" he asked, eyeing up the whisky bottle.

"I think you could add a couple more greats, but after two does it matter anymore?"

"Have you been to the cinema lately?"

"Don't make small talk, it's not the time."

He poured himself a drink. As he held the glass he used his energy to frost it.

"Plug the sass. I saw *The Three Faces of Eve* at the cinema a little while back. It reminded me of you."

"Are you comparing me to a mad woman with multiple personalities? How is that a flattering comparison?"

"Hear me out. You may not have three separate personalities, but you do have three distinct ways in which you deal with different people; three faces if you will. There's your public face, the way you are presented in that hogwash book of yours, etcetera etcetera. You even edited out your own son from your life story. The second face is how you are around people you like, even those you love. Then there's the third face, your only real face. The woman I'm speaking to now, I would guess I'm one of the only people to actually know you. The real you. I watch you put on those faces as if they were masks and it's interesting to watch the different performances."

"You make me sound like a play within a play. How very *Hamlet*. Is this going to be a lecture on being true to who I really am?"

He took a swig, "Not in the slightest. I think it's brilliant. I encourage using those masks. You're great at it. I love the real you, Astrid, you know that. You are like a daughter to me and I see you as what you are. It's fitting that you used the rose as your symbol, as it's beautiful, sweet, and delicate.

Even the rose knows to grow thorns to protect itself. I would call my Jocelyn my Rose, before things went wrong."

He picked up the bottle and smiled, pointing at the label, "If you're drinking Jack Daniels, you must have known I was coming. You do know it's my favorite. You only drink it when I'm here."

"I never understood that. You have tasted and have access to some of the best spirits the world has to offer. But you claim Jack Daniels to be your favorite."

"Simple. People strive their whole lives for the pursuit of perfection. To iron out life's bumps and sand down the rough edges. The longer I've been around, I realize that beauty and life's meaning is in those imperfections. I've tasted the most expensive whiskeys in the world. But, they lack soul. The bite, the notes of bitter, the burn, which is where the soul is."

"You're comparing me to a crazy woman and saying Jack Daniels has...a soul? How much in the bag were you when you walked in?"

"Don't fault me for the needing of liquid courage to knock on your door. It has been decades since you abandoned your faithful lap dog and yours truly. It was quite cruel to leave him in the wind like that."

"Don't talk about Alan like that," she snapped. "How is he doing?"

"I kept tabs on him over the years on your behalf. He found love and did well in spite of the pain you caused him."

"It had to be done," she said wiping condensation from her glass.

"Are you quite done sulking? Flynn's suicide is not on your bill."

She took a long sip and set the glass down. She folded her legs and looked at him square.

"I wish to make a pledge with you. No, a vow. No more secrets between us, no more games, only the truth. We will protect those truths and each other. Agreed?" she said holding out her pinky.

"A pinky swear? You must be kidding?"

"Would you rather we do a blood oath?"

He put his glass down and reluctantly put out his pinky, "I feel like a right ass, but I agree to our vow."

She sat back and tucked her legs underneath herself again, "Flynn didn't kill himself."

He took a large swig, "Run that by me again. The whole reason you've been in God forsaken Kansas is that you were distraught over Flynn's suicide."

"That was a lie. Like I said, only truth from now on. His wife Anne didn't contact me about gambling debts or his commitment to an asylum. None of that was true, he had cancer and he didn't have long. We made peace at the end. I have so many regrets, but I will never regret going to see him that last time. I told him everything."

"Wait, what exactly did you confess to Flynn?"

"Like I said, I told him everything. That my father John Cooper was not the good man I made him out to be. He was a cruel drunk who beat and defiled me. Then I was married off to Nathaniel, who was just as twisted and cruel. I don't know what I would have done if it wasn't for you. You saved me."

"Astrid, you saved yourself, I just took care of the bodies."

"It was the first time I was honest with anyone, besides you. Even with you, there's the game we play. I pretend the bad things didn't happen, and you help me create the new story for the world. Like what happened to Seamus. The truth does not like to stay buried."

"You do remember what happened? Sometimes I didn't know if you believed your own fictions."

"I always remember. Flynn handled it better than expected."

"You didn't tell him how his father died, did you?"

She looked up with tears gathering in her eyes, "After telling him what really happened, Flynn's greatest kindness was not only his forgiveness, but he gave me the key to forgiving myself. For years I was paralyzed with the guilt. It was easy to say The Cleaver killed him. Many saw them fight and Seamus struck down. Only you actually saw. Even thinking of that P.G.I. bastard makes me sick, that man was pure evil. It took everything I had to kill him. When I was grabbed from behind I reacted. That's it. It was a heat of the battle reaction."

"I saw it all, there was nothing I could do," he said, choking up and wiping away a tear. "I wished when you said The Cleaver killed our Seamus that you actually believed it."

"After telling Flynn, he absolved me of blame. It wasn't Seamus' fault either. He had never been near that kind of violence. He trusted he could approach me from behind. He was wrong. I no longer carry the burden of guilt for his death. Out of the years upon years I've lived, I wish I could forget that moment. A moment of mere seconds. The moment I watched him clutching at his throat," she held her stomach and her body shook. "I can still smell the stench of his blood mixed with snow and gunpowder. I reacted to what I thought was someone attacking. But it was him, not an attacker, him. That fact destroyed me. You saved my life after that, too, you know. You took me under your wing, protected me, and turned me into an Everblood. But, Flynn, my son, he saved my soul."

She poured more whiskey and chilled the glass with her energy. She wiped her tears and paused as she took a long sip.

"It was his idea. All of this was his idea," she said with a smile. "I came to realize, as long as I was with Alan, he couldn't be happy. He needed a life of his own, at least for a while. He needed to fall in love. He needed his own Seamus. He needed his freedom."

Ben sat back and let out a massive sigh, "I didn't realize you really were such a martyr. Hiding alone in the middle of nowhere for years, without a word. Lying to everyone about Flynn's death. Are you quite done on your cross? We need the wood," he scoffed and threw back his whiskey.

"I never said I was alone," she said avoiding eye contact.

He winced, then poured more whiskey. He took a deep breath and then two sips. After gritting his teeth, he rolled his neck.

"Who?" he asked pointedly.

"You're not going to like the answer."

"Who?" he raised his volume.

She looked into her drink and whispered, "Jocelyn."

"Jocelyn. As in my ex-wife Jocelyn. The woman who destroyed me. The devil that...what she did....her evil betrayal...she was here...you..." he stammered as he stood.

Sobbing so hard she couldn't speak, she nodded. He threw his glass against the wall, shattering it. He let out a long, anguished roar. He stumbled. Then fell to the floor. She winced, and wrapped her arms around herself. He propped himself up against the couch. He put his hand in his hair and sighed.

"Okay, we can do this. We can do this. I can do this," he said looking up at her. "I'm ready. Tell me. I promise to stay as collected as possible. I honor our vow, tell me the truth. I can take it."

She took a deep breath and sat on the floor in front of him. She took his hand and the tears fell. She felt him shaking and touched his cheek.

"I know what she did. There is no excuse for what she did to you. For what she did to them..." Astrid paused as her voice cracked. "I knew you were protecting me from her. Now I understand why you didn't tell me she was my mother. She told me what that ultimately means, that she's my biological mother."

He rubbed his temple and tears flowed down his trembling cheeks, "I don't give credence to my mother's crackpot theory."

"But she believes it, which makes her dangerous. I shouldn't exist. You know Everblood women can't give birth after the transformation. It is impossible for us to conceive naturally. No one has ever been able to, except my mother. I don't believe in your mother's prophecy, but you can't deny what I am. I had a birth of impossibility."

"Jocelyn told you about the Star Woman prophecy I take it?" he said crossing his arms.

"The prophecy is that your mother's equal will be someone called the Star Woman. A woman with an impossible birth that has the strength of over thirty men and cradles the stars in her arm. The Star Woman will match her in power and all abilities. The choice will come for the Star Woman to either destroy or save her. But your mother desperately fears the former and wants to find the Star woman and kill her."

"It would only feed her delusions if she found out that Jocelyn is your mother," he said and wiped his tears. His eyes widened and he looked over at her in utter terror, "Where is Jocelyn now?"

Astrid cringed and her face contorted with heavy crying, "Danika's goons found her yesterday. She must have found out the truth because…that happened." She pointed to the headline on the newspaper about the massacre at Borrows Manor. "Ben, I'm frightened. I need you to forgive me, because I need you. I don't know what to do."

He took three deep breaths and looked over at her, "Remember the two rules I live by? I defend the people I love and I take life an hour at a time. What are we going to do this hour?"

She smiled and wiped her tears, "For this hour, we rest."

Chapter 12

Drink the Kool-Aid

Borrowstown, California
April 12th
1986

T he college lecture hall was a bustle with over two hundred students and faculty. A man in his late twenties walked in and felt the buzzing energy of the room. He sat in his seat and, refreshingly, no one seemed to notice him. A man in a sixties-era suit tapped the microphone, booming a shrill reverberation through the hall. People covered their ears and winced.

"We are about to start, will everyone please be seated quickly," he said and the crowd settled. "I would first off like to thank you all for attending this week's Borrowstown Community College Saturday lecture series. This hour we welcome four prominent members of the Mover community. Our first speaker was part of the team behind the first Mover history textbook, which many of you know we gladly assign here. Please welcome our esteemed guest, Doctor Jon Rose."

The audience applauded raucously as he stood. He nervously smoothed his chocolate-brown hair and looked over the crowd. He strategically arranged his notecards.

"How are you all doing today?" he said as the clapping died down. "I don't know why you all are here on a Saturday to hear me talk. You must lead boring lives," the crowd collectively chuckled. "Now, I want to get something out of the way. How many of you had heard about me before this

84

lecture?" The majority of the crowd raised their hands. "For those of you who don't know, all two of you, I'm the descendant of Astrid Borrows, or for those familiar, eighth generation. My mother, Evelyn Rose, is the current Keeper of the Astridians. Yes, my name was Hershel and is now Jon. There will be no more questions or answers about my family, especially my mother. Hit the lights."

The projector on a stand whirred and a photograph of Astrid appeared on the screen.

"As you all probably know this is a photograph of our beloved Astrid Borrows. This picture was taken right before her death in 19…um… I meant *18*, 1870," he cleared his throat and looked down at his feet.

He scanned the audience and saw a familiar man scowling at him from the third row.

"An Astridian is a follower of Astrid's teachings and the Astridian ideals. Astridianism has no affiliation with any religion and is not itself a religion, more of a community. How many of you here today are Astridians?" Most of the audience raised their hands. "That is about par for the course in this area. In the three cities that make up Borrows county 71 percent of inhabitants classify themselves as Astridians. Not all Movers are Astridians, nor are all Astridians Movers. There are a few non-gifted individuals who follow Astridianism. Those who choose to put up with us Movers voluntarily are braver souls than I."

"I'm now going to discuss a chapter of Mover history known as the Freedom Battle," a projection slide of Europe circa 1350 C.E. appeared. "Let's back up a step to the beginning. The first evidence of Movers was in the late 14th century, in the area we now know as East France and West Germany. Our gifts are now referred to as psychokinetic ability. This ability only emerges during the onset of puberty, as if being a teenager wasn't taxing enough," there was a ripple of muffled giggles. All Movers display a birthmark known as the Mark of Alessar."

The slide switched to a one-inch pink kidney bean shaped birthmark on the back of the neck. Jon turned around and pulled down his shirt collar revealing the same birthmark. Then turned back towards the audience.

"The birthmark in the 14th century was believed to be a sign of witchcraft. Many were put to death, as they were believed to be part of the occult. That is where the slur Satan's plague witch started, as many blamed the Movers for the onslaught of the black plague. However, in spite of this persecution and the decimation of Europe by the plague, our numbers grew. A French king, Henry of Navarre, declared the banishment of all Movers from his cities and villages. With other nations on the continent following suit, many emigrated to Britain. Established around this time was the radical organization Protectors of God and Innocence. They were in support of banning all Movers. For several decades Movers lived in neutral territories and even formed their own style of government. This uneasy truce did not last.

"The P.G.I. were ordered to wipe out the Mover settlements. It is believed that the infamous Cardinal Richelieu sent the order. This was a man who said 'If you give me six lines written by the most honest man, I will find something in them to hang him.' It cannot be proven that it was him, but historians have their suspicions."

The slide changed to a painting of a young man on a horse waving a sword valiantly. His long blonde hair blown back revealing his stalwart face.

"This was Benjamin Alessar IV, a decedent of one of the first Movers. You'll recognize him from those glorified bedtime stories we read as children. What we do know is that Benjamin Alessar IV led Movers in a fight against the attacking P.G.I. They won what is now known as the Freedom Battle." He looked into the crowd and the scowling man stood up to leave.

"When the first Mover settlement was established in this country they honored this well-loved folk hero of our history by naming it Alessaria. In 1855, Astrid Borrows established the West Coast's New Alessaria. I believe you've had enough out of me since you know the rest, Astrid was assassinated, birth of Astridianism, etcetera etcetera. Your next speaker is the esteemed virologist, and my dear friend, talking about the Daffodils, correct?" Jon looked over and got a thumbs up. "I will let Robbie, I mean the great Doctor Robert Delving Jr., take over the mic. Thank you for your time and ears on this lovely day," the audience applauded as the men shook hands.

"Thank you, Jon-boy, I mean Doctor Rose. I do love your brand of public speaking, Jon. Isn't he a hoot? We went to the same alma matter and the stories I could regale you with, stories that would put hair on your chest," Jon shook his head while laughing along with the audience. "Many of you may recognize my family name, as the Delvings were among the founding families of New Alessaria. My father developed the widely used Delving Ability Scale, for which I am proud to say he will be receiving an Apple award shortly for this achievement. Doctor Rose here will also be getting an Apple award. For me, always a bridesmaid, never a bride I suppose. Right, enough silliness."

"As it was said I'm Doctor Robert Delving Jr. and my field of study is virology. The science wing students may have been forced to read my paper on the Mover malady Daffodils. For that I sincerely apologize, but it does make a decent doorstop. Thanks to modern science, and the vaccine, the Daffodils disease was eradicated before many of us were born. Let's jump right in, shall we? Hope you all enjoyed your breakfast this morning," he clicked to the first slide and the audience groaned in disgust.

Jon looked at his watch and slipped out of the lecture hall. In the hallway, the scowling man from the third row approached him. He was a heavyset man, with balding grey hair and a gray mustache. His eyes peered out from large black-rimmed glasses. He was in his fifties, but looked at least twenty years older.

"Stuart Sark in the flesh. How's it going, S.S. Commander?" Jon said, laughing.

"Yes, I'm aware of my initials. That joke is not funny and never will be funny. I see you're wearing one of those newfangled watches. What do you think of it?"

"Stu, I've known you too long to buy your small talk. Cut the foreplay, what do you
want?"

"I heard through the grapevine that you are visiting your mother while in town. Possibly even lodging with her at Borrows Manor."

"You heard correctly, what of it?" Jon said, glancing again at his watch.

"Evie told me to remind you she has quite a few appointments over the week and may not always available to be the proper hostess."

"I lived with her for eighteen years, I remember that community comes first. I see you're still her faithful lap dog, eh?"

"I've known you from diapers, show some respect."

"Fine, I'm sorry."

Jon walked away and Stuart followed alongside. Jon always thought of Stuart as his mother's henchman, always at her disposal.

"Why are you following me? Don't you have anything better to do?"

"I'm worried about your mother."

"Okay, I'll bite. Why?" Jon said without breaking his stride.

"She's upset about the Apple Awards…that she can't go see you accept your award."

"She won't go."

"Semantics," Stuart growled.

They reached the end of the hallway and went out the double doors. The sunlight was fierce and Jon reached into his pocket to retrieve his sunglasses.

"You know what April 14th means to your mother. Hell, even to you. I think it is stupid for the awards to be on the same day as the massacre anniversary. It's just plain insensitive."

"My birthday," Jon said under his breath.

"Excuse me?"

"I said, my birthday. April 14th is also my birthday. Mother has told me for many years that she didn't have the strength to celebrate my birthday. Because of what that means. What kind of bullshit is that?"

"Listen to me you little twerp, you should respect what happened that day. Don't disrespect it with talk of lost birthdays."

Jon stopped at the bottom of the steps and looked at a twisted dying tree to his right. He wondered how it had become so gnarled. He wondered if it was wind, disease, or simple neglect. He put his hand in his pocket and felt his wallet, the worn leather seemed comforting. He recalled that it was the first present his wife gave him when they were dating.

"I can sympathize with what happened to my mother that night, but I will never understand it from her perspective. It took me many years to figure that one out, not to mention the time in therapy. I know that she won't be there when I accept my award. Besides, I don't think I deserve an A.P.L. award. I barely contributed to the textbook and I hate doing these lectures. They make me feel like a pompous know-it-all. Maybe I am a pompous know-it-all. I know the only reason I'm getting the damn award is because of who I am, well who I'm related to, to be exact."

"These awards are not just about the recipients, they help strengthen the Mover community," Stuart clasped his hands in a symbol of unity. "The Astridians for Peace League are good people, they help the cause."

"Whenever you talk about it as 'the cause' you make us sound like a cult."

"We are not a cult. Not even in the same universe as crackpots like The People's Temple. There's no Kool-Aid drinking going on here and your mother sure as hell isn't a Jim Jones. We are a legitimate community, unassociated with monotheistic religions. The awards are a form of outreach and encourage Movers to strive for greatness, but also give back."

Jon walked into the parking lot and Stuart followed, "Stu, how many times have you practiced that response in the mirror?"

Stuart put his hand on Jon's shoulder forcefully making him stop, "You of all people should believe in the prophecy. No more bullshit…I know."

Jon's stomach sank. He was afraid of where this conversation was going. He had flashes of his daughter's smiling face. Her auburn hair fluttering as she ran around the backyard, innocent and free.

"I don't know what you're talking about," Jon stared at his car wishing he could leave, but he felt frozen in place.

"It's amazing what we are capable of finding. Even getting medical records, talking to certain doctors, like pediatricians."

"Your Chosen are nothing more than the Mover mafia. You're hooligans. Why is my mother associating with you people?"

"Don't skirt the issue."

Jon knew he was against a wall, "Does my mother know?"

"No, but, eventually it will come out," Stuart handed him a photo of a young girl with a triangle-shaped birthmark on her back. "Was this why you never came to see your mother after Sarah was born?"

"What do you want from me? Money?"

"The facts are all I want. Don't you see what this means? Your daughter Sarah is Astrid reincarnated. The prophecy says that the reincarnation of Astrid would have a pyramid birthmark, red hair, and the strength of thirty-three men."

"My mother also had red hair, why jump to conclusions?"

"Your dear mother may have also had the red hair, but she does not bare the mark."

"Hell, even if you do believe in the prophecy, it's only true if she is a thirty-three on the Delving scale," Jon said, handing back the photo. "We won't know her full potential until after puberty. Why are you bringing this up now?"

"My reasons are my own. I will give you a chance to tell your mother yourself. Two days, if you don't tell her, I will."

"What game are you playing? This is my daughter's life we're talking about. Tell me why you haven't told mother and why only two days?"

"There's also the issue of the mystery woman. The one at the library."

Jon's complexion paled and he felt sick, "I don't know what you mean."

"I know you do. I want to know what she's up to and why you're involved."

"Tell mother, I don't care."

Jon unlocked his car door and sat inside. He put his shaking hand on the steering wheel and reached for the door handle.

"Two days," Stuart said before Jon closed the door.

He turned on the ignition and Falco's *Rock Me Amadeus* came on the radio. Jon crinkled his nose.

"I hate this song," he said as he drove away.

Evie sat in the back of a nearby town car with a tumbler of scotch in her hand. She wore a mint green business suit with large shoulder pads and her now gray hair was severely pulled up in a bun. Her demeanor was as tightly wound as her hair. She gently twirled the bloodstone keeper ring around her finger as Stuart sat down next to her. She gave a hand motion to the driver and he started the engine.

"He said he knows what a hard day it is for you and that you need space. He was quite understanding."

"Stu, thank you."

"It's my job and I'm good at my job."

A woman in her late twenties stood in black slacks and bra wondering if she was forgetting anything for the trip. Her long red hair up in rollers. The smell of Old Spice wafted over her and she smiled. Strong arms wrapped around her midsection.

"How was the lecture?" she asked.

"We've got to talk," Jon said slightly stammering and crossing his arms.

She sat on the bed next to the suitcase. Jon closed the bedroom door and paced.

"What happened? You're frightening me."

He stopped pacing, "Stuart Sark paid me a visit. He knows."

"Okay, stay cool, he knows what?"

"About Sarah. He knows about Sarah. I'm not sure how much he knows, but he knows about her mark and "the mysterious woman from the library.'"

Her mouth gaped open and then she crossed her arms, "He's fishing for information, that's all. How could he find out?"

"It doesn't matter, he knows something. He gave me two days to 'tell the truth' or else. What are we going to do?"

"What did he threaten to do if you don't tell?"

"Tell my mother himself I guess. I called his bluff, was that wrong?" he said, pacing again.

There was a long pause, "Let's call his bluff."

"What if he tells her?"

"Let him tell her. We couldn't have controlled this secret for much longer," she said wrapping her arms around him. "We are going to leave tomorrow to go to your mother's and we will pretend that this doesn't exist. Alright?" she said and kissed his cheek.

He nodded, "I'm going to check on Sarah."

He tapped on the bedroom door and entered. In the middle of the floor Sarah had surrounded herself with her dolls. Her pigtails bounced as she played. She looked up and smiled. He melted at her deep dimples and freckles galore. He knelt down and kissed the top of her head.

"Hi, Daddy," she said as she continued to play with her dolls.

"Did you pack all your things, Princess?"

"Yep, Mommy helped me," she said, pointing to a pink striped suitcase.

"Are you excited to meet Grandma?" Sarah nodded her head eagerly. "Remember what we told you? That you shouldn't let Grandma see your birthmark?"

"I remember, Daddy."

"Good girl."

Jon left slowly, watching Sarah playing with her dolls. He wished that he could keep her five-years-old forever.

Chapter 13

A Rose by Any Other Name

New Alessaria, California
April 13th
1986

Evie walked into her office and saw a tall imposing man with white hair. The man smiled and shook her hand firmly.

"Sorry to keep you waiting, Doctor Delving," Evie said as she took her place behind the desk.

He sat down, "You can call me Bob. We've known each other for how many years? Must it always be business with you?"

"That's a very good point, Bob. How's the family?"

"They're doing very well, thank you for asking. The wife and I are quite proud of our boys. They're officially men now, but I still call them the boys. My eldest, Jack, just got lead homicide detective. Robbie's just been offered a job through the CDC, not sure how I feel about him going clear across the country. What about your son?"

"He's coming home shortly, I'm quite pleased," she looked at her watch. "I can't get over this new watch. Progress, eh?"

"Yes, it was always unfortunate that psychokinetic fields interfered with watches, so it is a welcomed new technology. I know the scientists behind the patent, distinguished gentlemen. We had lunch just the other day.

The scientific community is a small wading pool, especially Mover science."

"My son will be here any moment now. Not to rush you along, but why did you need me to meet with you? It sounded urgent."

"I know you are a busy woman and I appreciate you making time for me at this late juncture. It is urgent, Evie. This is the first time I really thought my life's work could be used against the entire American Mover population, maybe even worldwide."

"Aren't you being a little catastrophic?"

"You know how the Delving Ability Scale measures Movers' abilities. I only wanted to prove that the majority of Movers are good people, not these out-of-control mutants…" his voice trailed off. "It was meant to help."

"The Delving scale is such an important step in understanding what makes us Movers. You even made the connection that a Thirty-three on the scale is the third sign of the reincarnation. You are receiving an A.P.L. Award because of the good it does."

"Senator Walker is drafting a new registration bill. The new bill would not only register all Movers, but use the scale to isolate possible "dangers to society." Anyone who is a twenty-five or above could be legally locked up against his or her will. This would include the possible reincarnation of Astrid, I would add. All I have to say is over my dead body. You know that son-of-a-bitch head piggy is behind this. Damn P.G.I. is infiltrating the government."

"Why is this the first I'm hearing about this registration bill?"

"I just found out about it and you were the first person I called. You must help me fight this, Evie."

"You can count on me to do what needs to be done, that bill will not pass," there came a timid knock at the door, "What is it?" Evie barked.

The door opened revealing the new maid, "Your son and family are here, Mrs. Rose."

Doctor Delving stood and straightened his tie, "I must be going, as should you. Family is important."

"I will take care of this matter, Bob," she turned to the maid and said, "Tell my son I have something to take care of, but I will be down in just a moment."

"Yes ma'am."

Jon watched the wonder in Sarah's eyes as she twirled around the Borrows' manor foyer. He turned towards the sound of thudding footsteps on the west staircase. Doctor Delving Sr. walked quickly towards them with an outstretched hand.

The two men shook hands forcefully, "How are you?" the doctor asked.

"Good," Jon said tersely.

"We have an appointment next week, don't we?"

"You must be thinking of someone else."

"If you don't mind, I'll be off." Jon nodded and waved goodbye. They watched as he flew out and down the front steps.

"Mr. and Mrs. Rose?" the new maid said meekly.

"Yes?" Jon said turning. He saw an elderly maid standing next to the new maid and immediately embraced her.

"Judy, this is Cordelia. She practically raised me along with my nanny, Alice."

"So good to see you, Hershel. Look at you a grown man. "Would you like me to take Sarah to the playroom before dinner?"

"I think she would enjoy that, thank you, and I go by Jon now," he said as he put his arm around his wife.

They watched as the maid took Sarah by the hand and led her up the east staircase. After she took Sarah upstairs, Jon took Judy in his arms and spun her.

"I love you, my little red fox," he said and kissed her deeply.

She giggled as he kissed her neck. The sound of throat clearing startled them. Evie stood at the foot of the west staircase. She smiled and then walked towards them. The sound of her heels echoed in the large foyer. Jon felt frozen in place, unable to speak, the same feeling he had experienced from earlier that day with Stuart.

"It's been a long time," Jon said.

"Almost six years," Evie said slowly.

Evie smiled and gave Jon a tight hug, "Welcome home," she said. She turned to Judy and gave her a short one-arm hug, "How about we go into the parlor, kids?"

They nodded and followed Evie across the hallway. Evie walked over to the heavily stocked bar and started to make martinis.

"What's your poison?"

"I don't want anything, Mom," Jon said.

"None for me either," Judy said.

"Well, more for me," she laughed hardily.

Jon cringed and Judy took his hand in hers. She gave him a reassuring look and squeezed his hand.

"So, Judith, how is life?"

"Wonderful, although frustrating at times between work and being a mother. You can call me Judy, we are family after all."

"That we are...that we are. So, Hershel, how are things with you?"

"Mom, nobody calls me Hershel anymore. It's Jon, just Jon."

"Ah yes, Jon with no h. Jon and Judy. I'm surprised you didn't name the child with a 'J'. Well, you will always be Hershel to me. It is the name I gave you, after all. You are named after your father. Hershel is a beautiful name."

"Maybe I will have a drink," he said.

Evie took a martini glass from the cabinet and poured. She topped off her own drink with the leftover mixed martini. She stabbed two olives with stir sticks and dropped one in each drink. He picked up his drink and watched the olive bob side to side. He took a sip and coughed violently.

Evie laughed uproariously, "Too strong for you?" She turned to Judy, "He never could hold his liquor. How about we get comfortable? I know I would like to sit."

They sat on the couch, while Evie sat in an oversized armchair.

"Where is Sarah?"

Jon was not surprised that it took her this long to figure out that Sarah was not with them.

"In the playroom with the maid," Judy said.

"Cordelia, her name is Cordelia. Hershel was always bad with names, too. Oops, I meant Jon. I just had her pick up some new toys for Sarah."

"You didn't have to do that," Judy said.

"I didn't know if it would be another six years before I would see my granddaughter again. Oh well, let bygones be bygones, I always say."

She finished her martini with a long gulp. The butler entered the room. Evie handed her glass to him and then pointed her finger at Jon.

"You want a refresher?"

"No, thank you. How are you, Hank?" he said to the butler.

"I'm fine, Mr. Hershel."

"It's Jon now."

"Sorry, Mr. Jon, I forgot."

"Well, it's okay; it has been a while since I've been back."

Hank took Evie's glass to the bar and started making a martini. Silence settled like a fog among them. Jon looked back into his full martini glass and watched the olive bob around.

"I'm actually pretty beat, Mom. I'm going to take a nap."

"I'll join you honey," Judy said quickly.

"Well, should I have Hank call you down for dinner time?"

"Sure," Jon said as he set down his glass.

They stood and walked out of the room. After they left, Evie looked at the full martini on the table and picked it up. She drank it down and gave the glass to Hank.

"Here you go. Are you almost finished?"

"Here is your drink ma'am," he said as he handed a fresh martini to her.

"Good man," she said before she took a sip.

Evie opened the playroom door and saw Sarah playing with dolls. She had three dolls and a stuffed bear at a miniature table. There were five miniature teacups and a plastic kettle on the table. Sarah took a mock sip from her teacup. She looked up and saw Evie in the doorway.

"Hi, Sarah, do you know who I am?"

"You're Grandma, Daddy's mommy. I saw your picture; you were very pretty and a lot younger. Would you like tea, Grandma?"

Evie looked at her watch and smiled, "Would you like to have real tea and cookies?"

"Oh, yes, yes, yes," Sarah jumped up and down.

The maid walked by and Evie flagged her down, "I would like to have tea and cookies with my granddaughter."

Evie gave Sarah a wink and a smile.

"Alright, Mrs. Rose, where would you like to have tea?"

"In the dinette, I suppose. Yes, the dinette would be splendid. Oh, and will you freshen up my tea? Also, bring Sarah a pillow to sit on."

"Yes, Mrs. Rose."

After the maid left, Evie walked over to the doorway. She put her left hand on her hip and reached for Sarah to come to her.

"Follow me," She said and Sarah skipped over. She looked back at the dolls longingly. "Would you like to bring a doll with you?"

"Can I?" Sarah's face lit up.

"Sure, pick out your favorite and bring her down for tea."

Sarah looked at the dolls thoughtfully. She picked a doll with a pink silk dress and pink hat. She again skipped back, her hair bouncing.

"This is Elizabeth, Daddy bought her when he was in London. Isn't she beautiful?"

"Yes, she is."

"He also got me this," She pointed to the pink dress she was wearing. "It matches, see?"

Sarah held the doll next to her side and pointed to herself and then the doll. Evie put her hand out and they walked out of the playroom. After descending the stairs, they went down a hallway to the dinette. Evie lifted Sarah up onto the plush green pillow on one of the chairs. In the kitchen, the maid reached into a cabinet and pulled out a bottle of vodka. She filled about a quarter of Evie's teacup and put away the bottle. She then poured the tea.

"Is your favorite color pink?" Evie asked.

"Uh-huh."

"Do you like me?" Evie asked as the maid was serving the tea and cookies.

"The one with the spoon is yours ma'am."

"I like you. You don't talk to me like I'm a baby. Most grown-ups do that. You sure have a nice house. Big!" She threw her arms wide to emphasize her point. "You bought me toys, too."

"I'm glad you like me." Evie took a sip of her tea.

"Why are the men outside?"

"What men?"

"I saw 'em outside walkin' around. They look mean."

"Those men protect Grandma."

"From what?"

"Bad people, but nothing you have to worry about. Have a cookie."

"Will Mommy be mad? She always says 'no sweets before dinner, it will ruin your ap-ap-appe-kite.'"

"This will be our little secret."

Sarah took a cookie and smiled.

In the bed, Jon was on his side and Judy was on her back. She tapped her fingers on her arm and she let out a long sigh.

"Jon?" she said.

"What? I'm trying to take a nap," Jon groaned without opening his eyes.

"I'm worried about your mother."

"I'm trying to take a nap."

"This is serious. I think she's an alcoholic. You know my parents were alcoholics and I can spot one a mile away. She's a functioning one, I'll give you that, but an alcoholic none the less."

"I know she drinks like a fish. She always has and always will. I've accepted it, so should you. Can we go back to napping now?"

"This is serious, Jon."

"No it isn't."

"She is killing herself."

"That's her choice."

"How could you be so cold? She is your mother for Christ's sake."

"I don't care, I'm trying to take a nap," he said slowly, with his eyes still shut.

"Fine, I give up."

The large house was quiet in the middle of the night. Judy finished eating a piece of chicken she had snagged from the kitchen. With enthusiasm, she licked her fingers. She walked out of the kitchen and down the hallway. She entered the foyer and noticed a figure in the dim moonlight. She squinted and realized it was Evie in a flowing nightgown. She was standing and staring at the locked doors of the ballroom. The moonlight made the glass in her hand glint. Judy was about to talk, but something told her that it was not the time. She crept up the west staircase and went into the dark room. She slid off her slippers and nestled herself into bed with the haunting image of the silver-haired Evie standing in the moonlight.

"You smell like chicken," Jon moaned.

"I'm so sorry I woke you up."

"What's wrong? I can hear it in your voice."

"Your mother…" Judy's voice trailed off.

Jon sat up in the bed and waved at the bedside lamp, turning it on.

"What about my mother?" he sighed.

"She was standing in the foyer. Just, standing there."

"She does that every night, it's a ritual or something."

"It's kind of strange don't you think?"

"Look, she's allowed to be strange. She saw her entire family slaughtered, in this very house. To live in this place, with all the ghosts of the past and memories…it would make anyone a little off-kilter. So, understand that when she drinks too much, or stands in the foyer every night, she's just trying to survive. She's surviving the only way she can, so give her a break."

"How can you be this…what is the word…accepting?"

"The secret is, I still do have hope she'll change. I try not to admit it, that I want her to be different. Maybe that's why I put her name down as my other plus one guest for the award ceremony. I do wish she would come, but I know she won't. Do we have to do this right now? It's something o'clock in the morning. What time is it?" he reached for his watch and looked at it. "It's one in the morning."

"Alright, let's go to sleep."

"Thank you," he said, frustrated.

Jon looked over and turned off the bedside lamp with a little wave. He had a dream about living in India and having a pet mongoose that could talk.

Chapter 14

The Wrong One

Alexandria, Virginia
April 14th
1986

A man leaned back in his office chair, deep in thought. The fluorescent lighting made his brown hair seem more blonde and dark-brown eyes darker. He wore a white shirt with a black and white striped tie. The office contained only a desk and chair. The walls had old wood paneling from the 1950s and the carpet was stained.

A young boy opened the door, "Dad, it's some man with a briefcase to see you."

"Let him in, Sander."

The little boy scampered off down the hallway.

"Are you Alexander Bram?" the man with the briefcase asked.

"You seem to know my name, but I don't know yours."

"My name is not important."

"So, we're playing that game are we? Is that my money?" Alexander nodded towards the briefcase.

The short man nodded and handed it to him.

"I'll take it that it's all here?" Alexander asked as he opened it and looked upon the cash with an approving expression. "Will she keep her end of the bargain?"

"I'm not sure whom you are referring to, but my employer is a woman of her word."

"So, she's going to have our organization taken off the terrorist watch list and give me the rest of the money after I do this thing? Don't worry, I'm not wired, just had this place checked for bugs."

The man seemed to relax a little and there was a long pause. "It's none of my business, but why did you agree to this?"

"A dish best served cold is hard to pass up, especially when I can get paid to do it."

"Revenge?"

"See, that Satan's Plague Witch murdered my father in 1958. I made a promise to my father's memory to kill that bitch. That is what I get out of it," Alexander spoke in a cool collected way that gave the short man chills. "Pleasure doing business with you," he said with a smile.

The man nodded and left the room quickly. Alexander stroked the briefcase and then gave it a gentle kiss.

New Alessaria, California
April 14th
1986

Judy gave Jon a peck on the cheek as he was straightening his tie. He was dressed in his best tuxedo fresh from the dry cleaners and his shoes shined by a maid that day. Judy was dressed in a designer black dress that shimmered in the light. She picked up her antique hairbrush with an ivory handle and brushed down a wispy fly away.

"How do I look?" Jon said, still fiddling with his tie.

"You look amazing...but the tie."

"What's wrong with the tie?"

"It's the wrong one. You should wear a bow tie tonight, it's more special."

"Alright, you would know these things better than me."

After changing ties, Jon turned around and looked his wife up and down. He let out a long whistle in approval. He gave her an okay hand gesture and winked.

"Hot mama. You still look amazing, even after popping out a brat."

"You really know how to create a romantic mood Jon-boy."

"I hate it when you call me that."

"I'm going to check on our brat, as you so lovingly called her."

"Yes dear," he said in a mocking tone.

She opened the door and saw Evie reading to Sarah.

"Ah, Judy I meant to ask you something. What channel is the award ceremony on?" Evie asked.

"The local channel, I forget what number. What are you two reading?"

"We're reading a charming book, called *The Hobbit*."

"Isn't that a little advanced for her?"

"Oh, we're having a ball, aren't we?" Evie said as she set the book down on her lap and clasped her hands.

"It's really good so far, Mommy. Grandma tells me what all the big words mean."

"We were waiting to start chapter books."

"Well, that is one way to raise a child," Evie said as she took a long sip of her martini.

"Are you at least going to an anniversary party tonight? Tonight is a celebration of Astrid."

"Today has too many anniversaries. I just want to stay home with a martini and my granddaughter."

"In that order?"

"Don't be smart with me. Can I help you with anything else?"

"I came in here to say that we were leaving soon. Also, I hope you will wish your son a happy birthday."

"He knows my feelings on that subject."

"Um, okay then. Honey, you need to practice your piano tonight."

"I don't have the piano."

106

"Your Grandma has one."

"I have three. I would love to hear you play."

"Sarah is very talented. I know I'm biased, but her piano teacher told me that she is the most talented child she has ever taught."

"How impressive. When did she start the lessons?"

"She started last year, so not very long. But she plays wonderfully for her age."

Jon knocked on the door, "We should leave."

"You look all nice and spiffy," Evie exclaimed.

"Yeah Daddy, you look handsome."

"Thank you, ladies."

He took a short bow before he walked over to the bed and gave Sarah a kiss on her forehead.

"Will you be good for Grandma?" he asked. Sarah nodded vigorously. "Good-night," he said as he gave her a tight hug.

"Happy birthday, Daddy," Sarah said.

"Thanks, Princess."

"We're running late," Judy said pointing at the wall clock.

"Alright," he said as he released himself from Sarah's grip.

"Good-night, my little princess," Judy said and kissed Sarah on the cheek.

"Have fun kids," Evie said.

"We will and we'll be in late so see you in the morning," Jon said, and looked at his mother with a smile, but there was disappointment in his eyes. They left and Evie shook off the look he gave her.

"So, do you want to read some more, Sarah? Or would you like to play the piano for me? I would really like you to play for me."

"I guess I could play."

Sarah sat at the parlor grand piano and Evie sat in a chair facing the piano.

"Wuddaya want me to play?"

"Something pretty, what have you been practicing?"

"I just learned this one, but I only know the start of it."

Sarah placed her fingers on the keys and music poured out from the piano. Evie instantly recognized the butchered piece she was attempting to play. It was Beethoven's *Moonlight Sonata.*

"Stop," Evie shrieked, shaking her fists in the air. "For the love of God, stop, stop, stop."

Sarah halted her playing and looked at Evie with wide eyes. Evie panted, her chest heaving up and down. She stopped waving her fists around and sat down.

"I'm sorry, Sarah. I love your playing, it's wonderful. But, don't play that song. Anything, just don't play that. Do you know anything else, that isn't Beethoven?"

"Yes," Sarah paused with her hands over the keys and looked over at Evie.

"It's alright, you can play," she said as she unclenched her fists.

Sarah attempted to play Chopin's *Prelude in E Minor* as Evie bit her finger to slow her breathing.

Later that evening, Evie sat up in her bed watching the award ceremony on television. Sarah was asleep next to her. The audience clapped as they announced Jon's name. She thought about waking Sarah, but she seemed so peaceful. Jon accepted a gold statue in the shape of an apple. Evie smiled and wished she was there. The channel suddenly snowed out. She kept changing the channel and noticed all the others were coming in fine. She stayed on the news and watched the pretty weather girl talking about the current storm forecast. The phone rang. She looked over, but Sarah barely stirred. She floated the phone over and answered it.

"Hello?" she said in a hushed voice and headed to the doorway.

"Evie, it's Stu, were you watching?"

"Yes, there's something wrong with the local signal. I'm missing my son's speech."

"Hold on, my other phone is ringing."

She noticed the newscaster announced breaking news.

"We have initial reports that there has been some type of explosion at the Astridians for Peace Awards tonight in Borrowstown. We will report more when new information comes in."

Evie gasped and backed up against the wall. She shook and slowly slid to the floor. She looked over at Sarah, who was still asleep.

"Evie, are you there?" Stuart's voice returned. She forgot she still had the phone to her ear.

"Stu," was all she could whisper.

"I'm on my way to find out what happened. No one really knows the full details yet. I'll know more when I get there. Stay put, I'm sending more of my men over and Phyllis is on her way to keep you company."

"He's dead," she said flat and sure.

"Stop that right now. I'm leaving, I'll call you soon."

She turned off her wireless phone and looked down at it. Time seemed to stop. She looked up and saw Phyllis standing over her. She had no idea how much time had passed. Phyllis was a white-haired woman in her 50s, with blue eye shadow and sizable shoulder pads. She knelt down and Evie looked into her kind almond eyes. Without a word, Phyllis helped Evie to her feet and they both looked over at the sleeping Sarah.

"Let her sleep, her life might completely change when she wakes up. She deserves happy dreams," Phyllis said and motioned for them to leave the room.

Evie watched the fireplace in the sitting room as they silently sipped the scotch Phyllis had brought over.

109

"Thank you, Phyllis, I couldn't imagine being alone right now."

"Did I ever tell you about my father?" Phyllis asked, touching the condensation on her tumbler of scotch.

"No, but I'm not sure this is the time for stories. I'm not in the mood for such talk."

"Hear me out, honey. My father was a prohibition agent back in the day. What would he think of me with this drink in my hand? I was about Sarah's age actually, when my father's boss came knocking on our door. I watched my mother turn to ash. She hollered like nothing I had ever heard. It was an animal sound. He was murdered by a bootlegger. She lost my two brothers to the great war, my sister to influenza, and then her husband to a meaningless criminal's gun."

"Why are you telling me this? It's not helpful," Evie said with her palm on her forehead.

"Because, my dear Evie, my mother was not a strong woman. She simply cracked up. I went to stay with my aunt and would visit my mother in an asylum. I never could imagine what my mother had gone through until I had my son."

"I didn't know you have children."

"Yes, Stu and I were blessed with a beautiful baby boy. When I held him the first time I felt like I would never be alone again." Evie cried and took a tissue from the box on the coffee table. "I know you understand. I remember when I met you with baby Hershel in your arms. I saw that look in your eyes, that your baby boy was the answer to your prayers and your reason for living. You lost everyone, but you had him. When my son died of the crib death," she paused and took a deep breath. "I thought I would die, too. I wished God had taken me instead," a tear fell from her eye and she wiped it away.

"I know he's dead. They killed my baby. I feel like…he was the wrong one. They should have just killed me," Evie choked out and mournfully wailed.

Phyllis took Evie into her arms and held her, "I know you, Evie. You are the strongest bitch I know," Evie let out a little laugh through her tears. "It's true. There is no one I would rather have in my corner than Evelyn Rose. There's a little girl upstairs and her life is going to possibly change in a moment. She needs her grandmother. I don't care how you do it, but you don't have the luxury of falling apart. My mother gave up, I know what it's like to watch someone after they give up. You cannot give them the pleasure. You fight, like you always do."

"I heard it in Stu's voice. The fear."

"I know. He really is a poor liar sometimes."

"God, I should be holding out hope. I should believe there's hope he's still alive. I'm a horrible mother."

"You are not a horrible mother. Whatever happens, you will carry on," Phyllis said and stroked Evie's hair.

Phyllis noticed Stu outside the window talking to a patrolling Chosen member.

"You should try to rest, waiting up won't make the answers come quicker. Go up to Sarah, I'll hold down the fort."

Evie nodded and threw back her scotch. They walked out of the room. Evie stopped at the foot of the stairs and placed her hand on her chest.

"Thank you," she whispered and Phyllis nodded.

She watched her walk up the stairs and turned to see Stu standing in the front doorway. She gave him a tight hug and he led her into the sitting room.

"How is she?" he asked.

"How do you think?" she snapped. "What's going on, Stu?"

"It's a God damn mess. The place was blown to hell. They are finding very few survivors and most are kitchen

111

staff. Nothing official, but the bomb squad is sure the explosives were located under the stage."

She remembered Jon was accepting his award right before the channel snowed out.

"Dear lord," she gasped.

"There's more. The information I'm about to share with you stays between us. My men informed me that they stopped an assassination attempt here at the house coordinated with the bombing."

"They were going to kill Evie?" Phyllis asked in disbelief.

"There was an accident with the assassins and they're dead. I use the word accident loosely of course. One was tore up pretty bad but told our patrolmen the target was Sarah. Evie was on the list as a guest at the awards. Their job was to kill Sarah."

"We have to tell Evie," she said with urgency in her voice.

"No," Stu said and looked down at his shoes.

"But, she must know the danger she and..."

"No one, especially Evie, can know."

"But, how are you going to explain the dead assassins?"

"Dick Sparkman at the crematorium owed me a favor."

She recoiled in disgust, "How could you be so cold?"

"I'm doing my job. As my wife, you should be less emotional."

Phyllis slapped him and walked away.

Chapter 15

Cure for Sadness

New Alessaria, California
April 15th
1986

There was a predictable thud of the morning newspaper on the front porch and the sound of the squeaky front door opening and closing. The Victorian house kept no squeak or creak a secret. A man was in a bedroom buttoning his shirt. He caught the scent of coffee brewing and smiled. Midway through tucking in his shirt, he heard a bellowing cry and a loud crash. He rushed out of the room, shirt half tucked.

He saw a shattered coffee mug at the base of a wall, coffee dripping down the wallpaper. He saw her crumpled on the floor sobbing uncontrollably. He knelt down and held her, feeling her body lurch with every sob.

"What's wrong, Mongoose?" he asked, pushing back the strands of her hair that had adhered to her damp cheeks.

She could not stop crying long enough to say a word. Not knowing what to do or say he carried her to the couch. He went back to clean up the coffee mess. The newspaper was on the table. He looked down at it and froze. The front page displayed all the names of the victims of a bombing; the sheer number was hard to digest. He noticed Jon and Judith Rose were listed as two of the prominent victims. A sickness overwhelmed him and he vomited in the sink.

Borrowstown, California
April 20th
1986

The overcast day cast a literal dark cloud above the memorial service for victims from the bombing. On the other side of Remembrance Park, Sarah sat on a bench next to a tree. She was dressed in black and nibbling on a chocolate bar. She looked up from her candy and saw a boy about her age walking towards her. The boy sat down next to her and sighed.

"Do you want some chocolate?" she asked him.

"No," the boy said, she noticed he had been crying.

"My grandma said that it would cure my sadness, maybe it will help you."

"Is it working?"

"No."

"Well, it's silly. How can chocolate make you feel not sad?"

"I dunno. What's your name?"

"Brian Delving. You're Sarah Rose, right?"

"How did you know?"

"We studied you in school."

"Why?"

"You're important or something."

"How old are you?"

"Six. You sure ask a lot of questions," he said, annoyed.

"My daddy says that questions are good."

"I think it's just nosey," he said standing up and walked away.

"Sarah," she turned and saw her grandmother walking towards her. "There you are. You just vanished."

"Sorry, it's just that it was making me sad and I don't like being sad. I thought if I ate the chocolate it would make me feel better, like you said. Are you sad Grandma?"

Evie sat down on the bench next to Sarah and her eyes welled up with tears.

"Yes, I'm sad." A tear fell down her cheek. She put her arm around Sarah. "But I have you."

"Are Mommy and Daddy in heaven?"

"God damn right they are. Your parents were good people and they are definitely in heaven."

"You said a bad word."

Evie took out a pack of menthol cigarettes from her purse and lit one. She took a long, deep drag and let it out slowly.

"Sorry, I didn't mean to say a bad word."

"Daddy says smoking is bad."

"When you are older, you'll understand why I need to smoke at this moment in time. Don't worry yourself about this stuff. But, if I catch you smoking you will get a spanking. Promise me you won't ever smoke."

"I promise," she said quickly.

"Good girl, let's go home."

After the memorial service, Sarah watched from the hallway as the maid packed up her parent's things from the guest room. Sarah snuck into the bathroom and looked around the counter. Her eyes landed on her mother's antique hairbrush and she picked it up. She then saw a half used bottle of Old Spice aftershave and grabbed it.

"What are you doing in here?" the maid said, standing outside the bathroom.

Sarah had a sad and guilty expression on her face as she turned around.

"What are you doing with my parent's things?"

The maid looked at what Sarah had in her hands. She slowly looked both ways.

"I won't tell your grandmother if you leave and hide those things right now."

Sarah went to her room, just as the maid told her to. The stench of fresh pink paint hung in the air. She slid under her bed where there was a makeshift shelf created by the bed frame. She placed the bottle of Old Spice aftershave and the hairbrush on the shelf.

Chapter 16

How to Make God Laugh

New Alessaria, California
September 23rd
1996

Sarah sat at the vanity brushing her long auburn hair with her mother's antique hairbrush with the ivory handle. She remembered her mother brushing her hair and smiled. The memories of both her parents were beginning to fade more and more every year. After she finished brushing her hair, she knelt down next to the bed and put the brush back on the hidden shelf. She dusted off her uniform and sat back down at the vanity. She picked up a white gold locket with a rose etched into the front. She put the necklace on. Evie hurriedly came into the bedroom with a piece of paper in her hand.

"Is that my permission slip?" Sarah asked

"It is, but I won't sign it. I don't think that you should be going so far away from home."

"That isn't fair," Sarah stood up from the vanity and crossed her arms.

"Life isn't fair. You are young and should be close to home, where you can be protected."

"I have a chance to go to Las Vegas to be with the dance team and you won't let me go. This is bullshit."

"Watch your language little girl."

"I'm not a little girl, I'm fifteen."

"I don't want to fight with you," Evie shook her head. She looked at her watch, "You're going to be late for school. The driver is waiting for you."

Sarah picked up her backpack from the bed and stomped out of the room.

The driver tipped his hat to Sarah and she nodded. He opened the door and she sat inside. She buckled her seatbelt and then looked up to see her grandmother staring down at the car from a second-floor window. Sarah sighed in frustration as the driver drove the car down the long driveway. She recognized the classical music pouring from the car stereo as Beethoven's *Fur Elise*. The driver was new, so he didn't know the Beethoven ban. She was tempted to warn him of Evie's wrath if she heard Beethoven.

"Is something wrong Miss Rose?" the driver asked.

"It's Grandma, she's just being such a pain in the ass. I mean, I know she cares about me and all, but she shows it in very stupid ways."

"Cheer up, Miss Rose. Everything is done in your best interest."

"For once I wished people would ask me what I want, not what is 'in my best interest.' I don't want to talk anymore."

"Yes, Miss Rose."

"Please don't call me Miss Rose. Call me Sarah. It's my name after all."

"Mrs. Rose told me…"

"Oh, my grandmother has everyone spooked," she paused. "I just want someone to listen to me, really listen. Even my friends don't listen, if they really are friends. I think the only reason I have friends is because of who I am. I bet this is boring you, huh?"

"No, Miss Rose, I'm very interested."

"Hell, you're only saying that because my grandma pays your salary."

"Don't say that Miss Rose."

"It's true. Sorry if I'm being a bitch, I'm just upset."

"All is forgiven, Miss Rose."

After the car stopped, she looked out the window at the high school kids walking around. She listened to the end of Beethoven's *Moonlight Sonata* and opened the door.

"Have a nice day, Miss Rose. I'll be here to pick you up after school."

She walked a couple yards and heard a loud popping sound. She turned and saw the driver slumped over the wheel with blood oozing down his forehead. Then she felt a sharp pinch in her neck and felt woozy. Everything went black and she collapsed onto the ground. A gray van pulled up to the curb and two masked men jumped out. One man was pointing a gun wildly around and shouting for everyone to stay away. Another man scooped up the limp Sarah. The two men returned to the van and peeled away down the street.

Across town the elegant Borrowstown hotel lobby was bustling with people coming and going. Many did not even notice Evie in the midst of what they were doing. The manager did notice her and approached her eagerly.

"Hello, Mrs. Rose, how good to see you."

"I'm here to meet someone."

"Yes, Mrs. Simmons is waiting for you at the hotel bar."

"Thank you."

She walked into the bar and saw Mrs. Simmons waving to her.

"Hello, Mrs. Rose, good to see you."

"Hello."

Mrs. Simmons wore a dress that was not appropriate for the caliber of the hotel. After studying her accessories, Evie realized it was probably the nicest dress she owned and that she was trying to make a good impression on a frugal budget. Evie admired the effort; she knew not everyone was as fortunate as she was.

A waiter came over to them and asked, "Would you like a drink Mrs. Rose?"

"Yes, my usual," the waiter nodded.

Mrs. Simmons cleared her throat, "You are probably concerned as to why Sarah's gift coach is calling you into a meeting."

"You would be right," a martini was promptly set in front of Evie and she took a sip. "What was so sensitive that we could not discuss this over the phone?"

"Sarah is holding back."

"What do you mean?" Evie asked, but knew exactly where this conversation was going. On the outside, she was full composure. However, on the inside she was on full alert and panicked.

"I think Sarah needs to be retested," Mrs. Simmons gingerly suggested.

"She's a twenty on the D.A.S. which is perfectly normal."

"I think she's pretending to be a twenty. I can feel her holding back her power. If that power is not exercised and controlled, who knows what could happen."

"She does not need to be retested, end of story."

"I'm sorry, but you must understand the situation. If she is anything over a twenty, it could be disastrous. If a power like that is not harnessed, it can be deadly for those around her."

"I'm a drunk, not an idiot, Mrs. Simmons. I know what is in Sarah's best interest."

"Dear lord, you know. You know she's been holding back," she gasped. She looked around the bar and in a hushed tone said, "I've seen the birthmark."

Anger started to boil inside Evie and she considered committing an act of homicide for a split second. She took a sip of her martini and placed both palms on the table.

"Now, listen very closely, because I will not say this again. My granddaughter is the most important thing in my life. If you are saying what I think you are, you and I know she's not mature enough to handle it. Not now."

"If she's a 30 on the Delving Ability Scale…along with the mark, the hair…she's the reincarnation of Astrid."

"Say that ever again and I will destroy you. Mark my words."

A man from the hotel desk approached the table. Noticing the tension and the stare he received from Evie, he gulped and wrung his hands.

"I'm sorry to interrupt, but there is a phone call for you, Mrs. Rose."

"A phone call, from whom?"

"All they said was that it was urgent."

"Excuse me," Evie said as she stood and followed the man to the front desk. She picked up the phone receiver. "Hello?"

"Evie, its Stuart…there's been…something has happened."

"What?"

Color drained from her face. The last time she heard Stu in this much of a panic, her son had died. She gripped the counter, bracing for bad news.

"Sarah's been kidnapped," there was a long pause. "Are you there?"

"I'm here," she said, as her legs started to quiver.

"Well, thank God she was wearing the necklace. We tracked her to a warehouse downtown. I sent my best men in to get her. Don't worry. I've got everything under control."

"What do I do?" she said quietly, but in a panicked tone.

"Just go home and wait."

"I can't just…"

"Go home Evie," he said before hanging up.

After counting to ten and composing herself, Evie turned to the manager and tapped him on the shoulder.

"Yes, Mrs. Rose, what can I do for you?"

"Have my driver fetch the car and bring it out front, quickly."

"Certainly," he said before speeding off.

In a haze of confusion Evie made her way to the bar and picked up her purse from the table. After looking at Mrs. Simmons, she downed the rest of her drink.

"I have to go."

"We'll just have to finish this another time."

"No, I think we're done here. Good bye," Evie said before rushing off.

Astridian Community Hospital
Borrowstown, California
September 23rd
1996

The hospital room was dim and quiet. Evie sat in a chair next to Sarah's bed looking at her as she slept. She watched as her chest went up and down with every breath. She looked at Sarah's auburn hair flowing against the stark white pillow. The door opened revealing Stuart Sark. He motioned for Evie to come meet with him in the hall and she reluctantly obliged. Stuart looked back and forth down the hallway. His body movements were edgy.

"Anything new?" he asked, crossing his arms.

"She woke up a little while ago. She says that she doesn't remember what happened. The doctor says that memory loss is normal when someone has gone through traumatic stress. I just want to know what happened to her, Stu. The doctor said the rape kit was negative and she had no wounds of any kind. Just a couple minor scratches. What happened?"

Stuart sighed, "All I know is that we traced her to that warehouse with the necklace tracker. When my men got

122

there, she was already in shock. Without getting into gory details, all of the kidnappers were already dead. My men said it was a nasty scene. There was no sign anyone but Sarah and the kidnappers were in that warehouse."

"You don't think it was Sarah that killed them, do you?" Evie gazed down the hallway. "I don't believe it's as bad as your men said."

"Look at me," he wrapped his hands around her wrists and jerked her towards him. "I didn't either, so I went to see for myself. I don't want you to know what I saw, it's that bad. I know you are not being fully honest with me. What did the test say? What number is she on the Delving Ability Scale? What is her real D.A.S. score?"

"She's a twenty."

"Answer me honestly now, is she really a 30? Only a 30 can snap the necks of five men. One had his head nearly ripped off. I can only help you if you are honest with me. Is she a 30?" Evie nodded her head and cried. "So, it's true then. The prophecy is true, she is the reincarnation. Why would you hide this from me?"

"I was protecting her."

"From me?"

"You know as well as I do that this will ruin her life, her hopes, her dreams. Do you know how long it took to have her grasp onto a passion and build those hopes and dreams? You've seen her dance. She dreams of a future away from all this. I have no desire to destroy that. She deserves a normal life."

"I don't think you understand the gravity of the situation, Evie. Dark times are coming and I don't know if I can stop it. Our people need a point of light to follow or all will be lost. I'm sorry, but the future of our people is more important than Sarah's little dreams."

"That is nothing but cruelty hiding behind virtue."

"You talk of cruelty as if it's something you don't know. You sent a razor blade into a man's throat, killing him. Do you regret your cruelty?"

"That is an unfair comparison. I was fighting for my life and my baby's life. I had to."

"The truth is that you valued your life over his. You were willing to take his life from him to save your own."

"There is morality in this world, Stu. Look at the law of the land and the Ten Commandments."

"Thou shalt not murder."

"It was not murder, it was self-defense and you know it, you son-of-a-bitch."

"But you did take his life, whatever the reason. You made a decision to save your life and that took courage. To make the right choice is sometimes not easy, or popular. My job is to make the hard choices. I get to take on the choices no one wants to make. Sarah will be announced as the reincarnation, because it is the right choice."

"She has been through so much with all this," she said, motioning to the hospital room.

"At least she has no memory of the event. Let's just hope she never remembers what happened. You must hold a news conference after this and tell the world what she is."

"I can't…she can't handle something like that."

"She has to handle it. She just has to."

"What happened to the bodies? The police…" "There are no bodies."

"I thought you said that you found the kidnappers dead."

He repeated slowly, "There are no bodies." Evie simply nodded and wiped away her tears. He said, "This is for the good of all of us. I believe she will be the one to save us all one day."

Alexandria, Virginia
September 23rd
1996

124

Alexander Bram stood over a sheepish young man slumped in a chair. Alex flexed his hand and let it rest on the back of the chair. He looked from the young man in the chair to an intimidating man standing in the corner of the room. Alexander took in a deep breath and let out a light chuckle.

He walked over to the man in the corner, "So, Brother Greg, what are we going to do about this little S.O.B.?"

"I'm not sure, Brother Alex, I think this little S.O.B. deserves to have his throat sliced, but that's just my opinion."

"Brother Alex, I was just following orders," the sheepish young man sniveled.

"Whose orders? Not mine, that's for damn sure. What got into your thick skull thinking that my son Sander had any authority in this organization to lead such a shoddy operation?"

The young man in the chair quivered and beads of sweat ran down his forehead.

"How was it you and Sander escaped when five of my men   didn't?"

    "We were outside sm-sm-smoking."

"Hear that Brother Greg? Smoking saved this twerp's life. Isn't that precious?"

"Completely precious."

"So, let me go over this again, just so I get it straight in my own head. My crackpot son decides to show off and convinces you and five of my men to kidnap that mutant princess from school. She was tranquilized, taken by van to a warehouse which, due to the property records, can in a roundabout way be linked back to me. While you and my son were smoking, she murdered my men. Then you both take off as her cow of a grandmother's henchmen found her. Did I get all that right or did I miss something?" the young man let out a little whimper.

"Since I'm in an Armani suit right now, I've decided to not get rid of you," the young man in the chair let out a sigh of relief. "Brother Greg is going to do it for me, aren't you Greg?"

"With pleasure," Brother Greg cracked his knuckles and the young man wept.

"Well, I have a plane to catch and I don't want to get in his way, so I bid you both adieu," Alexander walked out the door and closed it behind him.

He went into a common room and all the men looked up from the television. The ticker on the bottom of the screen read: *Astridian Leader Evelyn Rose to make important announcement.*

"Where is Sander?" Alexander said in a steady voice.

All of the men pointed down towards the basement. He nodded and slowly descended the basement stairs. Sander was at the pool table lining up the cue ball to the eight ball.

Alexander picked up the eight ball and shook it, "I think it's broken, no fortune."

"Dad, I'm sorry. I…"

"Sander, you know the only reason I'm not having my men get rid of you like that twerp upstairs is that you are my son, and your mother would then kill me."

"I'm so sorry, I just wanted you to be proud of me and I wanted to be important."

"This is your first lesson in being a leader. Know when not to act. I do have to say, I admire your balls, son. But, never do anything like this again or you won't be so lucky. Am I clear?" Sander nodded.

"Rack 'em up. I have enough time for one game before my flight."

Astridian Community Hospital
Borrowstown, California
September 23rd
1996

Evie sat in the hospital room reading a tabloid magazine when she heard a soft moan. She looked over to the bed and

126

saw Sarah squirming. Evie rushed to the bed and held her hand. Sarah opened her eyes and looked up sleepily. She looked around the room and then back at Evie.

"It's alright, Sarah, it was only a nightmare."

"Where am I?"

"You're in the hospital for observation, remember?" a look of realization came over her face and she nodded.

"Do you know what happened to me, Grandma?"

"All we know is that you are safe now," Evie smiled reassuringly. "I'm pulling you out of school and placing you in home school."

"I don't have a choice, do I?"

"No."

"I guess it's for my own good," Sarah said with a tinge of anger.

"I'm going to have one of Stuart's men take the position of your body guard."

"I don't know if I feel comfortable with that."

"You need to be protected. I wasn't going to tell you this just yet but I need to. Tomorrow I will be announcing that we believe you are the reincarnation of Astrid."

Sarah bolted up in the bed. Tears filled her eyes, "No. This isn't…this can't be happening."

"I know you have been holding back."

Sarah cried and balled her fists. She looked at the window at her reflection, "I'm not."

Evie pulled Sarah's face gently so their gaze lined up. She stared into her eyes and nodded, "Sarah, I know that you are a D.A.S thirty-three."

"I tested as a twenty," her voice quivering.

Evie stroked Sarah's hair and smiled, "You have my hair. I remember before I went gray so soon, I had hair like yours. At one time there were rumors I was Astrid reincarnated. But I didn't nearly have the strength or the mark," Evie took a breath and touched Sarah's triangle birthmark.

127

"Please, no, I'm not her. I'm Sarah," she hit her chest. "I'm me, Sarah Rose, your granddaughter. You know me."

"Haven't you realized that the signs line up? You're a smart girl. You have the birthmark, the hair, and you are a thirty-three on the Delving scale."

"How do you know I'm a thirty-three, not like a little over a twenty?"

"When you were tested, you tested the highest they had ever seen. I paid them off to change it to a twenty and never told you."

"But, that can't be, I was holding back…"

"They have never seen a Mover holding back and still register as a thirty-three. You are the only one for a reason, you are Astrid reincarnated."

"I can't, it's too much responsibility. I have dreams of my own. You know that."

"I know, I know. Sometimes it helps to feel like a soldier, a general even. Leading our people is an important job. Duty to serve our people is a privilege."

Sarah let out a whimper through her ever-flowing tears, "I don't want it."

"I realize that. But you have it."

"Please don't make me."

"Honey, we don't have a choice. This is who you are."

"I hate you," Sarah said and buried her face in the pillow.

"I know, and I'm okay with that," Evie walked out of the room and saw Stuart in the hall. As she passed him she said, "We will make the announcement tomorrow."

"Thank you for your cooperation, Evie."

She turned and wiped her tears, "I'm a good soldier," she said bitterly and walked away.

New Alessaria, California

September 24th
1996

Sarah walked into her personal dance studio dressed in her black leotard, black tights, and ballerina slippers. After stretching, she placed a cassette into the boom box. The room reverberated with The Rolling Stone's *Paint it Black*. She danced along to the music. Her grandmother had turned one of the bedrooms into a dance studio when Sarah took to ballet. She cried as she danced, knowing that her dream of being a professional dancer would never come true. Evie looked on from the doorway and clapped at the end of the song. Sarah looked over her shoulder at Evie and willed the boom box to power off. She put her leg on the barr to stretch.

"Go take a shower and get ready for the press conference."

"I will go on one condition."

"Which is what?" Evie crossed her arms.

"I want to go back to school and not start home school."

"Out of the question," Evie scoffed.

Sarah continued to stretch and avoided eye contact, "If you do this for me and let me go to school, I will do the tricks and speeches. But, if you don't do this for me, you will never see me again, because I will leave and never look back."

"You think you can leave? You must have become delusional overnight."

"I'm powerful and you should listen to me. You can't control me. I think you would be stupid to not listen to me."

"How dare you speak to me that way? You should be ashamed."

"I love you and I don't want to leave. You're all I have. But if you want to try to control me, then I'm leaving."

Evie walked towards her and Sarah put up her hand. Evie felt like she hit a wall and struggled to move forward. Sarah lifted her hand slowly and Evie started to levitate

129

against her will. She looked at Sarah and tried to speak, but could not. Sarah slowly put her hand down and Evie returned to the ground. She regained her motion and ability to speak.

"You don't give me many options now do you?" Evie put her hands on her hips and took a deep breath. "Okay, I don't like it, but you have a deal. Never do that again, young lady. You may be powerful, but I can make your life a living hell if you push me. I promise you that. You will have a body guard at all times, which is my only condition. The press conference is in two hours."

Evie rushed out of the dance studio. After she left, Sarah turned around with a satisfied smile. She did a pirouette and walked out of the room.

On the way to the community center, Sarah sat in the limo watching Evie sipping at her martini. Evie was in her signature green business suit nicknamed "the battle-suit" and a mask of makeup. Sarah was dressed all in black, as if it were a funeral. She felt like it was a funeral and her outward demeanor was befitting her dark mood. Stuart opened the door to the limo; Sarah hadn't noticed they had stopped.

"Showtime," Evie said as she put the glass down and checked her lipstick in the mirror.

Evie left the limo and there was a roar from the crowd and reporters. Sarah took a deep breath as the wall of sound and energy nearly paralyzed her with fear. She followed Evie into the community center and as the doors closed, the wall of sound quieted. They made their way to the stage and she heard the same noise grow louder. Evie turned back, smiled at Sarah, and took her hand. After a nod from a man on the side of the stage, Evie motioned with her head for Sarah to come on stage with her.

The lights, shouting, and clapping all seemed too overwhelming. She looked at Evie who was taking it in stride, as if she was born to do this. Evie walked up to the podium filled with microphones of different news stations.

The flashing lights were blinding to Sarah. Evie gave Sarah a hug and whispered, "Look past the lights and smile."

"Hello, Astridians, Movers, and not forgetting you non-gifted people out there. I think I see two or three," a little chuckle went through the crowd. "I have called you all here today to share some amazing news. After consulting with officials and scholars in our community, we have come to a momentous decision. We have at long last found Astrid's reincarnation," a great commotion spread through the crowd. Evie made motions with her hands for people to settle down, "We believe beyond a shadow of a doubt, that my beloved granddaughter, Sarah Alice Rose, fulfils the great prophecy of Astrid's return to us. She is Astrid's reincarnation."

As Sarah stood beside her grandmother, her teeth hurt from clenching. Her hands shook and she wanted to run off the stage.

"She fulfills the prophecy left to us by Astrid herself. Let me read it to you to refresh your memory. 'I shall be reborn anew into my bloodline. They will have hair the color of fire, the mark of a great pyramid upon the flesh and the strength of thirty-three men. My reincarnation will lead you with their light.'

"Not only did Sarah officially test as a thirty-three on the Delving Ability Scale, but she is the first to test beyond a thirty." She nodded again and turned towards the crowd. The crowd sat in silence among the flashing of the cameras as they watched her lift into the air and float twenty feet above the stage. "Only a thirty or above can do that." There was a great applause as Sarah came down to the stage. "I will now take questions."

Chapter 17

Adolescence Already Sucks

Astridian Academy Private High School
Astridia, California
September 19th
1997

Sarah stood in front of her locker with three friends. Katie brushed her hair in front of her locker mirror, softly singing the Spice Girl's *Wannabe*. Katie's father, Richard Sparkman, owned the most prestigious funeral home and crematorium in the county. The twins joined in on the chorus of the song. The twins Hazel and Charley Ashwin, were new to the school. Their father was the new leader of The Chosen, since Stuart Sark had passed away that March. They were originally from India, but had both lost their accents.

"Dad is being super grumpy lately. It's that stupid registration bill thing, I think," Charley said, eating from a bag of chips.

"Oh yeah, what's going on with that bill? Grandma won't talk about it," Sarah said.

"It looks like it's going to happen and become a real thing," Charley said and handed Sarah the bag.

"That blows," Katie said.

"I know, but he wants me to be just as upset as he is. But we have the recital tonight, I can't focus on this stuff."

"You're being completely juvenile," Hazel said. "This could seriously change our lives."

"I'll show you juvenile," Charley threw a chip at her.

"Really? I can't believe you just did that," she pouted.

"Katie, speaking of things we can't believe you did…did you and Chad…?" Sarah asked.

"Let's just say I'm officially a woman," Katie said.

"Eww. Wait, did it hurt?" Hazel asked looking away from her magazine.

"It was beyond romantic. He was sweet and gentle."

"He's also too old, thirty is freaking ancient," Hazel said putting her magazine in her

backpack.

"At least he knew what he was doing, you know older means experienced," she said with

a grin. "Most high school boys don't know anything about life, let alone how to please a woman. No offense, Charley."

"None taken. I'm a high school boy and I can tell you that's 100 percent true," he said and passed Sarah the chip bag.

"Be careful, I don't want you to get hurt," Sarah said and ate a chip.

"You guys should be happy for me."

"We are," Sarah said. "Right guys?"

"Whatever. I'm thirsty, I need a soda. I'm going to the snack bar before class."

Charley said and left.

"Wait up," Hazel said and took off after her brother.

"It doesn't matter, I'm going to ditch this stupid town as soon as high school is over."

"I wish I could leave," Sarah said looking down at her feet.

"But you're famous," Katie said. She put up her hairbrush as a mock microphone, "Sarah Rose, what is it like being the most powerful Mover in the entire world?" she asked. The class bell rang, "Stay tuned for her riveting answer later on the ten o'clock news," they both giggled.

"Shut up, Katie. I've got to go to class."

133

"I'm just messing around. I'll see you at the recital tonight."

Sarah took her history book from her locker and walked down the hall to class. The teacher Mr. Gold stood at the front of the room handing out the graded weekly response papers. As he gave her the graded paper, he gave her a thumbs up. She looked down and saw a large red A+.

"Ok class, here is how this works," Mr. Gold said as he wrote grade ranges and tally marks on the board. "If you haven't figured it out, these numbers are you and how many of you earned a specific grade. As you can see, the majority of you fell into average territory and only one of you did what I asked. Sarah Rose, can you please read your response paper so everyone knows what I'm looking for?"

"He's looking for a kiss ass," Tommy Field shouted from the back row.

"Shut up Tommy, I so am not a kiss ass," Sarah yelled back.

"Decorum in my class room is sacred and required," Mr. Gold said calmly, but assertively.

"He called me a..."

"I know, but it does not have to provoke you to anger. As for you Tommy, go to the principal's office. I warned you yesterday that one more outburst would not be excused."

On his way out, Tommy bumped into Sarah and muttered, "Stuck up bitch."

Sarah fumed with anger. She thrust a large amount of energy at him, knocking him to the ground. She was sure his nose broke in the process due to the awful sound and gushing blood.

"Both of you go to the principal's office immediately. Tommy, you go to the nurse's office first."

As Sarah sat outside the principal's office, a whimpering Tommy shuffled out of the nurse's office. He sped past her and avoided eye contact. She heard her grandmother assert her influence without even raising her

134

voice. Sometimes Sarah enjoyed the perks of being from the most powerful family in town. As Evie exited the office, the principal shook his head. She motioned for Sarah to follow her out of the office.

As they walked down the hallway, she chuckled, "Sounds like you can hold your own."

"Wait, you're not mad?"

"Not in the least. From what I gathered, the boy had it coming."

"What's going to happen? The principal said…"

"Never mind what he said. Your bodyguard, Buzz, told me you enjoy dancing during your free class period. I know you might want to practice before the recital tonight. I have meetings this afternoon, but I'll see you at dinner." Evie walked away and turned back, "I'm proud of you, Princess."

"For what?"

"For standing up for yourself, not letting him take away your power. I respect you for that. Rose women shouldn't be messed with," she said and winked.

The class of 1976 had painted murals in the dance studio of famous ballets and dance styles. Her favorite was *The Nutcracker* mural, since the student who painted it had the most skill. She wondered sometimes who he was and where he was now. She liked to think of him following his artistic passion and painting in Paris. As she left for the locker room, she heard someone pounding the punching bag in the weight room. Curious, she peered in and saw a shirtless young man taking jabs at the bag. With each punch, a ripple went through his lean muscular frame. She found secretly watching him thrilling. Suddenly, he stopped and turned towards her.

"I'm sorry that I was staring at you," she said. "I'll go now."

He smiled and took his gloves off, "Hey, wait. I'm Brian, and you are?" he asked and extended his hand.

As she shook his hand she blushed and lightly bit her lower lip, "You're sweaty."

"Oh, God, shit, I'm so sorry," he said and wiped her hand with a towel.

"Sarah, to answer your question. I'm Sarah."

"I know who you are, I was trying to be cool and I just got sweat on you."

"It's okay. Do you do this often?"

"What? Get sweat on Sarah Rose often?" he said with an embarrassed smile.

She gave him a little shove, "That's not what I meant."

"Hit the bag you mean? I come in here a lot, to think."

"And hitting that thing helps with thinking?"

"You should know…I heard through the grapevine you gave that Tommy Field a knocking down."

"You heard about that?" she said, shuffling her feet.

"Well, duh, everyone knows that you gave Tommy what he deserved."

"I should let you get back to thinking," she said pointing at the bag.

"Wait. Do you drink coffee?"

"Yes, why?"

"Why do you think?" he said with a sweet and coy smile. "Are you blushing?"

"No," she said as she quickly covered her cheeks.

"I didn't mean to embarrass you."

"You didn't, I just have never been asked to coffee before."

"Really? How can that be?"

"I'm not sure; maybe boys don't think it's an option."

"Is it an option?"

"I'm considering it."

"Alright," he did a little victory dance. She laughed quietly and covered her mouth.

"I'm going to go get changed and if I decide to get coffee, I'll see you at the corner coffee shop," she said and left down the hall.

The corner coffee shop was across the street from the high school. It was a local hang out for a mostly high school crowd. In the midst of the chatter sat Sarah and Brian.

"I have a question for you, Brian."

"Shoot."

"You know me, but you haven't even told me your last name."

"I don't want to tell you," he said and sipped his coffee.

"That's weird...I thought it was Delving."

"Wait, how did you know?"

"I'm very powerful and all knowing," she said and laughed.

"I know my family is important around here, but I want you to like me for me and not my last name. I'm more than who I'm related to."

"You must be joking. Look who you're talking to."

"Good point," he said and looked down into his coffee.

"Brian," she said and touched his hand. "Nice to meet you."

She looked past him and saw the bodyguard she ditched.

"Oh, man," she muttered,

"What?" he said and looked over his shoulder. "Who's that?"

The bodyguard walked up to the table with arms crossed, and he motioned for her to come with him.

"Buzz, can I have just one more minute, please?" she clasped her hands. "Pretty please with a cherry on top?"

"You can have two minutes, just don't tell the boss," Buzz said and stood over by the exit.

Sarah smiled at Brian and shook her head, "I don't know why it surprises me when he tracks me down."

"I'm sure," he said and smiled. "Can we do this again?"

As she got up, she gave him a kiss on the cheek, "Totally," she said.

Later that night, Sarah stood off stage watching another girl dance in the recital. She did a beautiful program to Ravel's *Pavane for a Dead Princess*. Sarah started to doubt her choice in music, that it was not traditional. She anxiously smoothed a little crease in her long flowing white dress. Charley was standing next to her. He was dressed in black pants, a black dress shirt, and a red crushed velvet vest. In his hand was a devil mask. Sarah heard loud applause from the audience and the girl performing took a bow. Mrs. Nightingale, the dance teacher, whispered "Good luck" in Sarah's ear. The stagehand, also known as Mrs. Nightingale's husband, pushed out a short prop staircase onto the stage and motioned to Sarah that it was her turn.

With a deep breath, she went to center stage. As she moved into position, she turned to Mr. Nightingale and gave a little nod. Jerry, a pimple-laden freshman from the AV department started the music. Led Zeppelin's *Stairway to Heaven* poured into the auditorium. Her dancing was mesmerizing. As the music changed to the faster tempo, Charley joined her on stage wearing the devil mask. She danced with him behind her but did not acknowledge his presence on stage until right before the guitar solo. Then they played out through dance the devil pursuing her and her trying to fight back. A moment before the last section of the song where it slows down, they climbed the short staircase. She kissed him and lied down on the steps as the song slowed to a close. The audience broke into thunderous applause and rose to their feet. Sarah and Charley took a bow and left the stage.

"We killed them," Charley said and hugged Sarah, lifting her off the ground and spinning with her in his arms.

"Very good guys, now go backstage and get ready for the reception party," Mrs. Nightingale said.

At the reception party, Sarah stood with Evie at the punch bowl. Evie awkwardly held her cup and gazed into the bright red liquid.

"It's punch Grandma, you drink it,"

"Don't be a smart ass."

"Sarah, you were amazing," Katie came up with Hazel and all three hugged. "Your brother wasn't half bad," she said to Hazel.

"Hey Satan, come over here," Hazel called out to Charley and he walked over.

He was holding a plate with a mixture of cookies and baby carrots.

"Hi, Mrs. Rose," he said and smiled.

"Hello, Charles," Evie said. "I see someone I want to have a word with, excuse me," she said and walked off to the other side of the room.

"Someone important was in the audience," he said to the girls.

"What have I told you about being vague?" Hazel said and elbowed him gently.

"Some guy from The Alessaria Dance Academy."

"Shut up," Sarah said and gave him a little punch. "Which guy is it?" she said looking around.

"That guy," he said while pointing in the direction of two men talking to Mrs. Nightingale.

"Which one? The bald guy or the cute one," Katie asked.

"The bald guy."

"Sarah," Mrs. Nightingale called out and waved her over.

"Wish me luck," she said giddily.

Sarah walked over as quickly as she could without running.

139

"Sarah, this is Mr. Dalton. He is a teacher at The Alessaria Dance Academy, in New York."

"Hi," was all she could muster.

"Pleased to meet you, Ms. Rose. Your dancing was superb tonight." Sarah blushed. "Not only are you the future leader of our people, you are one of the most beautiful and skilled dancers I've seen in a while. I would like to invite you to come study in New York when you graduate."

"Oh my God, are you serious?" she exclaimed feeling the excitement pumping through her veins.

"Out of the question," Sarah heard behind her. She turned to see Evie standing with her arms crossed and wearing a scowl.

"Well, hello Mrs. Rose."

"Oh, shut up. How dare you ask her something like that without checking with me first?"

"I thought you would be thrilled,"

"You thought wrong,"

"Enough," Sarah screamed and the whole room turned their eyes towards her.

"Hush, Sarah, you're making a scene."

"There's no future for me here. I can have a life of my own, which is what Mom and Dad would have wanted. I wish Mom and Dad were alive, I wouldn't be stuck with you."

"Well, they're dead and you are stuck with me. We're leaving. You better come with me and stop being a spoiled brat."

Evie turned and left the room and Sarah followed with her arms crossed. The room was so quiet no one dared to even whisper.

Brian felt like he was floating after being on a date with Sarah. When he arrived home, he set his keys in his key jar and walked in to see a man bleeding on the dining room table. He took off his jacket and grabbed an apron from the closet. A man came from the kitchen with a boiling pot of water and towels. The man on the table was unconscious and there were a few puddles of blood on the tile floor.

"We're going to have to have that cleaning agency come out again. They were just here, damn it. Hey, Brian, how was your date?"

"It was good, I like her a lot. She's pretty and smart."

"That's a good combo. My Mary has both brains and beauty."

"Thanks, hon," Mary said as she walked in with more towels.

"So, what happened to Josh?"

"He was a grade-A moron this time. He tripped and fell onto a knife in a bar fight. I say tripped loosely of course. It took everything in my power to not let the cops take him into custody."

"I guess that's the perk of being a cop..." Brian said as he washed his hands.

"Brian, can you do your magic? I don't want Mary to do it and I'm out of my league here."

"Hey, just because I'm carrying your child does not make me useless," Mary protested.

"I wasn't saying that, dear. You just don't want to make yourself too tired."

"He's right Mary; you don't want to get too tired."

"Fine, I'll go make something to munch on. I have to do something."

"That's a good idea, I'm starved."

Brian rubbed his hands together and held them over the man on the table. After a half an hour of working to seal the wound, the final sizzle came. He rinsed the wound with a clean sanitized cloth and sighed in relief. He took the apron off and went into the kitchen. Mary had prepared fried zucchini sticks. He took one and bit into it, and softly moaned.

"I need a wife."

Mary smiled and gave him a light kiss on the cheek. She sat down at the kitchen table and placed her hands on her ever-growing belly.

"Jackson says you came home late because you went on a date. What's the scoop on that?"

"Mary, don't give the kid a hard time."

"I'm just asking."

"It's okay, cous'. This girl...she's so beautiful, funny, and smart."

"What's her name? Do we know her family?"

"Sarah," Brian grabbed a beer from the fridge.

"Sarah what?" Mary asked and there was a long pause.

"Rose," Brian said nonchalantly.

"Shut the front door. You went on a date with Sarah Rose?"

"Yeah, she's a person too you know. Don't make a big deal out of it."

"Does she know about the project?" Jackson asked.

"Nope, and she won't," Brian reached for another zucchini stick.

"Good boy."

Josh, the man on the table, moaned and grunted before sitting up. He reached for his chest and rubbed where the knife wound was.

"What happened?"

"You, apparently, were a grade-A moron and got stabbed," Brian said with half a mouth full of zucchini.

"Where's Ethan?"

"You know he can't stand the sight of blood. He went to Hooters for some chicken wings."

"Ha ha, very funny."

"I just called him to let him know the carnage was over and your dumbass was okay," Jackson said with the phone in his hand.

The front door opened to a man holding a bouquet of flowers wearing worn jeans and a Metallica t-shirt. He looked worried and rushed to the table.

"Oh my God, are you okay?" Ethan asked.

"Yeah, thanks for the flowers, I ain't dead," Josh said and rolled his eyes.

"Who said they're for you, asshole?"

They embraced and shared a long, deeply loving kiss. Josh patted Ethan on the butt and got off the kitchen table.

"I need something to drink," Josh said.

"I don't think you should be drinking, dude," Brian said.

"That is between me, myself, and I...and the beer in my hand."

"I'll make you something to eat instead," Ethan said, walking towards the kitchen.

"You worked at the restaurant all day, let me just call for a pizza."

"Mr. Josh Delving, I want to cook for you, damn it," Ethan said with a quiver in his voice.

"Fine," Josh said and rubbed his chest. "This time it's really sore."

"You did have a freaking knife in there dude. You better smarten up, or I might not be able to fix your ass next time."

"Brian, are you going tomorrow night?" Jackson asked.

"What's tomorrow night?" Brian said after taking a sip of beer.

"I told you, the guy taking Stuart Sark's place. His name is...something...Ashwin. He called a meeting."

"Yeah, I'll be there."

"You'd better, since he specifically asked for you."

"Why?"

"Didn't say, just said for you to be there. Oh and this came special delivery for you," he said and handed him a padded envelope. "Who do you know in England?"

Brian opened it and poured out a St. Margaret medal, "I ordered this."

"We're not Catholic."

"Stuart Sark had one just like this," Mary said as she looked at it.

"I still miss Stuart, even if he was a pain in the ass," Josh said.

"I'll toast to that," Brian raised his beer and everyone raised a glass in turn. "To Stu, the best Chosen leader and brother in arms."

"Amen," they all said in response.

"Now, Josh, you better help clean up your mess," Mary said.

"Wait, when did I have to start cleaning my own blood off the floor?"

"If you don't remember, you're the dumbass who got stabbed," Jackson said and handed him a mop and bucket.

Chapter 18

Jump into the Deep End

New Alessaria, California
October 10th
1997

Sarah was in her room putting on her strawberry lip gloss when she heard the doorbell. Excitement pumped through her. She looked in the mirror before grabbing her purse and going downstairs. She saw Brian in the foyer and she smiled. His face lit up when he saw her.

"Hi," he said.

"Hi back," she said. "Oh, I forgot something. I'll be right back."

"Okay."

He looked around at the foyer when he heard the clicking of heels coming behind him. He spun around and Evie was there with a martini in hand.

"Hi, I'm Brian," he said and did a little wave.

"I know who you are dear. Ashwin only speaks your praises." Brian's face turned into one of panic and he looked around nervously.

"Just so you know, your secret is fine with me," she said. "I know Ashwin has you on the mission. I heard you are his best fixer, and loyal. He even asked if I would put you through medical school. So, please don't take me for a fool."

"Ready to go?" Sarah said as she bounded down the staircase.

"Have a good time you two," Evie said leaving the foyer.

Brian drove a new black pickup truck. He opened the door for Sarah and then walked around to the driver's seat. While he was going around the truck, Sarah was searching for a lever to move her seat back. As she felt around, she found a cold metal object. She took it from under the seat and was shocked to see a gun in her hand. Brian sat down, started the truck and looked over only to find Sarah holding his revolver. The Verve's *Bittersweet Symphony* started to play on the radio.

"I can explain," he said.

"I would like to know what you're doing with this under the seat."

"I can tell you, but not in front of your house."

"Turn the truck off."

The only sound breaking the silence was his finger tapping on the wheel.

"Okay, I'm kind of a member of The Chosen."

"Why are you telling me this just now?"

He reached over, took the gun from her lap, and put it in the glove compartment.

"I was told not to by Ashwin."

"Wow, what could you do with The Chosen? You're seventeen."

"Okay. I'm only telling you because I really like you, Sarah. I'm what they call a fixer."

"What do you fix? Cars?"

"People."

"What do you mean you fix people?"

"I'm kind of like their doctor or surgeon."

"Wait, you can do that stuff already? You told me you were going to go to medical school. I didn't know you were pretty much already a doctor. What else are you hiding from me?"

146

"Sarah, I'm sorry. I was afraid to tell you."

"Why do you have a gun?"

"My brother gave it to me for protection."

"Have you used it?"

"No, I haven't and I don't plan on it. Jackson's a cop so he's on the paranoid side."

"Does he approve of all this?"

"Well, he's in all of this, too. But, you know we're the good guys."

"I need to think about this stuff. I'm going back inside," she said and Brian sighed.

Sarah stormed out of the truck, slamming the door. As she walked into the house, she noticed that music was playing in the parlor. She walked in and saw Evie on the floor face down. She screamed and went to her.

Brian had noticed halfway down the driveway that Sarah had left her purse. He did a three-point turn and returned to the front of the house. He knocked but there was no response. Then he heard Sarah scream. He opened the door and rushed in. He heard Sarah pleading with Evie to wake up in the parlor. As he went into the room he saw Sarah shaking Evie on the floor.

"What's going on?" he said as he knelt down.

"I don't know," Sarah said in a panic.

"Move," he said. He listened to her chest. "Ok, she's breathing." He raised her turtleneck sleeve to check for a pulse and noticed her skin had begun to yellow. "I don't know how to fix this; she needs to go to the hospital right now." He picked Evie up and headed to the door.

Sarah and Brian were in the waiting room of the hospital. The other people were staring at Sarah, pointing and whispering.

"Thank you for being here," she said as he rubbed her back.

"I'm glad you forgot your purse."

Sarah looked at him and nodded.

"I'm sorry I yelled at you."

"It's okay. We can deal with all that later."

A nurse opened the door to the emergency room and motioned for Sarah to come in.

"Only family," The nurse said pointing to Sarah.

"Do you know who I am? I want him with me and he's coming in," Sarah said.

The nurse pursed her lips in response.

"Fine. She's in bed three and the doctor will be in shortly."

Brian grabbed hold of Sarah's hand as they walked into the room. Evie was still unconscious. Sarah sat down in a chair and pulled it towards the bed. She clasped her hands around Evie's hand.

"Miss Rose, I'm Doctor Garcia," the doctor said upon entering the room. She shook his hand. "And you are?" he asked as he put out his hand to Brian.

"He's my boyfriend. It's ok to talk in front of him."

"Your grandmother has suffered significant liver damage and we are giving her care until she can be transferred to the intensive care unit. I can't guarantee she won't need a liver transplant, but we are trying to avoid that. We found high amounts of alcohol and benzodiazepine medications in her system. How long has she been abusing these?"

"She always has," she said. She looked back down at Evie, "Why won't she wake up?" she asked in a quiet voice.

"She's in a coma."

"For how long?"

"It's hard to tell you when she will come around. Go home and rest. We will keep you updated if you leave your phone number with the nurse. We will do the best we can," the doctor said and left the room.

Shortly after, the nurse came in and took down Sarah's information. As they walked to the truck, Sarah

148

looked up at the stars. She thought about how she always took them for granted and forgot how beautiful they are.

"I don't know if this is weird, but you can stay at my house so you don't have to be alone," Brian said when they got into the car.

"I think that's a good idea. Thank you."

"So, I noticed you told the doctor I'm your boyfriend."

"Yeah, sorry about that."

"Yeah, I'm not sorry you did." He leaned in and kissed her, "Ready to meet my family?"

As Brian and Sarah approached his front door, Brian noticed Jackson was yelling.

"Is this a good time?" Sarah said cautiously.

"Oh, if you're going to be my girlfriend you'll have to get used to yelling. It's how we show we care about each other."

They entered the living room and saw Jackson and Josh yelling at each other. Mary was on the couch flipping through a magazine.

"You are such a douche bag," Josh yelled. "You need to tell Brian."

"Tell me what?" Brian said. All he saw were blank looks and there was long pause.

"Hey, Brian," Mary said trying to break the awkwardness. "Oh my God, Sarah? Sarah Rose, that's you...here...in my house."

Sarah gave a little wave. Mary jumped up and gave her a hug.

"What does he need to tell me?" Brian reiterated.

"Dude, not a good time," Josh said and looked over at Sarah.

"I can go," Sarah said.

"No, Sarah can stay. Will someone tell me?"

"Okay, Brian it's about Liz. You might want to sit for this one." Brian did as instructed and sat down. "She came into lock-up today."

A long silence hung in the air.

"I would bet she deserves to be there. Karma's a bitch."

"Brian, you shouldn't be such a dick," Josh said.

"Hey Sarah, would you mind helping a pregnant lady fix some refreshments?"

"Uh, sure," Sarah said.

After getting into the kitchen out of earshot, Mary turned to Sarah.

"Okay, what I'm going to tell you is woman to woman. You're no ditz, so you probably figured out that Liz is Brian's ex. Hand me that bowl. The simple boiled down version is that she was Brian's first flame and she broke his heart, bad. She's Ethan's sister and she came off as a nice girl. We all liked her. But, she got in with a bad crowd. Poor Brian was willing to put up with the drugs, until he found out she was cheating on him."

"Wow, how did he find out?"

"Well, this is where it gets a little complicated. Fill this pitcher with water. Spigot is right there. He caught her red handed. I thought it would be best if you weren't in the room for the really bad news. Put those chips in that bowl." Mary paused, "I don't know specifics, but she was brought in for drugs and prostitution. She made bail somehow." Mary took a bag of baby carrots out of the fridge. Holding the bag in her hands, she sighed. "They don't know if it was an intentional overdose or not."

"Wait, she's okay right?" she asked. Mary shook her head no.

"They haven't told him yet."

"How do you know?"

At that moment they heard a loud bang and both ran to the living room. Brian had punched the wall and had made contact with a wood stud. Mary left and came back with ice in a dishtowel.

"Dude, I think it's broken," Josh said inspecting the hand.

"No shit," Brian said.

"You can fix it, right?" Sarah asked and all eyes looked to her.

"Who do you suppose will do it? Mary's pregnant, Josh and I are only fifteens, and our fixer is the one who needs to be fixed. We need at least a twenty; I guess I can try Jeff."

"Jeff sucks, you know that," Josh said.

"Can you show me how? I mean, I am like over a 30," Sarah said, Josh threw his hands in the air.

"That's not a bad idea," Brian said.

"Wait, you're going to let her fix you?" Josh balked.

"Josh, you need to leave right now. Get some fresh air," Jackson said pointing to the backyard.

Sarah went to Brian, looked at his hand, and gulped.

"So, step one, survey the injury. You'll feel through my hand for the broken bone or I think there may be more than one."

Sarah closed her eyes, focused her power on his good hand. Then as she switched to the right hand, she did the same process and found he had three broken fingers and a bone in a knuckle.

"Four are broken; two seem to have little pieces where it's broken."

"Oh, shit. This will take a while. You up for it?" Brian asked wincing.

She looked down at the hand and then up at Brian. She looked him in the eyes and nodded.

"So, I just make all the bones go where they should go, like the good hand?"

"Yeah. After that you will speed up the collagen production of the bones. You put a large charge into the osteoblasts and osteoclasts."

"You're going over my head."

"She can't do this, Brian," Jackson said.

"Sarah, forget the jargon. You are going to feel closely and there are cells that you can feel. It almost feels like they are flexing and seeping stuff out. Feel them?"

She held her hands over his hand and she could feel them.

"Yeah, I can feel them. Now what?"

"You are going to move the bones into their right placement and then energize the cells to produce faster. This might take a while but…"

At that moment, she put all the bones back into place at once. Brian wailed in excruciating pain. She then used all her energy and focused it on those cells. She could feel them rebuilding the bones. Almost like little spiders building a web. After less than a minute, the bones were set and fused back together.

"Brian, are you okay?" Jackson rushed over and pushed Sarah away.

Brian was dripping sweat from the pain and was rhythmically moaning. Mary came over and gave him a painkiller injection. After a couple minutes, his color returned and he opened his eyes. She didn't know if she had succeeded or caused more harm. Brian held his hand up and slowly flexed it. The look of awe on his face spoke volumes.

"You did it," Mary whispered.

"I'm glad it worked," Sarah said.

Jackson put his hand on her shoulder and looked in her eyes.

"You don't understand. It takes Brian at least half an hour to set one bone. You set four in less than a minute. I didn't think that was even humanly possible," his voice trailed off.

"Brian, how about you go lie down and rest? Sarah, would you mind staying with him? I gave him a good shot of morphine and he could get a bit loopy."

"What a night," he said as he flopped onto the bed.

"For both of us. I almost forgot about Grandma while I was helping you. How could I do that? She's lying in a hospital bed and I don't know if…"

"Your Grandma is going to be okay, she's a survivor."

"I hope you're right. I'm sorry about Liz. If you feel like it, you can tell me about her."

Brian sighed and looked up at the ceiling.

"Even though I knew this was coming, it doesn't feel real. I loved her, she was my first girlfriend after all."

"Was she pretty?"

"That's not what you want to know, you want to know if we did it. The answer is no. We were going to wait until summer vacation. The drugs I could have dealt with. I knew she liked to smoke weed and had a drug dealer. I honestly thought that was it. Then she started with the pills, which turned to shooting up. I remember she said the track marks were mosquito bites. God, I'm not a moron. The final straw was catching her with my brother at a party. She said it was an accident. I was so pissed I punched him, he has a couple fake teeth to prove it."

"You have a brother?" she asked with surprise.

"Yeah, Michael. He's my twin, but we're fraternal so we don't look alike. He lives with our Grandma. He and I don't get along, since he screwed my girlfriend and all."

"I'm sorry they did that to you."

He shifted and looked at her. He brushed his hand against her cheek and smiled slightly.

"Don't be. I know we haven't been together for long, but I know I can trust you."

153

She smiled gently and looked into his green eyes. She could not look away. She put her palm on his chest and felt his heart beating.

"I know what you mean."

He leaned in and kissed her. When he went to pull away, she held his head so he could not. He kissed her more passionately and rapidly. She touched his hand and moved it to her breast.

"Oh, we need to slow down," he said and pulled his hand away. By the look on her face, he felt like she needed an explanation. "It's not you or anything."

"What do you mean? Don't you want to fool around?"

"I do, of course. But I can't. It's embarrassing." She looked at him with confusion and he sighed. "I'm too excited."

"Oh," she said and bit her bottom lip.

"I have something else we can do,"

He went into his closet and pulled out a Hungry, Hungry Hippos game.

"Really? How old are we?"

"Where is your sense of fun, Princess?"

"My parents called me Princess," she said with a sad smile.

"Sorry,"

"No, don't be, I like it," she said. She grabbed the game from him. "But I'm always the pink hippo and I'm going to kick your ass."

"Trash talk has begun."

Mary came into the room, "Sarah, the nurse from the hospital was on the phone. Your Grandma is awake and responding well to the drugs."

"I told you, she's a survivor," Brian said and held her in his arms.

"She's going to be okay," Mary said as she left the room.

Chapter 19

Halloween Fisticuffs

Sarah hummed along to the radio and adjusted her Princess Leia Buns.

"I get knocked down, but I get up again," she sang along.

She sat at her vanity putting on lipstick when there was a knock at the bedroom door. She willed the door open to a frazzled maid.

"What's she doing now?" Sarah asked as she finished her lipstick.

"Throwing one of her tantrums. Can you deal with her, Sarah? I'm at my wits end. I wish she would just start drinking again."

"I'll be right down."

Sarah could hear Evie yelling in the study as she walked down the stairs. She looked into the room and saw Evie yelling at the chauffeur.

"Grandma?"

Evie turned and put her hands on her hips, "I've rested long enough, and I can't take this anymore."

"Please rest. I don't want you yelling at everyone and working yourself up."

Evie let out an exasperated sigh and sat down in a huff. She ran her fingers through her hair and teared up.

156

"It's like I don't know how to handle life," Evie said and Sarah sat next to her. "I'm so sorry, Princess, I'm supposed to be the adult right now. I'm failing you."

She cried and Sarah held her. She motioned to the driver that he was free to leave.

"I love you, Grandma. I just want you to get better. I can stay here and not go to the party."

Evie pulled away and looked at Sarah's costume. For the first time, Evie realized Sarah had a woman's body and was officially growing up. She touched Sarah's buns and smiled.

"Go   to   the   party,   have   a   good   time."

"Are you sure?"

"Yes. Is Brian picking you up soon?"

"Any minute," she said. Her face lit up at the mention of his name.

"You really like him, don't you?" Evie said with a smile.

"I'm not talking about this with you."

"It's okay, I can tell."

The doorbell rang and Sarah did a celebratory motion with her hands.

A maid came to the door of the study, "Miss Sarah, Brian is at the door."

"Have fun, your curfew is midnight tonight."

"Thanks, Grandma."

Sarah walked out of the study and saw Brian in his Han Solo costume.

"Wow you look great," she said and they shared a quick kiss. "Turn around for me."

He did an exaggerated catwalk turn, "Hot stuff, right?"

"You do look great; your tush looks pretty good without the wallet bulge."

He slapped his forehead, "My wallet, I forgot it."

"You don't have your wallet?"

"No big deal, we can swing by my house on the way to the party."

"What if we get pulled over?"

He started laughing as he walked out the door, without answering her question.

As they arrived at his house, Brian saw an unfamiliar car in the driveway.

"Huh, I wonder who's here," Brian said with a tone of concern. "You can stay here; I'll just go in and get my wallet."

"I'll come in. I have to use the powder room."

"It kills me that you call it that, so prim and proper."

"Whatever," she said as they got out of the car.

As they walked in, Sarah saw there was a strange young man in the living room before Brian noticed. They made eye contact, and she recognized him. Instantly, she felt the terror of the secret they shared. She prayed that only she remembered, until he gave a particular smile and nod proving she was not that lucky. He had feathery brown hair and brown eyes. He had a scar on his forehead and a slightly crooked nose from being broken more than once.

Brian turned and saw the young man and his demeanor changed drastically. Brian went at him fist first, but Jackson pushed him back.

"Nice to see you, too, bro," said the young man.

"Fuck you," Brian said.

"Go in the backyard and cool off," Jackson ordered.

"Why is he here?" Brian shouted, pointing at the young man.

"Go outside, I'll be right behind you," Jackson said. After Brian left he said, "Sarah, I think it's a good idea to let him cool off, stay here. Brian can have a slight temper problem sometimes."

She nodded and Jackson left. Turning, she looked at the young man and he smiled.

"Hi, I'm Sarah," she said, hoping he did not remember her secret.

"I know who you are, Sarah Rose," he said with a grin. She sat down across from him in the armchair. "I also know you remember me."

"I don't know what you mean."

"Cut the crap." She looked at him wide-eyed and full of worry; he smirked and rubbed his chin. "Don't worry I won't tell my brother."

"You're Michael, the twin?"

"Yeah, small world, right?" She sat in silence. "Sorry, I didn't mean to bust your balls. Does he know? I bet he doesn't, otherwise you wouldn't look so spooked."

"I haven't told anyone, no one knows."

"That's not true now, is it? I heard you claim you don't remember."

She started to cry, "I wish I didn't."

The sliding door to the backyard opened and shut. Sarah tried to stop crying and wiped away the tears. Brian and Jackson entered the living room and instantly noticed her tears.

"What did you do to her?" Brian yelled.

"I didn't do anything, bro," Michael said scrambling.

"It's nothing babe, let's just go to the party," Sarah pleaded

"You're crying, that's not 'nothing.'"

"It's Halloween, let's just go have fun."

"I want to know what's going on," Brian demanded.

"Look I can explain," Sarah said.

"No you don't," Michael said. "You don't have to tell him anything you don't want to."

"Just shut up," she yelled. "Let's go in the other room, okay?"

"You know him, don't you?" Brian asked and Sarah bit her lip. "You do know him. Did you sleep with him?"

"Oh, God no."

"Hey, I'm not chopped liver."

"Shut up, Mike, you're not helping," Jackson said.

"Can we talk about this…alone?"

Brian nodded, "But I still have to talk to him later," he said pointing to Michael.

They went into the bedroom and closed the door, Sarah sat on the bed and Brian paced.

"Sit down, you're making me nervous."

He sat on the end of the bed and rubbed his palms together.

"Tell me what the hell is going on."

"He was there when I was rescued," Sarah blurted out.

"Rescued?"

"Yeah, I was, um, kidnapped."

He sat up straight and put his hands on his knees.

"You said you didn't remember what happened."

"Wait, you know about the kidnapping?" she asked, mouth agape.

"I was a new member of The Chosen at that point and I was on cleanup detail. You were already taken to the hospital."

She realized he knew her deepest secret and saw what she did to those men. She realized he knew and in spite of it still wanted to be with her.

"I love you," she blurted out.

He smiled, "I know." Sarah looked down at their costumes and laughed. "In all the commotion I forgot to show you," he left with his car keys. Brian returned with a plastic red lightsaber, "I got this at the costume store."

"You're such a geek, Brian. Besides, Han Solo doesn't use a lightsaber, silly."

"Now who's the geek?"

He exaggeratedly waved the lightsaber around and made mock sound effects. The scene sent Sarah into a laughing fit.

Part III

Chapter 20

Mongoose and Shakespeare

New Alessaria, California
November 20th
1997

Deep Purple's *Smoke on the Water* blasted from the boom box. Sarah was on her bed staring at the ceiling while Katie sat on the edge of the bed with her hand on Sarah's ankle. It was Sarah's 17th birthday, but she had never enjoyed that she shared a birthday with Astrid. Most people treated the day like a holiday akin to St. Patrick's Day, where it is more about beer and food than the meaning behind it. Many referred to the day as Astrid's Birthday Celebration or A.B.C. There was also the common moniker of "Astridians get drunk day."

"Why are we listening to this old music stuff?" Katie asked.

Sarah sat up and tucked her legs before answering, "Every night before bed, my parents had a ritual. They would play a song and tell me a story behind it. I remember they told me this song was playing when my mom found out she was going to have me."

"Really?"

"Yeah. I guess they were at this bar watching a cover band and my mom completely upchucked on this one guy's jacket."

"Eww, gross."

"Well, turns out the dude wasn't pissed at all. He was a doctor and so was his wife. They gave my mom some water and said they thought she was pregnant."

"Wow, that's a funny story. Your parents sound pretty cool."

"They were," Sarah said as a timer went off.

"Want me to look?"

Sarah nodded and Katie went into the bathroom. She returned with the test stick and the box. Sarah looked at Katie, whose face was contorted with confusion.

"Give it to me, it isn't brain surgery."

Sarah looked at the stick. There was a pink plus sign. She referred to the box and saw that it meant she was pregnant. The floor felt like it fell out from under her and she almost couldn't breathe.

"You know those things aren't always right. Let's go to the clinic to find out for sure. It's not a for sure thing yet. So, I'll take you there tomorrow."

"This is not happening," Sarah said. She sat in the middle of the floor and put her face in her hands. She looked up, "Do you think I'm a slut?"

"No, God no. That's so stupid, don't even go there. You and Brian have been dating like two months and it was with the one guy, who you freaking love and he loves you. That is the opposite of slutishness."

"Grandma is going to kill me."

"It's your birthday, so try to not let this get you down."

"I want to go to the clinic today; I need to know for sure."

"Okay, when?" Katie asked. Without a word, Sarah got up, grabbed her purse, and left the room. "Now. I guess we are leaving now," Katie said rolling her eyes. "Hold on, I'm coming," she hollered.

As they went down the stairs, Evie called to Sarah from the study. Sarah ignored Evie's beckoning until she confronted her in the foyer.

"Did you hear me, young lady?"

"What do you want?" Sarah said with a noticeable edge to her voice.

"Don't take that tone with me, missy. Where are you both off to in such a hurry?"

"Mall, we're going to the mall. Might see a movie."

"How fun. Well, now that you have that cellular telephone I gave you for your birthday, you can keep in touch. Okay?"

"Okay. Can we go now? We're going to be late for the movie."

"Have fun, you two,"

"We will," Katie said as they left the house.

The sterile exam room was blinding white. One of the fluorescent lights had a slight annoying flicker and hum. Sarah was lying on the exam table in a paper gown, wondering what it would be like to be a teenage mother. She felt like her life was over.

The doctor came into the room, and she smiled.

"Hi, Sarah, good to see you. It seems like yesterday your mom came to see me, you were the size of a kidney bean," the doctor extended her hand to Katie. "Hi, I'm Dr. Frank."

"Wait, are you the up-chuck doctor?" Katie asked and the doctor chuckled.

"Shut up, Katie."

"It's okay, Sarah. No, that was my husband, poor thing. Even as a zygote, Sarah was never boring. But, down to why you are here today. I reviewed your tests and you are indeed pregnant. With your levels of H.C.G., I recommend an ultrasound. Nothing to worry about, it won't hurt. Is that okay?" Sarah nodded. "Okay then, I'll get set up."

165

The doctor left and Katie reached over and held Sarah's hand, "It's going to be okay."

Dr. Frank returned with the gel and put some on Sarah's exposed stomach. She placed the wand and a whooshing sound came from the machine.

"What's that sound?" Katie asked.

"The baby's heartbeat," the doctor said and Sarah burst into tears. "I know this must be overwhelming for you. I can set you up with a prenatal counselor and she can help you with your options. On a personal note, I know Evie can be hard to handle at times, but I know she loves you more than life itself."

"Oh God, I can't do this."

"You're stronger than you think. We all have strength within us and sometimes we have to be tested to know how strong we really are," Dr. Frank started to leave but turned and said delicately, "Oh, and happy birthday."

After Katie dropped her off at home, Sarah collapsed onto her bed and fell asleep. She dreamt she was on a strange street she had never been on before. Her hand was feeling the side of a brown brick building she did not recognize. The brick was cold and rough, worn from years of weathering. She stood in front of the building, she wanted to go inside, but she was afraid. She awoke suddenly to Evie gently shaking her.

"Sarah, wake up. Brian's here to take you to the party. Are you feeling okay?"

"Yeah, I'm fine. I need to get ready. Tell him sorry I'm running so late."

"Okay, I'll tell him," Evie said. She turned and asked, "Are you sure you're okay?"

"Yeah, just leave, I have to get ready, Grandma."

Evie flinched at Sarah's tone and gingerly left the room. Sarah quickly threw on her blush pink party dress. She looked in her vanity mirror and tenderly touched the locket around her neck. Because of that necklace, she was still alive. As she applied makeup, there was a knock at the door.

"What is it," she said and saw Brian enter the room. "I'm not ready," she shrieked.

"Like I care if you only have half your face done."

"Let me just finish, alright," she said and put on mascara.

"What crawled up your ass?"

"Nothing."

He gave a slight wince at her sharp tone. He sat on the bed and looked around her room. After she finished her makeup, she put her hair up in a bun. With bobby pins in her teeth, she looked in the mirror at Brian and saw him looking at a picture of her parents.

"Is that them?" he asked.

She put in her last bobby pin and turned around, "Yep, my mom and dad."

"Is it at some kind of hay ride?

"No, it was taken at the county fair when I was five, I think. I remember getting sick from the cotton candy. I still can't touch the stuff. I know I was really young when they died, but I miss them a lot. Maybe I miss the idea of them more than the people in the picture. I don't know if that makes sense."

"I get it. Look who you're talking to. I lost both my parents just like you did. I miss them all the freaking time."

"How do you deal with it?"

He sighed and gave her a sly grin, "Sadly, I lack the money to become Batman," he said and she laughed. "I don't know, this might sound corny, but since I met you, my life feels less empty. The hurt became a little less, I miss them still, but it's for different reasons. Like, I wish they could have met you."

"You are so sweet," she went over and kissed him. "Although, if you change your mind about becoming Batman, I think I have a few million dollars in a trust fund."

He laughed and shuffled his feet, "We should go, the party is going to be rocking and rolling soon."

"I want to tell you something," she said.

He looked at her with a goofy grin, "What?"

"It's just that, I love you, you dork," she said and he laughed.

As they drove to the party, Sarah looked at all the buildings and realized she had never been to this side of town before. The rundown area was the part of town referred to as eclectic. Many buildings were from the original inception of the town and protected by the local historical society. As she looked out the window, she saw the building from her dream and gasped loudly.

"What?" Brian said, startled.

"Pull over," she said and he pulled the car over to the curb.

She got out of the car and looked at the brick building from her dream. Brian rolled down the passenger window.

"What's going on?" Brian asked, half frustrated, half worried.

She went up to the building and felt the brick. It felt the same as in her dream.

"I dreamt about this place," she said quietly.

"So, maybe you remembered it for some reason. Can we go to the party now?"

"You don't understand. I've never been here. I've never even been to this side of town."

"Really?"

"Well, yeah. I've led a kind of sheltered life."

"Why would you dream about the Astridian Library?"

"I don't know," her voice trailed off as she went around the corner. She saw the entrance and looked at Brian, "But I want to find out."

She entered the library and Brian sighed, turning off the ignition. The library was small and musty, but nothing looked odd about it. It was old, but more shabby than decrepit. She looked up and saw a beautiful portrait of Astrid in an elaborate gaudy frame. She forgot how beautiful Astrid was. In the painting, she wore a vibrant blue dress, she was sitting with a book in her hand.

As they stood looking at the painting, a voice from behind them said, "Excuse me, we're closed."

They turned and saw a man appearing to be in his mid-thirties holding a couple books. He was wearing glasses, a plaid shirt, and pleated slacks. He dropped the books after he looked at Sarah. He looked startled as he picked them back up.

"Sarah Rose, I'm sorry I didn't know it was you. Oh dear me, excuse my rudeness."

He put the books on the counter and he put out his hand.

"Pleasure to see you here," he said as he shook both their hands. "And you must be Brian Delving."

"Yes, how did you know?" Brian said warily.

"I knew your grandfather and father before they, well, you know."

"Are you the librarian here?"

"Yes, one of my many titles. Excuse my manners, I'm Nick Meyers."

"The name sounds familiar. Do I know you?"

"It should sound familiar. Not to toot my own horn, but I helped write *The History of the Movers and Astridians,* along with two others, one of which was your father, Sarah."

"You knew my dad?"

"Yes, he was a good friend of ours."

"Ours?"

"Ah yes, Amy is my faithful counterpart here at the library." He turned and yelled, "Mongoose, can you come here a moment? We have people." He turned back to them and smiled awkwardly, "A silly little nickname."

Amy came out from the back and stopped as she saw Sarah and Brian. She also looked to be in her mid-thirties too with a long braid of black hair. She was dressed simply, jeans and a blue blouse. Sarah felt she had a familiar face but could not place her.

"Sarah, I haven't seen you since you were a little girl, maybe when you were five years old or so. So good to see you again," Amy said. She gave Sarah a big hug. It was a comfortable sort of hug, like a hug between family members. She suddenly pulled away with a large grin, "Congratulations," she squealed with excitement. "Six and a half weeks?"

Sarah turned pale and gulped.

"What do you mean?" Brian asked. Amy and Nick shared a glance, knowing that she made a blunder. "What does she mean, Sarah?"

"I was going to tell you. But, I wanted to figure things out first. I'm, um, kind of pregnant. I just found out today." She turned to Amy, "How did you know?"

"Oh, honey, I'm a soul reader."

"Wow, I just can't get over that you didn't tell me, why didn't you want to tell me?" Brian asked.

"I didn't want to disappoint you," Sarah said and her bottom lip quivered.

Brian paced back and forth for a couple seconds. He then took Sarah in his arms and whispered in her ear, "That is the opposite of how I feel."

"Let's celebrate, I don't really have anything fancy, but we have some soda in the break room. Or tea, I can make tea," Nick said.

"Shakespeare, look at them, they're dressed to the nines. They must be going to an A.B.C. party somewhere. They don't want to stay."

"A.B.C. party?" Nick asked.

"Shakespeare, it stands for Astrid's Birthday Celebration. It's just a glorified reason to party."

"I want to stay, if that's okay, Brian?" Sarah said looking at him with pleading eyes.

"I can drink a soda," he said.

"Actually, can I have some tea? My stomach is a bit gnarly right now."

"Perfect, you both can go sit in the reading lounge; it's those couches over there. Amy and I will be right back with refreshments."

Sarah and Brian went into the reading lounge. The assemblage of couches appeared to be thrift store finds, since all four were different. All had a common ambiance of previously belonging to octogenarian cat ladies.

Nick followed Amy into the kitchenette. She turned around suddenly, "Why are you acting so strange? And where did those glasses come from? You don't need glasses."

"I wanted to try something new. Nick was getting a little stale for me. I wanted to try the dorky librarian thing. What do you think?" Nick said and cocked his head in a humorous fashion.

"I think you are making a right ass of yourself, knock it off."

She floated the teakettle over her hand and used her gifts to boil the water. He started to assemble the china set on a tray.

"Remember when we bought this china?" he said.

"Of course I do. It was our last trip to England."

"Nope, it was our second trip to England."

"Are you sure? It was the same trip where we went to see Danika at the manor and Charles gave you that book of limericks."

"No, we bought the china the time before that. When we went to London and stayed in that flat by the park. We bought it at that shop, with the great cheese."

"You're right. How could I forget? The years must be catching up to me. How do you remember all these things, Shakespeare?"

171

"Honestly, I kept journals of all our capers and travels. I recently found a computer program to input dates and data, creating a searchable timeline."

"Computers have been a fascinating innovation."

"Hey Mongoose, when did we get old?"

She started to chuckle, "That ship sailed like five hundred years ago," she said with a laugh.

"I'm being serious. It sometimes feels that long though." She shot him a sour look. "Oh, Mongoose, I didn't mean it that way. Even though we're not married, you're still my soul mate."

"And you are mine. They are a cute little couple."

"I can't believe you spilled the beans on her being pregnant."

"I feel bad, but I didn't know she hadn't told him. I can't know everything for Christ's sake. I'm a soul reader not a mind reader. I would put money on that she hasn't told Evie yet."

"Oh God, I would love to be a fly on that wall when she finds out," he said with a chuckle.

The teakettle whistled. She poured the water into the teapot. Nick floated a couple sodas onto the tray. They went out to the reading lounge and Nick placed the tray on a coffee table.

"Sugar, honey, cream?" Amy asked.

"Honey please," Sarah said.

"I'll take lemon," Nick said.

"Hush up; I know how you take your tea."

"You guys are cute. How long have you been together?" Sarah asked.

They both laughed, "Oh honey, Nick is gay."

"Hey," Nick said, mock offended.

"Oh, I'm sorry, I assumed you were married or dating."

"It's okay; it's an easy mistake to make." She handed Sarah her tea. "What brings you to the library of all places tonight?"

Sarah took a sip of her tea, "I had a strange dream of the building and when we were driving by I recognized it."

Amy looked over at Nick and back at Sarah. "Interesting."

"You said you were a soul reader, what exactly is that?"

Amy put her teacup down and folded her hands on her knee, "It is a

Mover with a special gift of sight, a form of psychic ability. You have it as well. Didn't you know?"

"No way I'm a soul reader. You're pulling a joke on me or something."

"Do you have dreams like the one you had often? Can you tell someone's D.A.S. score just by feeling their energy? Things like that make us soul readers. It's almost as if everything and everyone has these impressions from experiences and it leaves a mark like Braille. We are people who know how to read it. If you would like, I can teach you how to hone it."

"This is a lot to take in right now; it's kind of blowing my mind." She turned to Brian and touched his hand, but she had nothing come in. "I don't think I'm doing it right."

"Oh, sometimes the ones we're closest to we get blocks and can't read them," Amy said. "What an interesting necklace, Brian, is that an antique St. Margaret's metal?"

"Uh, yeah. Are you Catholic?" Brian asked, shifting his weight.

"No."

There was a gap in the conversation. The only sound was the ticking of the antique walnut longcase grandfather clock.

"So, Brian, how did you snag Ms. Sarah here?" Nick asked.

173

Brian looked at Sarah and smiled, "Lucky. And I have amazing abs."

"That you do," Nick said and they all chuckled.

They all jumped at the sound of Sarah's cell phone ringing.

"Sorry, I'm so not used to having a phone all the time. I'm going to get this," Sarah said. "Hello?"

"Where are you guys? I'm getting worried over here," Katie scolded on the other end.

"Sorry, we stopped for a little detour. We'll be there soon."

"You better be coming, like right now."

"Don't worry, we're coming, Katie. Don't lose your shit. We're coming."

"Okay, but get your ass over here A.S.A.P."

"Bye."

Sarah hung up the phone and smiled awkwardly, "We need to go. They're expecting us at the A.B.C. party."

"It's your birthday too, Sarah?"

"Yep, every year."

"Happy birthday. Have a good time you kids and keep in touch," Amy said.

"Will do," Sarah said. They all exchanged hugs as Sarah and Brian left the library.

After they left, Nick turned to Amy and crossed his arms, "Do you think they suspected?"

"Him, not sure. That St. Margaret's metal has me suspicious. Sarah might have a feeling about us, although she might not understand quite yet what that feeling means."

She looked up at Astrid's portrait and sighed, "I miss that dress."

"You always do look stunning in blue, Mongoose."

"I know what you mean about being bored with Nick, I'm bored with Amy."

"Do you think it's time to change again?"

"I'm tired of changing...I want to be me."

174

"What do you mean?"

"I think it's time for a resurrection, don't you think, Alan?"

"Don't call me Alan, it's dangerous." He turned and crossed his arms, "You know full well we chose to abandon our true names to avoid slips."

"I miss being her, look at the confidence I had," she said, looking up at the portrait. She turned to him and gave a sly smile, "Let's bring Astrid and Alan back to life, shall we?"

"I don't think it's a good idea, Astrid. Damn, you got me to slip. This is definitely not a good idea."

"Alan, where is your sense of adventure?"

"Back in the 19th century where it belongs."

"I think I need to pay a visit to a current thorn in my side and really rattle his cage. The head of the P.G.I. found me out."

"Oh shit, what are you going to do?"

"He wants to find Astrid, so Astrid will find him."

"Astrid?"

"Yes, Alan?"

"Happy Birthday."

"Thank you. That reminds me," Astrid walked towards the supply closet. "I need to check on our oldest artifact."

Washington, DC
November 22nd
1997

Alexander Bram sat in a fancy steakhouse with his personal assistant sipping water with lemon slices in a fine crystal glass. He looked up from the menu as Astrid approached the table. He shot a glance at his two hidden security forces. She was in a seductive, but tasteful, blue dress and heels. She shot him a smile and sat at the table.

"Can I help you, miss?" he said half laughing at her presumptuous action.

175

"That is up to you, Mr. Bram," she said with a smile.

"May I ask who you might be?"

"That may seem like a reasonable request. But it's a tad complicated."

"Excuse me?" he said with a chuckle.

"I know you have been investigating me. The only reason you know anything is because I allowed it."

"I plead ignorance, my dear. If you would like to talk further, make an appointment. I would greatly like to enjoy my meal, in peace."

She smiled and gave a little snigger. He looked into her eyes and noticed a fire that contradicted her pleasant smile.

"I'm Amy Borne, or you could call me one of my many other aliases you know of."

He sat back in his chair as she said her name then took a long sip of water.

"Bold move, my dear. I have security present that is fully capable of taking care of the likes of you."

"Oh, you mean the bald man eating the lobster bisque and the young man posing as a waiter to the left?" she said, never relinquishing her smile. Alexander squirmed and looked perturbed. "You must be stupid to think I wouldn't notice. I'm disappointed," she said and clucked her tongue.

"You have my attention," he said. "I underestimated you. You must find great joy in that."

"Not really, it's hard to find joy in the predictable."

"Miss Borne, I..." he said. She gave a short laugh.

"I think we are past that. I know you know who I really am. I have been dealing with little twerps like you for over a century. Just because you are in a fancy suit does not hide your real identity from me. You are a bloodthirsty bigot. I know you had Stuart Sark murdered. I also know about Operation Sanitation."

176

The color drained from Alexander's face and he adjusted his tie. Looking around, he smiled.

"This is not the appropriate venue for such talk."

"Oh, I think it is. If you value your life, of course. I am curious if there is anything that will convince you to call it off?"

Alexander leaned forward, "Gloves off, I hate you and everything you stand for. It made me very sad to find out you were alive and well. I don't know where you got your information but I'll level with you. I had nothing to do with Stuart Sark's death. I would love to know where the leak in my boat is. I will tell you only that Operation Sanitation is not a plan for the future, it has already started. It is all in place and in motion, there's nothing you can do to stop it."

"But you need the bill to pass. It hasn't passed yet."

"Interesting, it seems you have underestimated me as well. That vote is a simple formality. I have more than enough votes bought and paid for. You would be surprised how many politicians either are on board with me ideologically or are easy to buy. Construction has already finished on the Public Safety Centers. The part that puts you at a disadvantage is that killing me will only make our progress stronger. You see, we have a saying 'Blood of the martyr is the seed of the church.' You know this well. As a leader, you were ineffective, but as a martyr, well that's a different story. You created a community that would follow you into hell. I'm just here to make that a reality."

"You're a monster," she said, abandoning her smile.

"I really don't care what you think of me. But, out of the kindness of my heart, if you leave and never show up on my radar again, your secret and your life will be safe."

"Even if I would do such a thing, you can't be trusted."

Alexander stood and motioned for his personal assistant to stand up. As he stood he loomed over her. He buttoned his

177

jacket and pulled out his wallet, throwing money on the table.

"We're done here. Enjoy a steak on me. I like mine rare, the flavor is in the blood. Consider my offer, Astrid," he said and drawing out her name with emphasis.

The men walked off. She glared at the money on the table. Waiting a moment, she stood and left the restaurant. She walked to the car where Ashwin was waiting in the driver's seat. He looked as distraught as she felt. She sat down and removed the wiretap from under her dress.

"It's as I feared," he said and punched the steering wheel. "But, I should thank you; I couldn't have done it without you."

"What should we do?" She put her hand on her forehead.

"I was afraid of this and had a backup plan set up for this very thing."

"You didn't tell me about this," she said.

"I prayed I wouldn't have to. This bill targets the strongest of us. If they are taken out, the rest of the Movers will soon follow. We can't let that happen. We can't hide, we must be able to defend ourselves. Whether we like it or not, we are now at war."

She looked down at her fingers and the back of her hands. She had not aged physically since she was in her thirties, but mentally she felt the weight of the years. She knew the path ahead was going to be hellish and did not know if she wanted to be a part of it. She thought about leaving her people to their destiny, whatever that may be. Then she thought of Sarah, the future. She decided that she could not abandon her people.

"What can we do?" she said looking at Ashwin.

"Hope is what these people need and you will give it to them. Hope is as vital as air and water. Any strong enemy knows that if you destroy hope, you win."

"Wait; are you seriously suggesting what I think you are?"

"Wake up. The P.G.I. knows who you are. But, they can't destroy you if their threat to reveal you is null and void. You know I'm right."

She took a deep breath and shook her head. Looking out the window, she saw the upper echelon of society entering and exiting the steak house.

"Okay."

"Alright, let's do it. But, I think we should tell Evie and Sarah first."

"No, first…I need a drink."

Astrid sat at The Drunken Fish bar drinking a scotch. This dive bar was about forgetting, rather than socializing. She felt very unsociable after her experience with Alexander Bram. At that moment, a man came over and sat next to her. He was in a slick business suit and looked very confident.

"Another for the lady," he said and smiled.

"No thanks," she said and sipped her drink without looking at him.

"Can't a man be nice to a pretty woman like you?"

She turned and put her hand on his and opened up her channel. She felt his energy, his memories, his hopes, and current desires.

"No thanks, Chad."

He seemed startled, "How do you know my name?"

"The same way I know about your wife, Nancy, married sixteen years and your two little girls, Jessica and Ashley. Go home to your family, you pig. A married skirt chaser doesn't work for me."

The man walked at such a fast pace he almost ran off in a cartoonish fashion.

Astrid then noticed a man laughing at the end of the bar. He had stacks of paper in front of him and a leather briefcase on the next barstool. He had on a buttoned collared shirt and jeans. A brown tweed jacket draped over the barstool gave off the stereotype of a young professor.

"What are you laughing at?" she said brusquely.

"You handled that well. It amused me. Forgive me for laughing. Don't worry, I'll stay out of your business. Enjoy your drinking."

She looked over and saw he was drinking from a can of soda.

"Who comes to a bar and doesn't drink?" she asked.

"I am drinking," he gave a coy smile and rubbed his 5 o'clock shadow, "My family owns the place. I find I make better progress here than alone in my apartment. I happen to not drink alcohol."

"You don't drink at all?"

"Nope, it numbs the senses, Amy."

This ruffled her and she went over and sat on the bar stool next to him, "What game are you playing? How do you know that name?" she asked.

He took a sip of his soda, "No game. I'm just observant."

She touched his hand and he smiled. She opened her channel, but no information came.

She was befuddled and tried again, but could not read him.

"How are you doing that?" she asked.

"Doing what?" he said in a tone that made it obvious he was toying with her.

"You're a soul reader," she said in awe. "You're very strong. I can't read you at all."

"Yes, but I can't read you either, so we're even. All I got out of you was your name, Amy, and that was because you told the bartender for the tab. How about we try talking like regular people?"

"Why would I want to do that?" she asked.

"Because I fascinate you," he said, with a flirting lilt in his voice.

180

She looked into his eyes and noticed they were very similar to her Seamus. They were a sparking clear blue and it was as if she were looking into his eyes again.

"Okay, I'll bite. Since you know my name, what's yours?"

"Doyle Quinn is what it says on my birth certificate. Everyone who knows me calls me Ducky."

"You must be kidding."

He laughed, "I wish I was. *Sixteen Candles* was very popular when I rushed a frat. It just never went away."

"What do you teach, Professor Quinn?" she said, motioning to the papers.

"Ah, I guess I am a dead give-away. I teach history at the community college."

"Interesting."

"I have many students who would disagree. Early in my collegiate career, I was an eager anthropology major. Once upon a time, I wanted to be a real-life Indiana Jones. But, I found I don't like to get dirty or travel, so I switched majors. History tends to lead you to libraries, instead of digging in a hole in the jungle with a toothbrush. I love artifacts, but I choose to just go to museums."

She shifted her weight and smiled. He was handsome and the more she tried to dislike him, she found him more fascinating. Besides, she was in want of someone in her bed that night.

"I have a similar inclination for artifacts."

"Do you now," he took a sip of his soda.

"I have an impressive collection back at my house, if you would like to see it."

"Tempting offer. But, I may need more information on what type of artifacts."

"My crown jewel, so to speak, is a map of Europe."

"And why is that impressive?"

"Because, the map dates back to the 15th century, nearly in its original condition."

His brows lifted and a twinkle came to his eye
"You better not be yanking my chain."
"There's only one way to find out."

They arrived at her home and he looked around at all her memorabilia that doubled as artifacts. She smiled at the sheer wonder in his eyes; he looked like a kid at Disneyland.

"Would you like something to drink?" she offered as she set down her purse.

"Coffee if you have it."

"I should probably tell you, I have a roommate so we should probably keep it down.

Including smells like coffee."

"Water will suffice," he said as he picked up a picture of her and Alan in London. "Huh," he said, with a tinge of puzzlement.

"What?" she asked.

"Good photo touch up job here. This picture," he said holding it up to her. She looked at him blankly, although she rightly knew that picture of her and Alan dated to right after the turn of the century. "The quality of the touch up is amazing. You're both even in period dress. Where did you have it done?"

"Some novelty booth at a fair or something. I'll be right back with your water."

She left the room and went into the kitchen. She paced a few steps and placed her hand on her chest. She felt like she was walking a tightrope and he might discover her secret before she got what she wanted. It both frightened and tantalized her to be on the edge and that he had the power to see her for who she was. After she quieted her nerves, she took a water bottle from the fridge. Upon entering the living room she saw him looking at one of the first pictures she sat for when photography was new and all the rage. The sepia photograph was over a century and a half old which gave her confidence he would not recognize her.

182

"Thanks," he said after she handed him the water bottle. "This must have set you back some change," he said as he pointed to the photograph.

"If you find that impressive, you'll love my map."

"I would love to see it," he said, trying to contain his glee.

"This way," she said. They went down the hallway into her bedroom.

He instantly zoned in on the framed 15th century map of Europe. He stood in awe and his mouth hung open while staring at the map. He turned around to speak and saw her lying on the bed with her fingers in her hair. He set his water down and sat on the bed next to her. She smiled and gently caressed his thigh with the back of her index finger. He looked at her with desire in his eyes. As they started kissing, she maneuvered on top of him and removed her shirt. He noticed the scar on her chest from the infamous bullet.

"What happened here?" he said, touching the scar.

"Do you want to interview me or get laid? You can't do both."

He laughed and flipped her onto her back. As they continued to kiss, they flung articles of clothing onto the floor piece by piece until completely nude. He stopped and looked into her eyes. She felt as if Seamus was looking through his eyes and shuddered.

"Are you okay?" he whispered.

"Yeah," she smiled and touched his hair.

He touched her face and suddenly she felt his energy searching to see if she was still resisting him reading her. She pushed him off and sat up in bed.

"What the hell?" he said in a raised frustrated voice.

"You were trying to read me, without my consent," she said in an angry hushed tone.

He sat up and sighed, "What are you so afraid of?"

"It is a violation."

"Like you wouldn't read me if given the chance. Hell, you tried in the bar."

"I…" she started, but then realized he was right.

He held out his hand, "I'll show you mine if you show me yours."

"I can't."

"Why?"

Tears welled up in her eyes and she looked away. He placed his hand reassuringly on her thigh and her channel opened. She was flooded with his memories. It was as if she was showered with a jumbled jigsaw puzzle. She saw him holding the hand of a pregnant woman in a totaled car. There was blood dripping from her forehead and he held her hand as she died. He placed a ring on the finger of the same woman at their wedding. The ultrasound of their daughter and the sound of the baby's heartbeat. The funeral of his wife and baby. Sitting in a courtroom while hearing the jury give out his guilty verdict of vehicular manslaughter. A scene of their first date at the local county fair. The glow of the Ferris wheel lights on her face and her equally illuminating smile. Him drinking at the restaurant and taking his keys from the valet.

Astrid opened her eyes. He looked deeply into hers, "Now you see me."

With a sigh, she let down her guard and placed his hand back on her thigh. He closed his eyes as she let him read her. She was in the dark as to what he was seeing of her. He closed his eyes as he read her. Suddenly his eyes snapped open and he grinned.

"Now was that so bad?"

She laughed, "That's all you have to say?"

He motioned with his finger and she went to him. As he kissed her, he placed his hand on the scar on her chest. As they made love she had never felt so trusting and at ease. She looked up into his eyes and no longer saw Seamus's eyes in

Doyle. After they finished he rolled off her and sat at the edge of the bed. He got up and she reached out for him.

"You can stay, if you want," she said biting her lower lip.

He got back into bed and she curled up next to him. He pointed to a scar on her hip.

"Where'd you get that one?"

She gently laughed, "Seriously?"

"It's called conversation."

"Bleeding Valley, bastard with a sword. Many of these are from the battle. Except for a few…"

"Which ones?"

She pointed to her stomach, "This is a c-section from Flynn." She pointed to her bullet wound scar, "Of course this one."

He smiled sweetly, "You are a survivor."

"Does that intimidate you? Me being who I am?"

"Should it? I don't think anyone is beyond humanity. Humans are fascinating and since I don't drink it helps me see that."

"Is the accident why you stopped drinking?" she asked and he winced.

"Yes."

"Sorry, I shouldn't have asked that."

"It's okay, there's so much I want to ask you but don't know where to start. What is it like being *the* Astrid Borrows?"

"It may sound strange but Astrid, as you know her, is someone I have not been in so long, I sometimes have a hard time remembering being her. She wasn't even really me, more like a skin I would wear." She looked down and gave a gentle smile, "I'm going to make some tea, if you would like some."

She got out of bed and put on her pale blue silk robe. He put on his boxers. They walked down the hall to the kitchen.

185

As they opened the door, they saw Alan sitting at the kitchen table drinking a cup of tea.

"Hello love birds, join me for a cup of tea?" Alan said and took a sip.

"Um, this is Doyle," she said and cleared her throat.

"Don't be shy, sit down."

They looked at each other and decided to sit. She poured two mugs of tea.

"You must be, Alan," Doyle said. Alan shot a look at Astrid and she shrugged. "I should explain. I'm a soul reader, too."

"Oh, interesting," he looked over at Astrid. "How's that going?"

"Don't be such a bitch Shakespeare," Astrid quipped. She noticed Doyle giving her an odd look. "Don't worry he's used to it."

"I've spent over a century taking this abuse," he said chuckling.

Astrid sighed, "I'm going to freshen up. Shakespeare, be nice to him."

"I'm always nice," he said as she left the kitchen. He looked over at Doyle and gave a gentle smile. "You like her."

"I do, what's not to like?"

"I'm not going to give you some speech on how not to hurt her or I'll kill you." Doyle laughed at this. "But, it would be true." Alan gave him a chilling stare.

Doyle sat up and glared back, "I have no intentions of hurting her."

"Good, we have an understanding then."

Astrid came back into the room, "Did you play nice?" she asked while glaring at Alan.

"As always."

She sat next to Doyle, "Alan, how dare you threaten Doyle."

"It never fails. You can't resist using your super powerful psychic abilities."

Doyle raised his hand, "Actually, it was me. As an experiment, I sent a message to Astrid without touch to see if it would work."

"It appears it did," Astrid said with a coy smile.

"Two soul readers. I'm in hell."

"Save that talk for when you go to Kansas in a few days," Astrid said and took a sip of tea.

Chapter 21

Kansas is Cool

New Alessaria, California
November 25th
1997

Astrid gazed up at the waning crescent moon as they drove up the driveway to the Borrows Manor. Ashwin and Alan exchanged a look of dread as they parked. Ashwin knocked on the door and a maid answered.

"Can you tell Mrs. Rose we are here to see her?" he said.

"Yes, Mr. Ashwin, come in."

As the maid left to inform Evie of her guests, another took their coats. After she whisked away their coats they went into the study. A fire was crackling in the fireplace. As they stood in the study, Sarah walked by and saw them.

"What are you guys doing here?" she said and hugged them.

"I'm glad you're here, Sarah. I was going to have you join us with your grandmother," Ashwin said.

"Is everything okay?" Sarah asked. From the look on their faces, she knew the answer was no.

Evie entered the room and stopped cold. Astrid approached her and gave her a hug.

"Hi, Evie," she said.

"Alice? Preston?" Evie seemed utterly stunned.

"No, Grandma. This is Amy and Nick, they work at the library," Sarah said.

Evie's glance turned to Alan and he gave a little wave.

"I don't understand," Evie said in an almost whisper and sat down.

Astrid sat beside Evie and took up her hand. Evie looked deep into Astrid's eyes and smiled.

"I would know those eyes anywhere. Alice had lovely sapphire eyes and one eye had a glint of gold. You have that gold streak, right there," Evie said and pointed at Astrid's eye. Shaking her head, she said, "But that can't be." Evie turned to Sarah. "Alice was your father's nanny. Preston her brother, a traveling priest, if my memory serves me well."

Ashwin snickered, "Really, Alan?"

"We kept trying to come up with identities that excused away a man and woman being together and not being married. We haven't had to do that since the late sixties, thank you sexual revolution," Alan said.

"I have not laid eyes on you since Hershel left for college. But, that was decades ago, you both haven't aged a day. How can that be?"

"Evie, I know you must be confused. I don't blame you for feeling that way. I have lived many years."

"But how can this be true? It's not possible."

"I can explain. I can trace my lack of aging back to when I fell very ill. My daughter was to be married and had to postpone the wedding. I was thirty-five."

"Thirty-five? How old were you when you had her?" Sarah asked.

"Sarah, don't be rude," Evie said.

"It's okay, Sarah can ask any question she wants. I was sixteen. We had children young in those days."

Sarah swallowed hard and crossed her arm over her belly. Astrid gave a nod and smiled in a way that let Sarah know her secret was safe.

"Before the wedding I had a bad case of the Daffodils. No one has experienced the Daffodils since they discovered the inoculation. Obviously, I recovered. The same happened to Alan. When I heard he'd fallen ill, I went to his side. I've stayed with him ever since."

Alan said, with a bittersweet smile, "I think it was when the '90s rolled around I realized I was forty-five and still looked thirty-three. Later, Doctor Robert Delving studied our cells, or something, and said our bodies were frozen in time." Alan said, trailing off.

"That doesn't make sense. Dr. Delving died in the 80's, the Apple bombing in 1986."

"Um, yeah, Amy, Alice, whatever, take this over," Alan said, crossing his arms.

"We should just come out with it. I was your Alice and I am Sarah's Amy. I have had

many names over the years, but my first was…Astrid. As in Astrid Borrows."

Silence drifted across the room as Evie worked hard to process this revelation. None was as dumbfounded as Sarah, who let out a gasp.

"You're saying you're Astrid? Like, our Astrid? *The* Astrid?" Sarah exclaimed.

"Yes, I'm Astrid Borrows and I know that is hard for you both to understand and accept. I will explain as much as I can to help you come to terms with this."

Sarah stood and angrily sobbed, "No. You said you were going to be reborn. Why would you let us all believe that if you're alive? They said I was you reborn. Why would you let them say that if you weren't dead? I have all the stupid signs…my life was turned upside-down because of your prophecy."

"Honey, sit down, please," Astrid said. "I'll explain it all to you."

"Astrid, can we have a moment in the other room?" Ashwin said.

"No, she should know the truth. Sarah, sit." Sarah glared at Astrid and sat as directed. "When your father went to college, Alan and I started our new lives as Nick and Amy.

190

We were able to take over the library and things were going relatively well. One day your father came into the library. He asked me pointblank if I was Astrid. I leveled with him."

"I never knew that was why; he never told me," Evie said and slowly shook her head in disbelief.

"About two years went by and I was at home with Alan on a Sunday morning. Jon stopped by. Sarah was just born. We talked for hours. He showed me his tattoo and I burst into tears."

"Dad had a tattoo?"

"Yes, he did. When he was growing up, he was about seven when I first read him *The Jungle Book,* and the story "Rikki-Tikki-Tavi." When he showed me his tattoo, it was a mongoose holding two dead cobras. Evie will remember he always had me call him Teddy and he called me Mongoose. He told me that he had realized I would always protect him and that I kept my secret for good reason."

Evie started crying, she dabbed her cheeks with a handkerchief, "Keep going, it's just hard to hear these things. I have not heard anything about my son in years."

"It was at that meeting that I convinced him to reconnect with you, Evie. I told him to change his name back, but he said he liked the rebellious image it gave him. You remember how he was," Evie nodded in agreement. "That was '82 wasn't it, Shakespeare?"

"No, it was '80. I remember it was right before John Lennon was shot."

"We lost our place, where were we? Oh, yes. Sarah, when you were born your father came to me with an idea. Dr. Delving had discovered a test that could predict an infant Mover's eventual D.A.S. number. He never shared it with the public and very few know about it. With your father's permission, you were tested and rated a D.A.S. 33. He told me that with your red hair and strength, you could be the prophesized reincarnation. He said our people were in need of something to believe in and he wanted it to be you."

"I was born with the mark too, which is the final sign."

"Honey that is not a birthmark. I'm sorry to tell you this, but your father had that placed to give you authenticity. It's a tattoo."

"No, my dad wouldn't do that to me. My mom wouldn't have done it for sure."

"I'm sorry, Sarah. It's true. It was your mother who sat with you while you got the tattoo. You can't understand her motives. Not yet. Not until you have a child of your own."

"That's not going to be for a while," Evie said in jest. Then she noticed a change in the room. Astrid looked at Alan and then at Sarah in an odd way. "What is it?"

"Tell her," Astrid said.

"Jeez. Now?" Sarah said wincing and Astrid nodded. "Okay fine. Grandma, you know how I've been dating Brian, well, don't freak out, but I'm pregnant. I was going to tell you, I swear. Don't be mad."

Silence fell on the room once more and no one could read Evie's reaction. A full minute passed before she lunged forward and held Sarah in her arms and wept.

"I'm so happy," Evie choked out, squeezing a startled Sarah. "Why didn't you tell me sooner?"

"I tried," Sarah squeaked out.

"I know this is a great moment, but we must get back to what is at hand. I cannot sit here and listen to the conversation meander anymore," Ashwin said sternly. "The Mover Limitation Bill is going to pass."

"We don't know that. I have many people fighting for votes in our favor," Evie protested.

"I'm sorry, but that effort is in vain, the vote is a mere formality. What we need to do now is prepare," Ashwin said.

"But how do you come to the conclusion?" Evie exclaimed.

"Straight from the snake's mouth," Alan muttered.

192

"We know the vote has been corrupted from Alexander Bram himself and our undercover informant has confirmed," Ashwin said.

Evie stood and paced, "We need a plan. This cannot happen."

"There is a plan we have in place, but we'll need your help. We will teach our Mover's from the titans right on down the scale, defensive and survival skills. Also, our ace up our sleeve is right in this room. Astrid will come out, so to speak. We are planning for it to happen soon. Also, Sarah will run away," Ashwin said matter-of-factly.

"Run away? Why?" Sarah asked.

"We have to keep Sarah safe," Astrid said. "I have a farm in Kansas no one knows about, we can place her there. Alan has volunteered to watch over her. Hopefully we will fix this horrible situation and bring her home shortly."

"Astrid will be exposed and will have to admit she was hiding all these years and go through testing and vetting. After we have established that she really is Astrid Borrows, we will place her in charge of the Astridians, alongside you Evie. Meanwhile, we will be training our people in self-defense," Ashwin said.

"But why should Astrid put herself at such risk?" Evie asked.

"The P.G.I. already know my secret," Astrid said. "It's best to take away their power, which would be to expose my secret for their own gain."

"Evie, what they are planning with this bill is worse than you can imagine. They named it Operation Sanitation. The plan is that the government will place all Movers with a D.A.S. score of twenty-five and up in those holding cells they dare to call, "Public Safety Centers." The unofficial plan we received from our mole is that they plan to murder all the detainees with an "accident," so to speak. We have yet to find direct damning proof that could be used to prosecute."

"Dear God," Evie gasped and shuddered.

"So, that is the path that lies before us. Are you with us?" Astrid said.

Sarah looked at Evie and then looked around the room. With a deep breath she said, "I'm in."

Evie reached over and grabbed Sarah's hand, "I'm so proud of you."

"Good. Now, who's hungry?" Alan said and everyone looked at him. "It's called levity people."

Brian sat in his living room, with Jackson, Josh, Mary, and Michael. Brian and Michael had come to a truce since he came back to live there. They were waiting for Brian to explain why he asked them there. Mary held the sleeping baby.

"So, I need to tell you guys a couple things. I have been talking with Ashwin and I'm going away on a trip."

"For how long?" Mary asked.

"That's where it gets complicated. See, what I'm about to tell you stays here. I'm not sure how, but Astrid, like *the* Astrid is still alive and is planning on coming out of hiding."

"What?" Josh cried out.

"Shh, you will wake the baby," Mary whispered.

"Yeah, I know, it's crazy. I guess they're worried about Sarah's safety. Especially with that bill vote. The plan is that she's going to leave, making it look like she ran away. She asked for me to go with her."

"But why would you do that? Why are you getting dragged into this? Is it that woman from England?" Jackson said.

"Jack, don't," Mary said.

"No, I want to know why Ashwin is allowing Brian to get involved. It's not right."

"Sarah's pregnant," Brian said rubbing his hands together. "There it is." There was a moment of silence and the baby started to fuss. "I'm doing this, and because of the danger, I can't keep in contact with you guys."

"Oh man," Josh said sitting back in his chair.

Jackson stood and walked up to Brian, "Stand up," he said.

Brian took a deep breath and stood. Jackson took Brian in his arms and gave him a long hug. After they separated, Jackson placed his hand on Brian's shoulder.

"I'm proud of you for stepping up as a man. I think I have a way for us to stay in contact, and no one will know. Let me know the name of the local paper where you are going. Leave messages in the paper for me with a code name only I will know. Understand?" Brian nodded. "Good boy."

"When are you leaving?" Mary asked.

"Sarah's on her way. There's this guy, Alan, I guess he's a friend of Astrid's. He's going with us to keep us safe. I call it babysitting. But we're leaving for Kansas when they get here."

"Kansas? They couldn't come up with a better place?" Michael scoffed.

"Hey, Kansas is cool. I don't really care where we go. As long as I'm with Sarah and we're safe."

Sarah sat in the passenger seat. All their bags were in the back of the station wagon. She looked over at Alan and noticed he still had tear marks on his face.

"Are you going to miss her?" she asked.

"Who, Astrid?"

"Yeah, it seemed like it was hard to say goodbye."

"You see, Kansas is a sensitive subject. Many years ago Astrid left to go to this farm we are going to. I lost her for forty years."

"Wow, why so long?"

"I guess that's how long it took to mend her broken heart. When you have all the time in the world, it's hard sometimes to live with such a thing as a broken heart. It took me a long time to understand that. I have not had to say goodbye to Astrid for a long time, but this time felt different, felt okay. She is my constant. I love her so deeply that we are always connected. She's my Mongoose," he said with a smile.

"You call her Mongoose, like Dad did?"

"Actually, I was calling her Mongoose before your Dad was even born. I remember she loved that silly story. This was before television mind you, even before radio. We would read for entertainment. A long time ago I started calling her Mongoose, to tease her. The nickname just seemed to stick. She calls me Shakespeare, since I was a writer when we met."

"They didn't have radio? How long have you been alive?"

"I was born July 13, 1845, so what is that? If I'm doing my arithmetic correctly, 152 years. I usually don't think of it all in one chunk. I've had a life like a book of short stories. Even though they are all in the same book, the stories have lives of their own so to speak. When we're in Kansas we will have plenty of time, I will bore you with all my tales and adventures then."

"His house is the last house on the left," Sarah said, pointing to Brian's house.

He stood in the driveway and gave a little wave. He placed his luggage in the backseat and sat next to it. His family waved from inside the house, as he requested no sloppy farewell scene to avoid suspicion.

"Road trip whoop, whoop," Alan said laughing.

As they drove, Sarah nodded off in the front seat. Brian shook her gently and pointed out the window. She saw the sign, "Reno: The Biggest Little City in the World." She looked back at Brian and grinned.

"Can we stop, Alan?" Sarah pleaded.

"No, too high profile. There are cameras everywhere and someone might recognize you."

Sarah watched Reno pass by her window and wished she could be normal. She closed her eyes and fell back to sleep. When she opened them again they were at a desolate gas station. She rubbed her eyes and sat up in her seat.

"Hey sleepyhead," Alan said from the backseat.

"Where are we?"

"We are near Salt Lake City. Brian took over the driving for me and is pumping the gas. I'm going to get some snacks and take a leak. You should do the same," he said as he got out of the car.

After Sarah used a less-than-hygienic bathroom, she entered the little food mart and picked up some snacks along with Alan. He microwaved a burrito while she searched the chip aisle.

From across the mini food mart she heard, "Sarah Rose?"

She froze in fear and slowly looked over to where the voice was coming from. It was a middle-aged man with a grin. The ghostly night clerk stood doe-eyed. She looked at Alan and he motioned for her to stay still. He walked up to the man.

"What is it to you?" Alan said in a menacing tone.

"I just didn't think I would see someone famous here of all places," the man said gleefully.

Alan looked down at the floor and sighed, "I'm sorry."

He cocked his head and snapped the man's neck. Sarah screamed and backed up into the row of chips. Alan turned his gaze to the frightened clerk. Sarah closed her eyes and heard the horrible sound of bone breaking and the body thudding to the floor. Alan grabbed her hand and she screamed again.

"Come on, we have to go," Alan said.

Brian came in twirling the car keys on his finger.

"Gas is officially pumped," he declared then noticed the bodies on the floor. "Holy shit," he said and looked at Alan and then Sarah. "Are you guys okay? What happened?"

"Good questions. All questions that can be answered when we're on the road driving away," Alan said. "But first, one detail I need to see to." He went behind the counter and ripped out the VHS recorder connected to the security camera system and melted the unit. He then opened the cash register.

"What are you doing?"

"Making it look like a robbery gone wrong." He put the cash in a plastic bag and wiped their fingerprints. "Now we should go. Don't touch anything."

Alan drove as fast as he could without drawing unwanted attention. Sarah eventually fell asleep in the backseat and had a nightmare full of flashbacks of her kidnapping. She screamed as she awoke from her nightmare, which startled Alan and he briefly swerved. Brian turned around in his seat, and placed his hand on her knee.

"Are you okay, Princess?" he asked with worry in his voice.

"Yeah, it was just a bad dream. I'm okay," she said and gave a forced smile.

"It's okay, you didn't miss much. Just most of Wyoming," Alan said and laughed.

"When are we getting to Kansas?" Brian asked.

"At this pace, we should get to the farm around noon, so about nine hours or so," Alan said.

"Alan, why did you do it?" Sarah asked quietly. Alan's smile faded.

"Sweetie, I'm here to keep you safe and make sure no one will compromise your safety. I hope you realize that I had to do it. You are an important person you know."

"I don't think any life is worth more than another," Sarah said.

"I realize you are young, full of hope and ideals. But, that isn't true. It's not fair, but there is a hierarchy of life value. When the Titanic sank, they put woman and children on the lifeboats first. It was always like that in those situations. Save the women and children first, right? Why? Because their lives were considered more valuable. Is it right? Hell no. But, it's the way it is. I mean, your life is more important than mine in the grand scheme of things. When you have your baby, that baby's life will be more important than yours."

"He has a good point Sarah," Brian chimed in.

"I'm not going to have this discussion with you guys," Sarah said crossing her arms.

Nine hours later, the car pulled up to the small abandoned farmhouse. The white paint was weathered and chipped; some of the siding was hanging off the house. The boarded up windows gave it a sad, decrepit look. The fields had nothing but weeds for decades. Sarah looked around and saw nothing for miles but earth and sky. Brian put his arm around her. Alan walked up beside them and smiled.

"There's no place like home," he said and walked up to the door.

Chapter 22

Buffalo Nickle Love Story

New Alessaria, California
February 14th
1998

Astrid walked into the gymnasium, looked around and saw it was full of high school students. Her high heels clicked on the floor, echoing in an ominous way that quieted the room. She crossed her arms and looked around the room at the forlorn faces.

"As you probably heard on the news, I am Astrid Borrows," she announced. She noticed a muscular young man in a green shirt rolling his eyes. "You," she said as she pointed at the young man. He looked around himself, "Yeah, you, the Jolly Green Giant, come here," the class rippled with gentle laughter.

"Why?" he asked.

Astrid walked up to him and smirked, "Rolling your eyes is a sure way to volunteer for class participation. What's your name?"

"Tommy Fields," he said and crossed his arms.

"Class, Tommy here will be helping me for today's lesson. You all are here for beginning self-defense for D.A.S. scale numbers up to and including eighteen. As you are hopefully aware, your twenty-five and above brothers and sisters are in trouble. You may feel since the bill that is about to be passed doesn't seem apply to you, why worry? You would be wrong. Not only is it wrong to abandon them

200

in their hour of need, but soon no one will be there in your hour of need. Which is coming, you can count on that."

Tommy scoffed. Astrid glared at him, "Would you care to tell us why you are having such a good chuckle?"

"Alright, Astrid, if I should even buy that you are actually a zombie Astrid, what the hell are you doing dressed like that if this is a real self-defense class?"

Astrid looked down at her black slacks, button-up blue silk blouse and patent leather high heels.

"What is wrong with it, Tommy? Not fashionable for your tastes?" the class broke out in giggles.

"I mean, how can you show us how to kick someone's ass in chick clothes?"

Astrid glowered at him, awkwardly silent and suddenly slapped her thigh. She laughed until she had to wipe away tears. She then put her hands on her hips.

"Thank you, Tommy. I needed a good laugh. Now, class, I will answer his question with a demonstration. Don't worry, Tommy, I promise I will not hurt you. Everyone gather around the center of the room. Tommy, follow me."

She walked to the center of the gym with Tommy in tow looking quite pale.

"Now, I am aware more than a few of you believe you can rely on your gifts as a mover in a fight. I am here to tell you that strategy is wrong. For one, there was a formula developed consisting of various toxins that can weaken any of us enough to wipe out our abilities. To have any chance, you must know what to do in such a case. For instance, I am a D.A.S. thirty-three." A wave of whispers went around the room. "So, because I am not a beginner I think it would be unfair for me to humiliate this young man on his first day here." She paused and grinned, "I will need another volunteer to do it for me."

"Oh come on," Tommy threw his arms up. "What is that going to prove?"

"My dear Tommy, this is going to prove that not only can I kick your ass, as you put it, but that I can teach anyone to do it. Let's begin. Any volunteers?" To Astrid's surprise ninety percent of the class raised their hands. "I see you are very popular," she said with a smirk.

She paced a few steps looking over the class. She stopped and pointed to a scrawny fourteen-year-old boy with a Teenage Mutant Ninja Turtles t-shirt and cargo khakis.

"What's your name?"

"Simon," he said, looking over at Tommy with a satisfied beam.

"Okay, Simon. This is for everyone to hear, so listen up. When you are about to spar with an adversary, you must make up your mind about a few variables before any punch is thrown. You must ask the purpose of the fight, defense or offense? Whether or not you are willing to harm the other person? The larger question being, are you willing to take their life if it comes down to you or them? Trust me, these are never easy questions. See Tommy there?"

She walked up to him and pointed. "If you merely want to stun him and run away, a quick punch to the kidney would do. Most people aim for the stomach, face, or testes, but this spot here by the kidney does not take a punch well and will give you a head start." She took off her right shoe. "Oh, and ladies, remember that a good pair of heels can be a great weapon. It can even be a deadly weapon. A stiletto heel to the neck, right about here," she pointed to Tommy's neck with the heel of the shoe. "With enough blunt force, it can puncture the external carotid artery. It will at least cause a great amount of blood loss," she said, then put her shoe back on.

"Simon, your lesson today is to do a gentle kidney maneuver on Tommy. Hold a fist and jab using your shoulder, not your wrist. Put most of the punch power at the contact point, rather than a running start so to speak."

Simon stood in front of Tommy and made his hand into a fist, swinging front and back a couple times. He swung again and made contact with a thud, forcing Tommy to the ground. Applause rippled through the auditorium. After regaining his breath, Tommy stood back up.

"Thank you Simon, that is all," she said and motioned for him to join the crowd of students.

"I think you are full of it, Astrid. I think you really aren't a D.A.S. thirty-three." Tommy shouted, his voice boomed around the cavernous gymnasium.

Astrid stood a foot in front of him. She stuck her tongue in her cheek and put her hands on her hips.

"You see, you are not the first of your ilk I've come across, Tommy. You think you're calling my bluff and you will come out in the right. I'm sorry to say, you are so very, very wrong."

She stepped back a couple feet and grounded her energy. The room buzzed with static electricity. She lifted her hand slowly and as she did so, Tommy lifted vertically in the air. A silence only awe can provide hushed the room. Tommy soon reached the ceiling, shaking and whimpering softly.

"Put me down," he cried out, the fear making his voice waiver.

"As you wish," she said and brought him down in one violently fast motion. She held him hovering face down an inch above the floor. She closed her fist releasing him and he gently thudded to the floor. He shakily stood back up appearing he might faint or vomit.

"The question you asked regarding how could I kick your ass in chick clothes, as you so eloquently phrased it, I would like to address that."

She leapt in the air, hooked her knee around his neck, spiraled, and pinned him to the floor. She finished the move with her black patent leather heel pressing into his chest. It was such a swift motion that many students missed the complexity of it.

"That is the end of our lesson for today," she said and the room of students applauded.

When Astrid arrived home, she took off her heels at the door. The smell of food cooking greeted her. She heard clanking in her kitchen and went in to investigate. Doyle stood at the stove stirring a pot. She crept up behind him and wrapped her arms around his middle. He gave a soft moan of delight.

"You forgot that you can't sneak up on a soul reader. Did you remember that it happens to be Valentine's Day?"

"I did know both of those things. What I don't know is what you're doing in my kitchen. Whatever that is, it smells amazing."

"I'm making my famous puttanesca recipe. This sauce is the food version of making love to a beautiful woman. How was the self-defense class?"

Astrid grabbed a bottle of water from the fridge. She took a swig and shrugged, "It was okay."

He turned and pointed the spoon at her, "Do I need to read you or can you just tell me about your day?"

"Why do you need to know about my day, anyway?"

"You are a perfect person to teach this class, you are always defensive."

"It's nothing personal, it's who I am. I've always had people trying to rip me apart. I'm not used to the sweet side yet."

"Are you calling me sweet?" he said lifting an eyebrow.

She smiled and gave his butt a slap as she walked by him, "You can bet this sweet ass."

He laughed, "I'm not a piece of meat."

"You're my piece of meat," she said as she left the room.

Flynn, Kansas
February 14th
1998

Sarah sat in the chair by the bay window looking out at the sky. In her hand was a book of short stories by O. Henry. The farm house had been through a facelift and finally felt finished. Between Alan and Brian, they had fixed everything. She was in charge of decorating. She found joy in learning to cook and even cleaning. Her first attempts at cooking were a disaster, but Brian and Alan were very patient. She had finally conquered macaroni and cheese. There was no television, so the week they arrived Alan had raided the local bookstore and brought back a box of books and board games, including Hungry, Hungry Hippos. She heard the truck pull up and smiled. Brian come in with arms full of groceries.

"Lucy, I'm home," he called out in a subpar Ricky Ricardo impersonation.

She stood up and followed him to the kitchen. He set down the bags and took her in his arms. As they kissed, Alan walked up and cleared his throat behind them.

"Sorry," Sarah said with a giggle.

"No, I get it, young love, yada yada."

Brian held his hand on her growing belly, "How's our little guy?"

"Good," she said with a smile.

"I didn't know if you love birds know, but today is Valentine's Day."

"Oh yeah, forgot that was today," Sarah said. "Being cooped up all the time I lose track of days."

"Well, you kids are going on a date tonight."

"Alan, what if I get recognized?" Sarah exclaimed.

"I thought of that," Alan pulled out a box of hair dye. "How do you feel about being a blonde?" he grinned as he shook the box at her.

Brian put on a gray collared shirt and black slacks. He put on some Old Spice and felt he was ready to go. Alan poked his head into the room with a grin.

"You need to check out your lady," he said and motioned for Brian to follow.

He followed Alan to the living room and saw Sarah. She had dyed her hair blonde. She was in a pink and green dress he had never seen. She was glowing and radiant.

"Wow," was all he could utter and Sarah giggled.

"That good eh?" she said. "Alan picked up this dress for me. It's a little big, but that won't be for long."

"I also picked these up," Alan said holding up wedding rings. "Before you freak out, they're for show. It's the kind of town where since Sarah's pregnant, people would talk if you don't have rings."

Brian took Sarah's ring and went down on one knee. Sarah started laughing until she saw the serious look on his face.

"Wait, is this for real?" she asked.

"Sarah, I know we did things ass backwards. But, I love you and I should have done this a while ago. Will you marry me?"

"But, can we even get married if we are in hiding?" Sarah exclaimed.

"Shut up and say yes. You'll figure it out later," Alan said. He pushed Sarah towards Brian's outstretched hand.

"I guess we can figure it out later," she said.

"Is that a yes?" Brian asked, still on his knee.

"Oh, well yeah, it's a yes," she answered and he kissed her.

"Now the ring goes on the finger," Alan coached.

"Like you're an expert," Brian chided.

"I have a lot of experience. I was fake married to Astrid several times after all."

Brian and Sarah were at an Italian restaurant in the downtown area of Flynn. Sarah looked at the ring and she smiled.

"It's so pretty," she said.

"I helped pick it out."

"Really?"

Brian laughed and squirmed, "I was there, does that count?" They both laughed. He reached out and held her hand. "I have a serious question," he said. "Do blondes really have more fun?" She giggled and let out a little snort.

The waiter served their pasta, she took a bite, "Oh my God this is way better than mine."

"Oh yeah," Brian saw the look on Sarah's face. "Oh, I meant, yours is good too."

"It's okay, don't wig out. I know my cooking needs a lot of help."

"You've been getting a lot better. Honest."

"I can't believe I didn't even know how to work a stove. Actually, I can believe it. We had people to do that stuff. I never had to. It's really nice to be learning life stuff,"

"You're cute," he said with a stifled chuckle. "Have you looked at that baby name book Alan gave you?"

"Yeah. It was saying, in the Jewish tradition, they name a baby after a dead family member."

"You're Jewish?" Brian said with surprise.

"Yeah, only a little. I didn't tell you?"

"You could have, I'm not sure," Brian said.

"What are you?" she said.

"I'm not sure actually," he looked away in thought. "I think Episcopal."

"That's a type of Christian right?"

"Yeah."

"What makes Episcopal different?"

"Not sure, never really thought about it."

"How are we going to raise this kid? I mean religion wise, it seems like we don't have a clue," she said rolling her eyes.

"Hey, we will figure all that out. First we have to name him."

"I was thinking, since it's a boy, to name him after our dads. Maybe Jonathan Robert."

"Wait, why can't it be Robert Jonathan?"

"Because I'm the mom."

"That's not fair."

"When you push a baby out of you, then you can name it whatever you want."

"If science ever makes that possible, I'm keeping you to your word. Wait, wasn't your dad born with a different name?"

"Do you really want a kid named Hershel?"

"Jonathan Robert is a nice name."

"Besides, my dad said that he wasn't Hershel anymore, like he was a different person and felt his name had to reflect it."

"I miss my parents at times like this."

"Yeah, me too. But, I really miss my grandma. I know we fought like constantly, but I love her. I don't know if I told her that enough."

She pushed a meatball around on her plate and watched as the candle on the table swayed.

"She knows, don't worry about that. My family is the same way. We bicker, but there is no doubt we love the shit out of each other. Even Michael."

"Lately, I've been thinking that I'm happier here. I feel normal."

"You don't want to be normal. You are an extraordinary person; you have great abilities. When Alan was training you I saw how wonderful your gifts are."

"I would trade them in a heartbeat if it means being happy."

"But that is who you are. Who I am. People try to make us feel bad for being special because they aren't. Remember that."

"How did you get to be so smart?" she said.

"I'm just a genius, what can I say?" he said grinning.

"Happy Valentine's Day," she said and lifted her glass of water.

"Ditto," he said and clinked his water glass with hers.

Sarah woke in the night and went to the restroom. On the way back to bed, she noticed a light on in the living room. She walked into the room and saw Alan crying in a chair. He looked up and wiped his tears.

"I didn't think anyone was up," he said.

"I had to pee and I saw the light on. Are you okay?" she asked and sat across from him.

"Yeah, I'm just thinking," he said. He saw that she noticed he was holding a coin. "Have you ever seen a buffalo nickel?"

"No," she said. He handed it to her and she looked at it under the light. She noticed the date imprinted on the coin. "1913?" she asked, fascinated.

"It's probably worth something, but I keep it for sentimental reasons."

She handed it back to him and he half smiled.

"What's the story with the coin?"

He flipped it into the air, "Valentine's day is a reminder of love. I loved the man who gave me this coin. That was many years ago."

"Tell me about him," she encouraged.

"Oh, boy, where do I start? Jeffery was a wonderful man. It was 1908 when Astrid had gone into her recluse stage and I could not find her. I searched for a couple years but gave up in late 1910, I think. I was in New York when I met him, a very handsome stockbroker. I told him I was thirty-three, so in his mind I was two years his junior."

"Did he love you?"

"Yes, he did," Alan smiled a sweet smile. "He only had love for me and basset hounds," he chuckled. "He was very stubborn and opinionated. Once he went off on one of his rants. I said that if he wanted to give me his two cents I wanted it in advance, with interest. Got to love Jeff, he put a buffalo nickel in my pocket and kept on ranting."

"How long were you together?"

Alan smiled, "Almost forty years."

"Wow," Sarah said with amazement.

"Yes, we had a beautiful life together."

"How did he not figure it out? I mean you not aging."

"Don't tell Astrid, but he knew all of my secrets. I kept nothing from him and he nothing from me. I am grateful to Jeff for showing me unconditional love and peace."

"Why did you guys break up?" Sarah asked and then realized the obvious answer.

"Forty years is a long time, people age. He smoked a pipe all day long. He got lung cancer and in those days it was a death sentence. After the doctors told him he was going to die, I brought him to the house in New Alessaria. We stayed there two months, a hospice of sorts. One spring day, I was reading by a beautiful bay window and he called to me. He asked me to read him some of my book, to take his mind off the pain. I was reading a book of limericks of all things. My friend George had given it to me on Astrid and I's last trip to England."

"What are limericks?" Sarah asked.

"They're little clever poems. Most of them are dirty but tame by today's standards. At the time they were very shocking. Let's see if I remember one. Ah, here's a tame one, 'there was a young lady of Niger, who smiled as she rode on a tiger, they returned from the ride, with the lady inside, and the smile on the face of the tiger.' I read limericks to him all afternoon and he would chuckle at most. Sometimes he would struggle to catch his breath. After a time, I noticed that he had stopped chuckling and looked up to see he had passed away. Yes, it was sad. Of course, I was broken up. But, when he died, he had a beautiful smile on his face. I will always treasure that in the last moment, the very last moment of the life of the man I loved, I gave him happiness and he died with a smile. He didn't have to die alone."

"That is so romantic," Sarah said, wiping away a tear.

"Yes, it is," he said.

"How did you deal after he died? That must have been so hard."

"Oh, Sarah, you are so young. You haven't known that kind of love. Even with Brian, it's different. After, I was in such a place of despair, I wanted to die or kill someone. I couldn't choose, so I enlisted," he laughed. "You would be surprised how easy it was to get into the army in those days."

"You fought in the army?" Sarah asked with surprise.

"Fairies can fight with the rest of 'em. But, yeah, I'm not the fighting type. I was stuck behind a desk the entire war. Never left Ohio," he laughed quietly.

"You guys having a good chat?" Brian said with a yawn.

"I'm sorry honey, did we wake you up?" Sarah stood and brushed Brian's stray hair behind his ear.

"Nah, I was having a hard time sleeping and heard you guys talking. Thought I would come check it out."

Alan let out a forced yawn and looked at the wall clock, "It's quite late, I'm off to hit the hay," he stood and walked to his bedroom.

Sarah craned her neck up and kissed Brian. He looked down at her and smiled.

"What was that for?" Brian asked.

"I just love you."

"Um, okay. I love you, too. Let's go back to bed. I have to work on that stupid fence tomorrow."

In that moment, Sarah was happy and she wished everything could stay just like this forever.

Chapter 23

Capacity for Evil

New Alessaria, California
May 28th
1998

Evie stood in her study staring at the television blankly. William Gondory came into the room.

"Tell me William, how's your family?"

"Very well, thank you."

The news was on mute and a picture of a man was on screen with the words "suspect in mall shooting" under his picture.

"Arthur Cowell, true evil right there?" she gave an exasperated chuckle. "It is surprising how one man can undo a lifetime of good. I don't think we will ever know if that bill would have passed or not if he hadn't done what he did."

"When are you going to visit the victims?"

"My plane leaves this evening. I will meet with the families and surviving victims. They are having the memorial tomorrow."

"Do they know what exactly happened? Do they know totals?"

"What I've been told, is Arthur Cowell was classified as a nineteen D.A.S. Fifty-three of the victims are expected to live. The final death total as of today is 33. They shot him fifteen times before he died."

She rubbed the back of her neck and wept, "How can anyone create such horror? It's hard to understand, let alone stomach that he could do this."

"Evie, please sit down," he sat next to her and smiled. "You've known me many years. I remember finding you in that bathtub like it was yesterday. I saw what was done in this house years ago. After that, I'll be honest; I didn't know how the Astridian people would go on."

"I remember it too well."

"But, somehow we all, even you, lived on with purpose. After the '86 bombing, I again lost hope. I came to comfort you and I met little Sarah. You told me of the signs, the mark and such. That day my hope was restored. Today, I have never been so frightened for our future, ever. I'm not alone. The community center is being flooded with people just as frightened. Evie, I consider you not only my leader, but also a very dear friend."

"William, you are one of my only true friends I have in this world. Without Sarah by my side, I feel like a boat without an anchor. I have no clue what to do now."

"You know I was in the army during the war, right?" he asked and Evie nodded. "I was eighteen when I was drafted. It's one thing to read in a history book about war and the Final Solution. I was there. I've seen what men can do to their fellow man. Once, we freed a camp, there was a man I spoke German with. He was so weak he could barely walk. We spoke at length that day. His name was Abraham and he was an inch from death. I asked him his profession before the war. He told me he was attending art school. You know that pencil drawing in my study of me. He asked if he could draw that. I gave him my parents' address in the states before we separated. I came home from the war to a letter and the portrait. Have I ever mentioned my friend Abe?"

"Many times, but you never told me this."

"I had sent him an urgent letter about recent events and said I never expected them to pass that bill, in this day

214

and age. I'll read you his response." He pulled out a paper and put on reading glasses.

"My dear friend Billy. I understand what you mean. I have known you many years and I know I never speak of the past. I feel it necessary to do so now. In 1938, they outlawed us Jews owning guns. My father sat before me and said the equivalent of what you just said. He was a smart man, a professor at the university. He said he believed in the goodness of men and that it was a temporary fervor. When we were relocated, they put us in a long line, shoulder to shoulder and announced that every third person would be shot. As they went down the line, families would fight over who would be the third.

There was a moment when counting I realized I would be the third one. I didn't pray to be saved, I prayed for it to be quick and painless. As they approached, my father pushed me aside and took my place in line. I am telling you this because there are times of darkness and people who commit evil acts. But, there is always light in the world. The Nazi with the gun watched my father take my place. I watched him shoot the gun and my father's body fall. I fell down to my knees in despair. That Nazi looked down at me trying to keep his tears from the other guards.

He looked to be about my own age. He extended his hand to me and helped me to my feet. Then he continued down the line.

It would be easy to say there are people born evil and that's how they can do such things. The truth is not easy and is hard to stomach. That Nazi who murdered my father was not born a Nazi. A man in a white sheet who hanged an innocent Negro man from a tree branch was not born with that kind of hate in his heart. What happened with that bill today I am afraid is only the beginning. I am an old man and have seen things that no human should ever see. I watch the news every night. For too long, I have stood by and not said a word. I cannot live through the trains again. People say it can't happen here that this is America.

Ask an old American Jap that question. I have a friend here, his name is John. Surprising to find a Jap named John. I vaguely knew him, I knew he was a retired teacher and his wife had died a couple years before. He and I didn't get along because I'm a Mets fan and he's a Dodger fan. One day he was talking about the war. He said he was third generation Japanese-American. He was a high school teacher during the internment. Someone asked him if he was still angry. I laughed. John turned to me

216

and with anger asked why I was laughing. You know I never show my arm, but at that moment, there were no words. I stood up and rolled up my sleeve. He looked at me for a long time. I was not sure how he was going to react. He got up and gave me a hug. John is now one of my greatest friends, even if he is a Dodger fan.

I'm old. I tend to ramble. The point of me telling you this is simple. We must not repeat the past. This must be stopped, but I am too old to fight the good fight myself. Please, do not give up on the goodness of people, but never underestimate their capacity for evil. God bless my friend."

Evie sat wiping away her tears. She looked at the television and gave a disgusted scoff.

"Oh William, I miss my Sarah. But, I'm not stupid, I know I can't contact her no matter what. It's tearing me up inside. I have been wanting to drink since she left."

"Evie, how long has it been since your last drink?"

"Seven months, I think."

"I can help you with your recovery, Evie."

"Thank you. You are a dear friend. I hope you know that after that horrible night forty years ago, the silver lining was you found me in that Godforsaken bathtub. I used to think that night a part of me died. That some of my goodness and proper qualities were destroyed by seeing such horror. But, I think that maybe all it did was give me an excuse to drink away my life. I have such regret, it is overwhelming at times."

"Don't be so hard on yourself. You are a good person. You need some well-deserved rest."

"I'll rest when I'm dead. I don't know, maybe I should just let her take it all over. Let the chips fall as they may. I'm tired," Evie said.

"Who, Astrid? You are our leader, Evie."

She turned her gaze to the television and shook her head.

"I might be our leader, but she might be our salvation."

Chapter 24

Theodore Rose-Delving

Flynn, Kansas
June 21
1998

Sarah held her baby boy in her arms and watched him sleep, his little hand wrapped around her finger. She beamed as she kissed his forehead, inhaling the sweet baby smell.

"Welcome to the world, my little guy. I love you so much already and we just met. Your name is Theodore. My dad hated the name he was born with and changed it to Jon. But he was never a Jon either. Astrid called him Teddy when he was young. He even had that tattoo of the mongoose. I wish I knew that version of my dad. I wish he could meet you," she kissed his hand. "I promise to love you, forever and ever. No one will ever hurt you."

Brian sat on the porch swing, startled when the front door opened. Alan sat down on the other end of the porch swing and sighed. He gave Brian a strong pat on the back and smiled.

"Seems appropriate you become a father on Father's day," Alan said and Brian burst into tears. "What did I say?"

"I'm so freaking happy," Brian said laughing with tears going down his face. "You must think I'm a pussy for crying."

"Nah, I've seen men cry for things that are not worthy of tears. My friend, enjoy this moment. You deserve it."

"I'm scared. I'm the man here. The father, the husband. Well, I'm going to be a husband soon at least." He looked over at Alan and clasped his hands, "What if I can't do it? What if I can't take care of them? What if something bad happens and I can't protect them?"

"Ah, I see. I could say that you are making much ado about nothing and tell you everything will be okay. But, you are smarter than people give you credit for. The shit is going to hit the fan. That's just life. When or how, I have no clue. I can assure you it will be a mess. There are things you can't prepare for. Hell, I've had times that I didn't know what was happening, let alone what the right thing to do was."

"Like what?"

Alan looked into the small field and then at the sky.

"Meeting Astrid for one. She was a force I had no idea how to classify, let alone understand. I was almost twenty-five when I met her. She neglected to inform me of her plan to stage her death for the masses. The woman I admired was shot in front of me. There was so much blood. No one tells you that you can smell blood. I can still smell it. I held her in my arms, believing she would die. Watching the blood pouring out of her chest, her white dress turned red. Imagine my surprise when she later showed up at my door."

He looked at Brian with a far off gaze, as if he were watching the past replay.

"But, they didn't actually shoot her though, right? It was faked."

"One thing about Astrid is that she goes all the way with everything. She took a bullet like a champ."

"She survived a gunshot to the chest?" Brian said looking away in dismay.

"I always pray for the soul of anyone who gets on her bad side. Luckily, I've never had the bad fortune to be on the receiving end."

"It was really lucky that you survived the Daffodils and became immortal and all that."

"Lucky," Alan whispered and stood from the swing. He stepped out onto the ground and kicked a small stone. As he stared off into the distance, he put his hands in his pockets.

"Did I say something wrong?" Brian asked gingerly.

Alan turned and walked back onto the porch, "No, kid, you said nothing wrong. Luck just had nothing to do with it."

"What do you mean?"

Alan sat back down on the swing and sighed, "After Astrid was assassinated, or so we thought, her followers worked to sell her autobiography that was ghost written by yours truly. Astrid was generous and left me a house downtown and money in a bank account. I got a job at the local newspaper. Nine years later a maid arrives, saying she was paid for by the foundation. Her name was Mary. I did not know she was newly infected with the Daffodils. Within the span of a day or two we both fell ill. I thought I was having visions when I opened my door to see Astrid on my stoop.

"It was touch and go for a while there, but two weeks later the fevers stopped. I knew I was not hallucinating, Astrid was very much alive. Soon after, I tended to the dying housekeeper. She asked for my forgiveness. You see, she was a patient in a daffodils ward the day before she came to work for me. Astrid paid her to come work for me and assured her the best medical care."

"Hold on. Do you believe Astrid gave you the Daffodils on purpose?"

"It is not what I believe, it's what happened."

"Why would she do that?"

"People will do anything when they are lonely and frightened."

"You could have died, man. That's hardcore. You must have been pissed."

"At first, you bet I was. I confronted Astrid, after Mary succumbed to her illness. I was furious beyond comprehension. She told me that it was to help me stay immortal. Of course I thought she was lying. But, she went on and on about the people she had met with the same condition years previous. There was a club of sorts located in England. It was a common thread that these people were alive for hundreds of years. She said she wanted me by her side. I think what I had a hard time understanding for many years was that she made the decision for me."

"It worked out in the end. You get to live forever."

"I won't lie, there have been many moments where I have enjoyed the length of my years. To be truthful, every single day I take a breath, I dream of the day I draw my last."

"Whoa, that's intense," Brian said shaking his head.

"I didn't mean to get intense, just having a moment. You have a beautiful baby boy. Be happy about that. I know you will do your best to take care of him and Sarah."

"Thanks man. I'm thinking of going into town to get Sarah and me some ice cream. Want some?"

"Sure. I think she will like it if you get some flowers, too."

"For a gay dude you know a lot about women."

"I've spent most of a century with a woman; it would be surprising if I didn't learn a thing or two."

"Why do you stay with Astrid? I mean find yourself a man, date, and get a life of your own."

"I've thought about it, but I've grown tired of heartache and needed a break for a decade or two."

"It's so freaky how that isn't a long time for you guys, living forever and all."

"Time is a funny thing, there's either too much or too

little. But, I recommend you go in and ask Sarah what flavor she wants. I want mint chip."

Brian got up then turned around, "Thanks man, I appreciate that you're here with us."

"You're welcome. Now, enough mushy stuff. Go get some ice cream for us. Chop, chop."

Brian stood at the counter filling out a newspaper ad form. A woman with tan-rimmed glasses tapped her pen rhythmically and periodically snapped her gum. He finished and handed her the card.

"Just to verify, your ad is as follows: Wanted crib for healthy newborn baby boy, name is Theodore. Contact: Jackson/Mary. Is that all correct?"

"Yes."

"Don't you want to put a contact phone number?"

"Nope, I'm good."

She looked at him and rolled her eyes, "Okay, good luck with that. It'll be in tomorrow's paper."

Chapter 25

Some Will Fall

Alexandria, Virginia
July 1st
1998

Michael Delving coughed up blood as he lay sprawled out on an expensive rug with a man's foot pressed hard on his chest. Dried blood from a broken nose flaked and itched. His hair dripped with sweat and his breathing was labored. He grabbed the shoe holding him down and tried desperately to push it away. Another man gave a kick to his side and Michael wailed. Tears rushed down his face as his body lurched from the pain.

"Enough," a voice bellowed.

All three men looked over to the source of the voice. The man kicking Michael crossed his arms behind his back. The man with his foot on Michael's chest released his hold. Michael coughed and rolled onto his side. He looked up at the sharp dressed man and winced. He would know that smirk and perfectly formed hair anywhere.

"Jesus, you're Alexander Bram, aren't you?" Michael asked.

Alexander crouched down, looked him in the eye and smirked, "Pleased to meet you, Mr. Michael Delving."

"What do you want? I don't know anything," Michael cried out.

"Tisk, tisk. Do you think I'm stupid? I don't like it when people call me stupid." He stood and walked over to a

224

table. He poured himself a scotch and slowly plopped in three ice cubes. "My men found you and three of your comrades in one of my warehouses downtown. Why would you trespass on my property?"

"I'm not going to tell you anything," Michael said and spat on the ground.

Alexander swirled his glass and took a sip.

"I doubt that," he looked at his men. "I know that you know things."

"I don't know anything, man. They sent all the information to the leader of the raid and that wasn't me."

"You see, dear Michael, I am looking for other information. Your brother is Brian Delving, is he not?"

Michael looked around and gulped, "Yeah, what's it to you?" he said in a low voice.

"Ah, I think you know where he might be these days."

"I don't know anything," Michael said slowly through clenched teeth.

"I suspect you do. I would prefer not to torture you, but I am willing and able to do so. Did you know a man could live without his testicles, or survive a mutilated dick? Sometimes with no dick at all. Rick here likes to take off a slice at a time, nice and slow."

Michael turned his head away, breathing hard and fast, "I'll tell you if you promise not to hurt me anymore."

"I am a man of my word and I give you my word that I, nor any of my men, will cause you anymore pain."

"He's in Kansas," Michael whispered.

"Where?" Alexander put his glass down.

"Near a place called Flynn, on a farm."

Alexander smiled and slapped his thigh, "Stupid bitch made it too easy. I should have seen it sooner." He looked down at Michael and nodded. "Good boy, this is the break we needed."

"What are you going to do to them?" Michael asked.

Alexander snapped his fingers and the two men took Michael by the arms and stood him up. Another man took out his revolver.

"Are you going to shoot me? After I told you what you wanted?" Michael sobbed.

"My dear boy, to answer your first question, you want a clear conscience so I won't tell you my plans. To answer your other questions, I'm not going to shoot you." Michael sighed in relief. "They can trace bullets."

Alexander nodded and the two men dragged Michael screaming to the balcony.

"Good-bye Mr. Delving. I thank you for your help this evening. I promise, this won't hurt. I'm a man of my word."

The two men tossed Michael off the tenth floor balcony. Alexander picked up his scotch glass and took a sip.

"What now, Alex?" one of the men asked.

"Call our cleaning crew. That body needs to disappear. Rick, I charge you with the most important job of all. Go find that little Astridian whore in Kansas. And her little dog Brian, too."

Ashwin threw his headphones across the van and ran out into the street. He put his hands on the back of his head and closed his eyes.

A man stood next to Ashwin and sighed, "We were lucky, at least they didn't find the wiretap we placed in there."

Ashwin lowered his arms and looked over at him with disgust, "I would not wish such shitty luck on anyone."

"I'm sorry if I said something wrong."

"Shit," Ashwin yelled and balled his hands into fists.

"Sarah's location has been compromised. What are we going to do? We are going to need to move fast."

"You think I don't know that?" Ashwin put his hand on his chin and sighed. "Get Evie on the phone, now."

226

New Alessaria, California
July 1st
1998

Evie sat in the study watching the fireplace spit and crackle. In recent years Evie was always cold. Evie smiled at the memory of Sarah chiding her about having a fire going in July. Astrid walked in and saw the shadows dance on Evie's face. She turned and smiled at Astrid.

"Come in," Evie said and sipped her tea.

Astrid sat next to her on the couch and looked at her wristwatch, "It is officially after midnight. You're not pacing the hallway."

Evie sighed and put out her hand. Astrid put her hand on Evie's and smiled.

"Does it ever get easier?" Evie asked, her eyes welling up.

"Sometimes," she said and gave a slight smile. "I keep the pain deep inside, away from the world."

"You and I are similar, our paths are from different times, but I feel a kinship beyond bloodlines and family trees. Do you agree?"

"I remember when I was employed as the nanny, many times I noted my admiration for you. You are strong, whether you realize it or not. Every night I would watch you walk the foyer and wait. I know that feeling well. You pray that the spirit of your loved ones would appear and you could say the things you wish you had while they lived. But, night after night, you only see an empty house of memory and scars."

Evie dabbed her tears with a handkerchief, "Sometimes I forget that you suffered so much loss, too."

Astrid took in a deep breath and looked into the fire. She stroked Evie's hand with her thumb.

"It has been a hundred and sixty three years since I held my Seamus' dead body in my arms. Not a single day passes that I don't miss him. That I don't mourn him. A day

227

does not pass that I don't regret that he died in pain. Yes, there are moments where I forgive. But, those are few and far between. After I realized I was cursed to carry the weight of this for eternity, I promised that I would distance myself from all I love. I said it was to protect them. But, now I know it was to protect me."

"I will forever be thankful that you rejoined our family after what happened in this house," Evie said.

"In truth, it is not you I was speaking of. You brought me back to life. Hershel taught me how to love another person again, a maternal kind of love, but still love. For that, I will always be grateful. You were a good mother, Evie. I admired that."

Evie looked down at her damp handkerchief and scoffed, "I was a drunk, not the mother he needed. I should have been better."

Astrid held her hand on her chest and looked at her with eyes full of sorrow.

"I will share something with you; the only other person I ever told was Alan. There are parts he doesn't even know. But, I feel like you need to know. I kept in touch with my son's wife, Anne, after I left the public life as Astrid."

"I didn't know you had a son."

"That was by design. Flynn was Seamus' and my child, he was born after Seamus died. We had never married. I was selfish and concealed the pregnancy. Publicly, I told people he was the child of a friend, but I told him the truth. He never forgave me for it. He was born without our gifts; he couldn't move a damn thing. He grew resentful and angry. I don't blame him. I was a shell of a mother.

"After Seamus died, I put myself away and created a persona. I became a performance of Astrid. I believed Flynn was weak and hated that he looked like his father. He reminded me daily of what I lost and I hated him for it." She took a deep breath, "I feared after I was gone, no one could or would protect him. I felt separating him from me and my family would ensure his survival. It was what in turn caused his death."

"You had him murdered?" Evie gasped.

"No, but I think it would have been an easier fate. As you know, after my public death everything went to my daughter, Nadine. I legally denied him using my family name. I did bequeath a spot of land in Alessaria, the home where I grew up. I provided a large amount of money in the will. He saw the will and was furious. I was so blinded I believed it was about the money. I see now, he felt I was abandoning him. Which was true, but the truth is I had abandoned my love for him long before. His wife Anne was aware of my plans and I left lines of communication open to her in case of financial need. In my will my request in return for the real estate and funds was for Flynn never to set foot in New Alessaria again. If he did come back, he would lose everything. I literally banished him."

"Wow," Evie said.

"There were assassination attempts on his life as well as mine he knew nothing of. I thought I was saving him. It was selfish and hurtful. One day, Anne sent me a telegram that he was in a mad house, and that he had ruined them financially with booze and gambling. Alan told me not to go, but I'm stubborn and went to help." Tears fell down her cheeks and she trembled. "When he saw me, he collapsed in my arms, weeping like a small child. I told him everything, as if confessing my sins to a priest. After we cried and held each other, he went in the other room. I heard the gunshot that took his life." Astrid put her trembling fingers to her lips. "I was no fool. I knew that I would outlive him. But, what I could not live with was that his death was on my hands."

"That wasn't your fault," Evie said and clasped Astrid's hand in hers.

"It took me nearly forty years in Kansas to figure out it was my fault. He didn't die because I came back, he died because he never had me to begin with. It took me a long time to forgive myself. In forgiveness, I found my freedom. It took some time. I know you feel like a disappointment as a mother. I know without a doubt, that isn't true. I know what it is to be a disgrace as a mother, that wasn't you. I want you to know the freedom from those shackles. I want to…" she looked off into the distance wide-eyed, trembling.

"What is it?" Evie asked, concerned.

"I don't know," she whispered. "But, it can't be good."

The butler entered the room and Evie bolted up, "Miss Evie, there is a phone call for you."

She rushed to the phone on the end table and picked up the receiver, "Hello?"

"Evie, it's Ashwin. They found the location of Sarah's safe house. The P.G.I. know where she is."

Evie's legs buckled, Astrid caught her and helped her sit in the nearby chair. She gently took the phone.

"What is your plan to fix this, Ashwin?" Astrid said with a tone of anger.

"That's why I'm calling you," Ashwin said with a disheartened sigh.

Astrid looked into Evie's eyes and took a deep breath, "Contact the proper authorities with an anonymous tip of Sarah's location."

"You can't do that, we must be able to move her without doing that," Evie cried out.

"We have no time, Evie. At least this way she has a chance. If the P.G.I. get there first she won't have a chance in hell. You know I'm right," Evie nodded and let out an exasperated sigh. "Ashwin, make the call. Alert the press. We want the world's eyes on this. Also, send out a message on my behalf for our volunteers to assemble."

"Assemble? Aren't we being hasty to start calling them in so soon?"

"If Alexander has Sarah, you know he is going to burn down the holding center they take her to as soon as he can. We need to get our people. They can't stop us if you get everyone to that center as soon as we can. Make sure you send enough volunteers. We don't know yet where they will send Sarah."

"Okay, if you plan on being our peoples' savior, you better do it now. Save our people, Astrid," Ashwin yelled and hung up.

"No pressure or anything," she said rolling her eyes. "Evie, strap on your ruby slippers, we're going to Kansas. We're bringing 'em home."

Chapter 26

Capturing the Princess

Flynn, Kansas
July 3rd
1998

The warm morning sun came in through the lace curtains. Sarah stood at the kitchen sink peeling a carrot. A cool cross breeze from the front door and back door gently fluttered her white cotton dress. She looked over at the basinet where baby Teddy slept soundly. She smiled and sighed happily. She heard the truck pull up. After wiping her hands on her apron, she headed to the front door. Before she made it across the living room, she heard several gunshots and shouting. She froze in place and shook uncontrollably. The front lace curtains flapped around and she caught a glimpse of Brian on his knees with his hands behind his head. Several men in SWAT uniforms pointed their guns at him and yelling things she could not make out.

"Sarah," she heard Alan's voice behind her.

He was about to say something, but a tear gas can crashed through the front window. Sarah screamed and coughed as gas plumed around her. She saw the SWAT team storming in through the back door. Turning, she watched Alan point a gun at the officers. Several of them opened fire. She screamed out as his body lurched with every bullet. She could hear Teddy's cries and ran to the kitchen. A familiar pinch came to her chest. She looked down and saw a dart.

As she drifted off into the blackness, all she could hear was her son crying.

Several hours later in a nearby hospital, Evie and Astrid walked briskly down the hallway. Astrid saw two police officers posted in front of a room and walked toward them.

"Let me pass," Astrid said sternly and tried to push past.

"We are under strict orders not to let anyone in this room."

"If you do not let me pass, you will not live long enough to regret it," Astrid barked.

Behind Astrid, a well-dressed man with an English accent said, "Let her pass, she is a friend of mine."

She turned and nodded her head to the Englishman before entering the room with Evie in tow. Evie looked at Alan in the hospital bed covered in gauze, tubes, and wires.

Astrid rushed to the bed and sat next to him. She took his hand in her hers as she blubbered.

"You're such a stupid asshole," she whispered. "You had to be a drama queen and get shot."

He let out a hoarse laugh, "I had to go down in style. I took a page from your book, my dear," he touched her face and she smiled. "Now you can't win the "I got shot" argument."

"How many times did they get you?" she asked wiping her tears with her sleeve.

"Seven. For a SWAT team, you would think they would be better marksmen."

Evie stepped towards the bed, "You are a lucky man."

Alan gave a bittersweet smile looking at Astrid, he said, "Luck has nothing to do with it."

The English man came in and put out his hand to Evie, "Pleasure to meet you, Mrs. Rose," he said.

Astrid stood and they embraced. After they parted, she kissed his cheek and took his face in her hands.

"I don't know how I can thank you enough. Send my thanks to Danika."

"I'm sure she'll find a way for you to make it up to her."

"Evie, this is Charles, an old friend," she said warmly. She turned back to him, "Was it hard to get him out undetected?"

"You don't want to know the details. My private plane is in a nearby airfield for extraction."

"What about Sarah and the baby?" Evie asked.

"The baby is safe. I placed a call to a trusted contact. He is on his way from CPS with Theodore."

Evie sat down and placed her hand over her heart, "Thank God," she whispered. She looked up at Charles with a tiny smile, "They named him Theodore." A look of realization washed over her. "What about my Sarah? And Brian?"

He pulled up a chair and held her hand, "They are okay. We must focus on getting you home with the baby."

Evie leaned in and hugged him. Astrid sent a channel asking him if he knew if Sarah and Brian actually were okay. He looked up at her and sent a channel back apologizing that he did not know. Astrid looked down with worry at Alan and squeezed his hand.

Sarah awoke in the back of a van. As she became more aware, she felt someone holding her and struggled.

"Sarah, it's okay, I'm here," she heard Brian's voice and turned to look up at him.

She cried and he held her closer, "Where's Teddy?" she asked looking around.

"They took him," Brian said trying to hold back tears.

"They killed Alan," she whispered, tears flowing down her face.

He brushed her hair from her face and wiped her tears with his finger, "I know." The van came to a sudden stop. They looked at each other, "Whatever happens, don't be afraid," he said then kissed her deeply.

The doors opened. Men dragged them out of the van. As they pulled Brian in a different direction, Sarah kicked and squirmed.

"Where are you taking him?" she hollered. "Brian!" She squirmed as one of the men picked her up and threw her over his shoulder.

"It's okay, Sarah. It's going to be okay, be strong," Brian shouted.

They took her into a building and went down a long poorly lit hallway. At the end of the hall, they set her down on the floor in a dark room and left. After the door closed, the lights flickered on. She looked around and saw two chairs and a table in the center of the room. It looked like the interrogation room from detective movies. A woman in a gray pantsuit came into the room and sat on one side of the table.

"Please sit," she said as Sarah just glared back. "You might want to make this easier for all involved, including yourself." She watched the woman turn on a tape recorder.

Sarah reluctantly sat, "Where am I?"

"Utah Detention Center for Public Safety."

"Where's my son and Brian?"

"Both are safe."

"Please let us go, we don't want to hurt anyone."

The woman sighed and relaxed her shoulders. She turned the recorder off. "If I could change your situation I would, mother to mother. I think this is bullshit."

"Then why are you helping them do this to me?" Sarah said with anger seething in her words.

235

"I have two children. I'm sorry but feeding them is more important to me than social causes like yours. You should understand now that you have your little boy. A mother does all she can for her children and this job comes with medical."

"How can you be such a cold bitch?"

"Wake up to the world. This is temporary. The worst that will happen is you will stay in a cell for a couple weeks, month tops. You are important, they'll get you out in time." She winced as she realized she had let information slip.

"What do you mean 'in time'?"

The woman stood and made her way to the door. Sarah tried to stop her, but she was still too weak from the dart.

"Good luck, Sarah. I really mean it." She went to leave then turned back. She whispered, barely moving her lips, "Don't eat or drink anything, they put stuff in the food. Don't tell anyone else or they will know I told you. Also, hide some food to make it appear you're eating or the gig is up," she said, her voice wavering. She shut the door behind her.

Chapter 27

Karma's a Bitch

The office door opened and Alexander Bram's personal assistant came in with a manila file. He stood, staring blankly. While waiting, the ticking clock put him on edge.

"Yeah, what is it?" Alexander snapped.

"The Chosen tipped off the authorities and they got to her first. There was a lot of media coverage."

"Son of a bitch," Alex yelled and threw a stapler across the room.

"But they do have her on lockdown in the Utah center. All guards are on alert and primed to start Operation Sanitation."

"Good, when will everything be in place?"

"Approximately one in the morning, as discussed. Our inside man is estimating that it will only take a couple more hours."

"I want this to go smoothly, no more fuck ups."

"Sir, I have something I need to tell you and you're not going to like it."

Alex rubbed his eyes, "Okay, out with it."

"You know how after Astrid contacted you, you knew we had a mole in our organization. As you requested, I did some digging into the phone records and financials.

237

Your accountant found a red flag while doing an expense report for your wife."

"What do you mean, 'a red flag'?"

"She booked flights to Santa Barbara several times this year."

"You moron, her Aunt Jocelyn lives out there."

"I did a little research and this Aunt was not the purpose of those trips. I actually couldn't find any information that Aunt Jocelyn is a real person."

Alex sat forward and rubbed his neck, "That makes no sense."

"As far back as two years, for every trip your wife took to Santa Barbara, the flight manifests showed a Jocelyn Clayton boarding a plane in Santa Barbara then flying to New Alessaria."

"Are you sure of this?" he felt his stomach tighten.

"I'm one hundred percent sure, Sir. I just got the rest of the information just now from a source we have in New Alessaria. I sent him a picture of your wife and he recognized her. She was meeting with The Chosen."

Alex stood up and stormed down the hallway to the kitchen. He saw his wife and son preparing dinner as he stood in the doorway. She instantly saw something was wrong. She stopped chopping and wiped her hands on her apron.

"What's wrong?" she asked.

"Did you do it?" he yelled.

"Do what? I…" she stammered.

"Are you the mole? Don't you dare lie to me."

She looked down and whispered, "Yes."

Alex punched the wall twice and she screamed in terror.

"How could you?" he bellowed. "You're my wife."

"Dad, stop yelling at her. She did it for me," Sander cried out.

"Don't Sander," she exclaimed.

"Let him talk. What are you saying Sander?"

"She was protecting me. She knew I killed Stuart Sark."

Alex backed into the kitchen counter and put his hand on his head, "Why in the hell would you do such a thing?"

"He knew I'm one of them."

The color drained from Alex's face.

He looked at his wife, "What is he saying?"

"Please, I was trying to protect both of you."

"What did you do?" he said, crying angry tears.

She choked out, "I never told you, but I was adopted. I didn't think it was important. I promise, I didn't know. I didn't know."

"Didn't know what?" he yelled.

"I was born without symptoms or the mark, but my birthparents were Movers. I didn't think it was an issue until Sander was born with the mark."

"I don't believe you," he spat out his words like they were knives. He pulled Sander over to him by the neck.

"Don't hurt him," she hollered.

Sander used his gifts to push his dad across the kitchen. Alex's face twisted with anger and horror. His personal assistant came rushing in and Sander threw him against the wall. The assistant fell into a limp heap on the floor.

"You aren't my son, you can't be," Alex shook his head. "You must have been fucking around behind my back. This monster isn't mine."

"He's your son, Alex. You're the only man I've been with."

"You betrayed me, how can I believe a word you say?"

Alex slipped down to the floor and punched a cabinet. Her body heaved with sobs. Sander looked down at his father with tears streaming down his face. Alex pulled himself up, holding onto the counter. He looked down at the knife with bits of celery stalk next to it. His nose flared and his lip curled. He picked up the knife and charged at her.

"Dad, no," Sander cried out trying to grab his father's arm.

Alex swung around and the knife sunk into Sander's chest at an upward angle. He looked at his father wide eyed and coughed. His body wobbled as Alex took the knife out and dropped it to the floor. Alex watched Sander collapse, blood gushing out of his chest onto the white tile floor. His skin paled and his lips turned purple. His wife cried out as she crawled to her son, cradling him. He made a gasping gurgling sound as his body lurched and jerked.

Alex knelt down and watched him take his last agonizing breath. He whispered, "I didn't mean to…"

"What have you done to our son? How could you?" she was shaking so hard it came out in her voice.

Alex sat on the floor and said calmly, "He wasn't my son. He was one of them, a monster. He wasn't mine. I didn't mean to, but it is no loss. The world is better for it."

She gasped, holding both hands on her chest as if stabbed by his words. As he looked out the window, she picked up the knife. After a deep breath, in a swift motion, she slashed his throat. He grabbed at his throat, slippery with cascading blood, and slumped forward. She stood and watched as his blood pooled with Sander's. She heard knocking at the front door and dropped the knife.

She ran out the open sliding glass door into the night. She ran across the yard and jumped a hedge, scraping her shin. She arrived at a house down the street and banged on the backdoor, leaving bloody fist marks.

A middle-aged woman opened the door and gasped, "What happened, Jocelyn?" She took off her apron to wipe the blood off her door.

"He…found…out," was all she managed choke out.

"Let's get you inside where it's safe," she said, guiding her into the house while looking both ways.

Chapter 28

Follow Her Light

Sarah looked up at the ceiling as she lay on the lumpy bed in her tiny cell. The cells were outfitted with new technology that severely curbed Mover powers. She had cried so much, her cheeks felt tight. A strange feeling washed over her and she looked towards the cell door where a guard looked at her. He put a piece of paper through the bars.

"Take it," was all he said.

As she took the message and read it.

"Listen carefully. My name is Doyle, Astrid sent me. You are in danger. Did you eat or drink anything?" she shook her head no.

He took the paper back and wrote. He handed it back to her.

"The guards have planned to stage an electrical fire. We are positioning outside to save you all. Wait until we cut the power and backup generator. You will hear the explosion. Free as many as you can, we will be helping. Be safe and head to the edge of the tree line," he looked up as the lights went out. He whispered, "Be safe."

A guard called up from the first floor, "Power's out."

Another guard yelled, "No biggie, backup power should kick in soon."

They heard a loud explosion from a different building. She heard Doyle's voice in her head, "Open the doors, now."

She grounded her energy and sent a power surge into the door mechanisms. All the doors snapped open.

"Everyone get out of here," Doyle yelled.

As the Movers left their cells, some saw Sarah and gasped. Doyle turned on two flashlights and handed one to Sarah.

"No time for gawking, let's move, move, move," he cried out. "Follow the flashlights."

"You heard the man, let's go," Sarah chimed in.

As they poured out onto the lawn between buildings, a few of the guards shot at them from the guard towers. They cowered next to the building as gun fire seemed to come from all directions. Soon, the firing slowed until there was eerie quiet.

"All clear," a familiar voice called out from across the lawn.

"Astrid?" Sarah called out.

Astrid ran over with a rifle and walkie-talkie. She gave Sarah a long hug and Sarah cried in relief.

"We have to leave. We have busses on standby to take people to safety. You all follow Doyle to the busses. Sarah, come with me," Astrid said while walking briskly away.

They arrived at a makeshift dirt airstrip where Charles stood next to his private jet.

"Sarah, this is Charles, he's a friend. He's here to take us home."

He shook her hand, "Pleasure to be of service."

"Home?" Sarah said in tone of disbelief as they boarded the jet.

"Home to New Alessaria, of course. Your grandmother has your son and Alan is recuperating," Charles said as he closed the door.

"We can't leave without Brian."

Astrid smiled and nudged Sarah. She looked over and saw Brian sitting with his leg haphazardly bandaged and a swollen lip. She rushed over to him and gave him a kiss. He winced in pain, but didn't stop her.

"I'm so happy to see you." She looked down at his leg, "You're hurt."

"Eh, it's not too bad. I'm sure one of you gals will fix me up." She cried as he put his arms around her.

Charles gave a quick clap, "Now that matter is settled I can inform the pilot we can shove off."

Once they were in the air, Astrid fixed Brian's leg. When she came back from washing the blood off her hands, she saw he was asleep in Sarah's arms.

"We did it," she said with a sigh of relief as she sat next to Sarah.

"What happens now?"

"We take a nap," Astrid covered them with a hand-knitted white blanket and closed her eyes.

"I mean, when we get home."

"Don't worry, it will be okay," Astrid said without opening her eyes.

"But are we going to be in danger from now on?"

"Sarah, honey, there are two rules I learned to live by. One, I always protect the people I love. Two, I only take life an hour at a time. This hour we rest."

Sarah decided to put her questions on hold. She knew the road ahead of them was not going to be easy, but she let the fear leave her as she felt Astrid's arm hold her. Serenity blanketed her as she placed her head on Brian's chest and drifted off to sleep.

Chapter 29

The First Movers

The fire glowed orange as she stoked the embers. She placed the pot of stew to simmer before she went outside. The morning air was sweet and refreshing. A slight breeze swept through her blonde hair and she felt the coolness on her face. She went to the pasture and looked at the small assortment of farm animals. She eyed the plumpest chicken then looked around to see if she was alone. She cocked her head and using her mind broke the chicken's neck.

She left the pasture gently swinging the chicken carcass. Before entering the cottage she looked down the road, expecting her son would be home shortly. As she plucked the chicken, she heard her husband hollering in the shed. In a huff, she stormed through the door. Smoke and the smell of burning flesh poured from the shed. He reached out his sizzling, smoking hand towards her.

"Danika, I need milk from the goat. It will stop the pain, hurry," he said wincing.

"Royd, what have you done? You know right well the church forbids alchemy.

Witchcraft it is," she reprimanded.

"Please, the milk."

245

"You're a good man, but I don't know if they will see that behind your potions," she pressed her lips and shook her head. "I'll go fetch your milk."

Later that afternoon, while stirring the stew on the fire, she caressed a scar on her right wrist. She looked over her shoulder with a smile, then rushed to the door. She flung it open to see her son in the doorway. She squealed with delight as they embraced and she showered him with kisses.

"I'm so glad your home, my little Benjamin."

"Mama, I was not gone long. I'm no longer a child."

"Hush, you may be a man, but you will forever be my little cub," she said as she released her embrace.

He inhaled the air deeply, "Smells delicious, I'm ravenous," he said looking around. He asked, "Where's papa?"

"Where he always is," with a disappointing sigh she pointed to the shed. "Stew still has some time on the fire. Let's speak of your journey."

An hour later, as she sat embroidering and her son whittling, her husband burst in, "You're home," he cried out and embraced his son.

"Good to see you, Papa."

"Did you get me what I asked for?" he said raising an eyebrow.

She put her hands on her hips, "You sent our son to buy your witchery?"

"Mama, it is okay, I was careful." He handed over a wrapped package.

She watched as her husband opened it with glee. It was an assortment of powders and herbs. He elatedly sped out of the cottage.

"Off to his shed without even a thank you," she said shaking her head and went to stir the stew.

"Mama, something is happening. I didn't want to tell you, but I think I must. There was news of a vast plague,

246

many people are said to be dying. They are saying it is the end of days."

"Hush now with that talk, especially around your papa."

The father came back in with a jug of honey wine and a large grin. He poured three cups and handed one to each of them.

"I'm glad to have you back home," he said ruffling his son's hair. "Drink up, for tonight is a night of celebrations. To family," he said and took a swig.

The son looked over at his mother, "To family," and took a sip.

She sighed and smiled at her husband, "God help me, I love you," she said then took a sip.

She went back to stirring the pot of stew. Her eyes watered from the smoke, so she rubbed them. After opening them, she was in bed. Confused, she looked up at her smiling son, tears of joy flowing down his face.

"Mama, you're awake. Can you hear me?"

"Yes, what's happening?" She felt her head spinning as she tried to sit up.

"Thank the heavens, awake at last. Don't try to get up just yet."

"What happened, I don't understand?"

She slowly sat up and looked around. There was an odd sense of quiet about the house. A sharp pain shot through her temples and she cradled her head waiting for it to pass.

"I was stirring the stew...why am I...?"

"You must rest, Mama,"

"Where is your Papa? Fetch him for me, he has that powder that helps the head pains." He shook his head.

She grabbed hold of his hand and memories flooded over her. Shortly after he had arrived home from town, one by one they fell ill from plague. Benjamin was the first to recover strength. He went to the shed to find his father missing. He feared the worst. He scoured the surrounding woods to no avail. He spent the remaining week nursing his

247

mother back to health. She snapped out of the inundation of memories.

"I saw it," she said. "Your soul spoke to me."

He shook his head in dismay, "I don't know what is happening."

"The last thing I remember is the night you returned. After he gave us the honey wine, I was stirring the stew," she gasped. "The honey wine. Your father must have put a hex on it."

"Maybe it was the Eden root."

"What is the Eden root?"

"I got it from a mystic in town for Papa. He said that before the Lord cast Adam and Eve out of Eden, they smuggled out a fruit from the tree of life. In exile, they planted a new crop from the seeds. The root of a tree from Eden is meant to give everlasting life."

"That cannot be."

He went to the shed and returned with a white root, "See, this is it."

She took it from him and shook her head, "A parsnip. He was a fool to believe a parsnip to be a magical thing. Such things are not real."

"Mama, we survived plague; there must be something that spared us his fate. What if the root is real?"

She took the root in her hand and scrunched her nose in deep thought, "We must go to town to see the mystic."

"You need to rest, Mama."

"We need answers and supplies, neither will we find if we stay."

The following morning they packed up their belongings. The nearest town was a day's journey by horse and wagon. When they arrived, it was apparent the plague had already came and went. They walked up and down the road calling out, but no one answered back. An eerie silence floated in the air.

"They cannot all be dead, can they?" the son asked, knowing the answer.

They looked inside a stable and saw a large wolf feeding on a corpse. The snarling wolf charged Benjamin. It bit his leg and he cried out in pain. A surge of energy flowed through him. He pointed his hand at the wolf and it flew across the stable. He looked down at the bloody bite and winced. His mother ripped part of her shawl and made a wound dressing.

"Oh no, not again," she muttered to herself.

"Mother, it is almost dark, let us go to the mystic's cottage. If he's there he can help us."

"But you're hurt. Let me go ask."

"No, he knows me. Wait here."

After he knocked a couple times, he limped into the cottage to see the twisted, bloated corpse of the mystic. He put the body in the neighboring baker's flour barrel, wheeled him across the alleyway to the butchery pigpen. A handful of the pigs were still alive. They hungrily rushed towards the body.

He went back to the stable, "He's not there. I think we should seek shelter. I'm sure he won't mind guests."

As they went to the cottage, his mother looked at him with suspicion. "What you did with the wolf, how did you learn that?" she probed.

"I can explain," he stammered.

Once inside the cottage, she lit candles as he took the makeshift bandage off his leg to look at the wound.

"Let me take a look at it," she said.

She knelt down and held her hand over the wound. He felt a surge of hot pain and jerked away. He fell backwards in the chair, protectively holding his leg to his body.

"What were you doing to me?"

"See for yourself," she said.

He looked down, the wound had sealed shut.

"I'm a witch, and now so are you," she said crying. He went to console her, but she put up her hand, "I'm frightened that I'll hurt you. I can't control it sometimes. What if I'm evil?" she whispered.

"Mama, you are a good woman. I cannot believe you are evil. You used your magic to heal me. Evil does not heal, it destroys. Now I know I'm not the only one."

She smiled and pointed to a small bowl. Focusing, she tried to push the bowl with her mind. Suddenly, it flew off and shattered against the wall.

"Perhaps you just need to practice." he said with a sly grin.

"I'm just glad we are both alive and well. If it is the end of time, I'm glad I'm with you, Son. It's just us my little cub."

Part IV

Chapter 30

I'll Rest When I'm Dead

New Alessaria, California
June 19
2000

A clock radio blasting Britney Spears' *Oops, I Did It Again* smashed against the wall. Sarah buried her face in her pillow and groaned. She heard gentle footsteps coming in the room. She looked up to see Brian with a mug of tea. He sat next to her.

She sat up in bed and he handed her the mug, "Sorry, I forgot to turn the alarm off. I know you need your rest."

She held back tears as she rubbed her finger around the rim of the mug.

"Brian, you have been so sweet. But, I'm not sick."

"Sarah it's okay to rest…"

"Don't. Just…don't. Grandma Evie was murdered in front of me, it's not like I have a cold," she saw the pain on his face and realized he was just trying to comfort her. "I'm sorry,   I   didn't   mean   to   snap."

Brian sighed and put his hand on her thigh, "I know, I want to make you feel better, let me help."

"Brian, you can't fix something like this. I need to be strong and I can't be if you keep reminding me I have a reason to fall apart."

"Why do you have to always be the strong one?" he took her hands in his. "Let me be your rock."

252

"I will, after today. Astrid said everyone is meeting in the parlor for the verdict. We need to be ready with a statement for the press. I think a black dress will do nicely, either way."

"Sarah, they will understand if you want to sit this one out after all that has happened."

"I need to tell you something, listen to me," she caressed his hand with her thumb, "I love you so much, I know we will be okay. I just know. We just need to be strong today and keep it together. We are leaders now and we need a brave front. Falling apart will not bring Grandma back to life."

"It scares me how calm you are with all this. It's like you are turning into your Grandma."

He realized instantly he said the worst possible thing. She slapped him and stormed out of the room. She walked down the hallway to the playroom. She looked in and saw Astrid playing with Teddy.

"Mama," he squealed and toddled to her.

She sat on the floor next to Astrid. She took a deep breath hugging her son close.

"I can't believe he's going to be two years old in two days." She felt a wave of grief and wished her grandmother could have seen him grow up. She had a flashback, complete with the horrifying feeling of the spray of blood and turning to see Evie collapse. The memory of feeling helpless was still fresh.

"Do you want to talk about it?" Astrid asked gingerly.

"I can't have any secrets around you can I?" Sarah said with an exasperated chuckle.

She released Teddy and he went to play with his toy cars.

"Princess, do you really want to keep all that pain inside?"

"I can't take much more of this," Sarah said and tears welling in her eyes. "But I have to be strong. I don't have a choice."

"I understand."

"You do? Brian sure didn't."

"Don't be so hard on him, Sarah. He's doing the best he can. The verdict will come back today in our favor and everything will go back to normal."

"It will never be normal without Grandma," Sarah declared, Astrid took her in her arms. "I want a break from people I love dying." Sarah pulled away, wiping her tears. "Astrid the great and powerful, you need to make people not die," she laughed out of frustration and wiped her tears on her sleeve. "I need a good day."

"I can promise, today will be fabulous."

"How can you know that? The Supreme Court might say the law was constitutional and we are at square one."

"Sarah, I am Astrid the Great and Powerful, I see all. Remember?" They both chuckled. "Just have faith that things will work out. Evie had miles of faith. Don't let that faith die with her."

"I miss her so much." Sarah shook as she held back tears.

"We all do, Princess," she smiled. "I have something for you."

She left and returned with a book. She handed her a vintage copy of *The First Movers: Danika and Benjamin Alessar*.

"It is a gift for your college graduation."

"It's just community college."

"Nothing is ever "just" anything. Celebrate yourself once in a while. Have you read it?"

"No, I heard it's good though."

"It is a creative account of the first of our kind. I know the author; he works in the archive department with the library."

"You are pulling my leg. I have been working at the library with you and there's no archive department."

"That's because you don't know where to look. She checked the time on the wall clock. "They're going to announce the verdict shortly, we should get dolled up. As Evie always said, 'Showtime.'"

Alan sat downstairs in the parlor sipping iced tea and watching the media circus covering the Supreme Court decision. Sarah came in and sat next to him.

She looked over and elbowed him, "Hey, does Astrid know something I don't?"

He laughed and rhythmically tapped his finger on the crystal ware.

"She always knows something you don't. Just accept it and move on."

"I mean about this verdict," Sarah pointed at the TV.

"Oh, that. You are smart enough to know that the answer is complicated."

The news switched to coverage of Evie's assassination, showing footage right before the shooting. Sarah felt pangs of sadness come over her and felt ill.

"I'm going upstairs, let me know when they give the verdict."

"Will do, Princess."

She flopped down on the bed and held her aching belly, wishing her grandma were there. A tiny knock came at the door, it was Mary.

"Is this an okay time?"

"Yeah," Sarah said, "I'm just tired."

Mary sat on the bed and put her hand on Sarah's ankle.

"Don't be mad, Brian told me what happened between you two."

Sarah sat up and tucked her legs under herself.

"I didn't mean to be such a bitch, but then he said what he said and I slapped him. It just got out of hand."

"Honey, do you know how Jackson and I met?"

Sarah thought and realized she never had heard that part of their story.

"No. But what does it have to do with this?"

"Just listen, sweetie. Like you, my family died in the '86 bombing. My mother and father were staff for the catering company. It was just us, so when they died, I didn't have any family to take care of me. I was put into the foster system."

"I'm sorry you had to go through that, I had no idea."

Mary looked off as if staring into the past. Sarah knew that look well.

"It was hard, but it got worse. When I was seventeen, P.G.I. radicals kidnapped me and held me in a basement with other girls. Put simply, it was hell on earth. They would hurt us for sport, to find our weakness." Sarah winced. "When one of us girls would die, we could smell them burning the body. One day, a group of The Chosen came to save us. One of them was Brian. He was there as a fixer, his very first day on the job in fact.

"I had aged out of the foster system during my stay in hell. I had no place to go. He offered me a place to stay while I got on my feet. That is when I met my Jackson. I thank my lucky stars for Brian not just for saving me from that hell, but for bringing me to the love of my life. Brian is a good man. He is a fixer not only by trade; it is who he is as a person. Sometimes, he needs to feel like he's fixing things, even if it's all nonsense. It brings sense to his world. Sometimes when you love someone unconditionally, you give them their peace, even if it isn't rational. Like letting him think he made you feel better. Understand?"

She nodded, "Thank you, I needed to hear that."

"What's family for?" she said and hugged Sarah.

Down in the parlor, Alan looked over to see Charles with his wife Dani in the doorway, and he stood to greet them. She was in her early thirties, with champagne-blonde hair. She wore a tasteful vintage Vivienne Westwood silver dress. Many said she resembled Grace Kelly.

"Alan, so good to see you," she said with a refined English accent.

"No more problems between us then?" Alan said. She laughed to break tension.

"One hand washes the other," she said. Her smile broke as she gave a quiet sigh, "I wish things could have worked out before Evie's, well, you know."

"Evie's murder you mean?" Astrid said from behind them.

Charles put his hand on Alan's shoulder, "How about we go out on the porch old chum, I think the ladies have some catching up to do."

The two men sat on the porch bench overlooking the garden.

"I'm worried that I shouldn't have left Astrid alone in there," Alan said.

Charles said gingerly, "If I tell you something, will you promise me to keep it in confidence?"

"Of course."

"I love my wife, you know that. But she is one of the most evil, sadistic bitches I've ever known. We have been together a long time and I have seen her go up against some downright evil people, and win. The only human being who has ever struck fear into her heart has been Astrid but I don't know why. Do you?" Alan looked up at him awe struck. "I guess that look speaks for itself."

Astrid poured herself some iced tea and took a long drink.

"I'm going to put Sarah to work in the archives department," she said.

"Out of the question," Dani balked.

"Just because we are being cordial doesn't mean you should be so stubborn."

She crossed her arms, "Astrid, you are being very disrespectful. Tread carefully."

"Look, Sarah is a good girl. I wish I was as good as her. Yet, she needs something to help her since Evie's sudden passing. It's been hard on her. She has a passion for history that I have only seen with Ben."

"You want her to work with Ben?" Dani rolled her eyes. "You know he likes to keep to himself. Good luck getting him to agree to that arrangement," she scoffed and looked at her watch. "I think we will be shoving off now. Places to go, people to see. If you really think Ben will go for that, you must be dafter than I thought. Best of luck," she cackled as she exited the room yelling for Charles.

Astrid looked at the TV and noticed the verdict had come back. The newscaster announced that the Supreme Court had declared the Mover Registration law unconstitutional. She looked around the empty room and raised her iced tea glass.

"Cheers."

Chapter 31

The Oldest Artifact

New Alessaria, California
June 21
2000

Sarah sat at the kitchen table putting sprinkles on the last of the baby blue cupcakes. She noticed a splotch of blue frosting on her shirt and let out a huff of frustration. A clean shirt hovered in front of her and she giggled. She turned to see Brian holding Teddy and a plate of buttered toast.

"This is why I love you," she said. She took off her dirty shirt and put on the clean one.

"You know the staff can make cupcakes."

"I'm his mother, I want to make him some cupcakes." Teddy rubbed his eyes, "How is my birthday boy?" she asked taking him in her arms.

"Open wide," Brian instructed and put a piece of toast in her mouth. "Bite and chew."

She looked at the clock and winced, "Damn it, I'm going to be late. It's my first day and I'm going to be late."

"You can eat your toast on the way, I made you a cup of coffee to go," Brian handed her a travel mug.

"You are my real savior Mr. Delving," she said and gave him a kiss.

"Have a great first day Mrs. Delving."

"Brian, you know I didn't take your name, only hyphenated. We talked about this."

"Can't you give me one morning without taking my balls? They do that enough at medical school."

"You signed over the ownership of your balls to me when you married me."

"Balls," Teddy said and they laughed.

"I forgot to watch my mouth around him. He's a little parrot."

"Say good-bye to mommy, she's going to work," he waved his little hand as she walked out the door.

When she arrived at the Astridian library, the chiming of the walnut longcase grandfather clock showed that she had barely arrived on time. When she passed the front desk, she heard clanking in the kitchenette. She went in and saw a young man of about twenty taking flavored creamer from the fridge. He had feathery champagne-blonde hair and a lean build. He wore dark denim jeans and a vintage 1970's Rolling Stones concert t-shirt.

"Hi, I'm Sarah," she said with a little wave.

"I know who you are," he said with an upper-crust English accent. He put out his hand, "I'm Ben. I work archives."

As she shook his hand, her channel opened slightly. She felt that he was very powerful and he jerked his hand away.

"Did I give you permission to read me?" he said in a huff.

"I'm so sorry; I still have trouble controlling it."

She was shocked knowing how strong he was. The strongest Mover she had met until now was Astrid, another thirty-three on the delving scale. He was much stronger.

"Wait, how did you know I was reading you?"

"I'm a soul reader, too. Astrid did a bang up job training you, didn't she?"

"She's been busy…"

"Busy with that dope Doyle you mean. Why do you of all people want to work in the archives? Is the estate having money trouble?"

"No, nothing like that. Astrid thought I might like it. I'm going to school for my history degree. I just want to be like my parents, I guess." He chuckled as he looked down in thought. "What?" she asked crossing her arms.

"Nothing. Let's get to work then. I'll give you a probationary trial period and can sack you at any moment. I'll show you around the archives or as I lovingly call it the "goody room.'" He bounced his rear end to imaginary rap music.

"I've been here for almost two years and never saw the archives."

"You just need to know where to look," he said and winked. He grabbed his Mona Lisa coffee mug and pointed down the hall. "Follow me."

He led her to the supply closet and she gave him a perturbed look. They stood before a cabinet holding office supplies.

"This is the supply closet, what kind of bullshit is going on?" Sarah asked accusingly

"Magic," he pivoted the cabinet revealing a hidden door. "Ta-da," he said dryly and took a sip of coffee.

"Wow," she said and nodded her head in approval. "I never would have known about the secret bat cave in the library."

"That's the idea," he put his hand on a biometric handprint reader while swiping an ID card."

"Do I get a card?"

"Nope," he said as the doors opened.

After walking through, the automatic doors quickly slammed shut, startling her. After going down a steep staircase she looked down a long gray corridor with many doors. The first room appeared to be an office.

"Each of these doors leads to a specific holding area for art and what not." The phone from the office rang and he winced, "I'll be right back."

261

After he left she noticed a lone painting at the end of the corridor and walked up to it. It was a large painting of a young man and his mother. She then recognized it as Leonardo da Vinci's painting of the first Movers. Although, she knew the real thing must be in a museum somewhere. She gently tapped the frame.

She was flooded with memories of where the painting had been, who had touched it, the secrets it held. This was no copy, it was the real painting. The painter was Leonardo Da Vinci. *The* Leonardo Da Vinci. He knew the first Movers; they were immortal, like Astrid. She then gasped as the knowledge came to her that Ben from archives was Benjamin Alessar from the painting. The boy she and young Movers heard stories about for generations. Shakily, she stepped back from the painting and turned to see Ben.

"You're…" was all she could muster and fainted into his arms.

Sarah awoke on a bed with a cool washcloth on her forehead. She looked around and saw she was in a small studio apartment. Ben sat on a couch watching television and eating Cap'n Crunch. He saw she was waking up and pointed to his bowl with his spoon.

"Sure beats gruel, had enough of that for centuries."

She took off the washcloth and sat on the side of the bed, "Where am I?"

"My flat."

"How long was I passed out?"

He looked at his watch, "A bit past three minutes." He smiled at her look of confusion, "My living quarters are on site."

"You live in the archives?"

"Astrid jokes that I'm the oldest artifact in here."

She laughed nervously and rubbed the back of her neck. He walked over to the kitchenette and washed out his cereal bowl. She watched him as if he were a zoo animal.

"If you stare like that I may have to charge you."

"How can you be so chill about all this?"

"Can you be a little less vague?" he said as he put the bowl in the dish drainer.

"I mean, I found out your secret."

He sat on the end of the bed and smiled, "It was my secret to find."

She looked at him and saw the boy she heard all the stories about from her youth.

"You wanted me to find out," she said with a slight gasp.

"The point was to ease you into the idea, but yes, you weren't meant to stay in the dark."

"How could you trust me with such a secret? You don't even know me."

"Your grandmother gave me this library and permission to build the archives in secret to house all Mover treasures many years before you were born. I knew your parents very well. I'm honored to say we were friends, best chaps with your dad. In photographs, I'm the longhaired best man at their wedding. I held you when you were three hours old." A smile came to his face only the joy of nostalgia can summon. "I know your history, Sarah. I know how you have grown, and lived. You have loved and you have suffered. You have a heart that is pure, don't you see that?"

"You're just soul reading me," she said with an edge of distrust.

"Did you feel me soul reading you?"

"Well, no, but…"

"Then, no. I will only tell you the truth."

"Wow, I'm kind of star struck."

"Just think of me as a regular bloke. Tell me something about you I may not know."

"I'm not that interesting," she said looking down.

"I disagree," he said. He sat close and gently pushed her chin up, "You are one of the most beautiful souls I've met."

They shared a long gaze, and she felt a connection she could not describe. She never even felt this connected to Brian and she loved him deeply. Her breath quickened, her palms started to perspire and she noticed a rhythmic thumping sound. She realized it was their synchronized heartbeats. She watched him lick his lips and she felt her chest tighten.

"Well, my life is crazy right now," she said to break the sexual tension.

"How so?"

"This morning I made cupcakes for my son's birthday party. He's two today."

He smiled, "Your face lights up when you talk about him."

"I love him so much. You should come to the party. I mean, I know it's just a silly kid's party but it's just going to be a family thing. Teddy tends to like the wrapping paper better than the presents anyway."

"I would be honored. What do you buy a two-year-old?"

"That little boy is so spoiled, the last thing he needs is another toy. I'm not sure, clothes are probably too practical."

"I'll figure it out."

There was a gap of silence and Sarah was about to say she would ask her grandmother. Then the reality that she could no longer ask her grandmother anything hit her. This caused a pain in the depths of her stomach. She remembered the feeling of Evie's blood splattering on her, sending a chill through her.

"You miss your nana don't you?"

"That time you were definitely soul reading me."

"No, I just know how to read people, not just their souls. I've been around a long time after all."

She wiped away a tear, "I keep this strong front but I can't tell people how I really feel," she laughed, "I can't believe I'm crying in front of you."

"I make many women spontaneously weep, it's a gift," he said and they both laughed.

"Tell me something," she said wiping her eyes.

"You need to work on this vague thing that you do."

"Like, how old are you?"

"Nineteen."

"Come on, I'm being serious.

"So am I. I've been nineteen for six hundred and fifty years."

"Wait, you're almost seven hundred years old?"

"Don't round up, it's insulting," he said with a sly grin. "But yes, I've been around a while."

"You must have had lots of girlfriends. You are the first Mover and all that must be a great pick-up line." He winced and looked away. "Did I say something wrong?"

"No, it's just that it's not exactly true. I had a wife, Jocelyn. We were together for over two hundred years. Then I lost her."

"I'm sorry, how did she die?"

"It's complicated."

"If you don't want to tell me, I understand. It was a rude question."

"No, it's okay. She went with my mother's lover Hugh, which did not bode well. Very *Days of our Lives*. Yes, I was heartbroken, but my mother…you don't want to ever be on her bad side."

"What did she do?" Sarah asked and put her hand on his.

"My mother, up until recently was the only one of us to permanently kill one of the Everbloods. That's what we call those of us given the gift of everlasting life. She had Jocelyn burned at the stake for witchcraft. Hugh, the coward that he is, fled."

"You couldn't stop her."

He laughed, "My mother is very powerful, it is enough that we are not on speaking terms at the moment. But if she wanted to press her hand, I would be powerless against her and her horde."

"What happened to Hugh? He just vanished?"

"Not quite," he crossed his arms. "He was not only my mother's lover, but an accomplished chemist. He created the Everblood elixir."

"Is that like a magic potion?"

"It is something we drink to help the change, but it isn't magic."

"Wait, you're telling me you drink this stuff and it makes you live forever."

"Not quite. It is a two-step process. We discovered it only works on the strongest of our people. What you would define as an eighteen or above on the Delving Ability Scale. We expose them to a contagion that would weaken the inductee to near death. Then give an infusion of regular blood and blood from us first movers, we are called The Hand."

"Sounds like vampires."

"Many vampire stories started because people were loose lipped about the ceremony. Vampires aren't real by the way. If an Everblood survives the process, which not all do, then they will have regenerative properties and will live forever. Well, death resistant at least. Hugh discovered this process and perfected it. When he fled, the first Daffodils epidemic cropped up. Somehow, he created a super plague and had it attached to the daffodils to target only Movers. It was his twisted message to my mother. A dangerous fellow who can hide on this planet from my mother. He is still missing. He blames me for not helping Jocelyn. To this day I still regret that I didn't save Jocelyn from burning at the steak."

There was a cloud of silence. She put her arms around him cradled him in her arms. She could smell something that she had not noticed before, Old Spice. She looked him in the eyes which told a tale of a sensitive man who had seen too

266

much heartache. As she felt his breath on her, she became aware of how aroused she was. Thoughts of Brian and Teddy melted from her mind. All she was aware of was his sweet Cap'n Crunch and milk breath.

He gently leaned down and kissed her. She did not push him back, but fell into the kiss. They lay on the bed together kissing and groping each other wildly. He undid her pants and put his hand in her panties. She moaned as he stroked her. She took off his Rolling Stones t-shirt and unbuttoned his pants. As they made love, she forgot all her worries and concerns. It was magical. Towards the moment of her climax, she noticed they were floating in the air. She was about to say something, but he gave her a reassuring kiss. As she climaxed, the room shook and several things fell off shelves. After he climaxed, they floated back to the bed. As they lied in the bed, he started to trace her left nipple.

"What are you doing?" she asked, giggling.

"This one is my favorite," he said with a puckish smile.

"What about righty?" she said with false indignation.

Her cell phone rang and she leapt from the bed to search the pile of discarded clothing.

"Hello?" she answered.

"Hey Sarah, Teddy has a high fever. I'm going to take him in to the pediatrician. I know it's your first day and all so if you can't make it down I think it would be okay."

She looked over at the bed and instantly felt pangs of guilt.

"Let me just ask my boss," she held the phone to her chest. "My baby is sick, can I go with him to the doctor?" Ben nodded. "Brian, he said sure, so I'll meet you there, okay."

"I can swing by, I have to drop Astrid off anyway, the nanny called her first."

"Um, okay. I'll wait up front to make things go quicker."

"Okay, love you."

267

"Love you, too."

She stood naked holding her pants and phone. The realization that she had just cheated on the man she loved hit her and she felt nauseated.

"I have to go, I'm sorry."

"Don't be, I understand, your baby is sick." He put on his boxers as she put on her clothes. "You think this was a mistake, don't you? Before you answer, I just want to say, I don't think it was. My soul knows your soul and your soul knew mine. It was as if we had known each other for centuries."

"It was amazing," she whispered as she put on her heels. "But I love Brian, he's a good guy."

"He doesn't have to know," he said holding her waist.

"I don't know if I can carry a secret like that," she said and he kissed her neck. She pushed him away, "Stop." She grabbed her purse and started to leave. She looked back. "I will call you later to tell you if I'm coming back tomorrow."

He only nodded in response and watched her leave. He made the bed and put the fallen items back on the shelves.

Sarah watched Teddy sleeping and Brian came up behind startling her. "Thank goodness his fever went down," he   whispered.

"I shouldn't leave him with a nanny, I should quit."

"No, don't do any such thing. This isn't your fault. I think the job will be good for you."

The maid knocked on the door, "Ma'am, you have a visitor."

She went downstairs with Brian and to her dismay, Ben was standing in the foyer.

"Who's that?" Brian asked.

"My new boss," she muttered.

"Hi I'm Ben," he said extending his hand. "You must be Brian."

"So you're Ben from archives."

"Here, I got this for the little chap." He handed over a toy dump truck. "I didn't have the foggiest clue of what to get   him."

"This is perfect, he's obsessed with trucks," Brian said.

"Is everything okay at the archives?" Sarah asked.

"Ah, I guess you are wondering why I'm really here. I wanted to plead with you to keep your job. I know you were worried about the little tyke. Is he okay?"

"How nice of you, yes just an ear infection," Brian said.

"Good to hear it's nothing more serious. Will I see you   tomorrow   then?"

Sarah looked at Brian and felt pangs of guilt, "Yes, I'll will be there."

Chapter 32

Oops, I Did It Again

New Alessaria, California
June 22
2000

Sarah entered the library and saw Doyle pushing the returned book cart.

"She's putting you to work, eh?" she teased.

"I'm just helping out while Alan is out of town."

"Is he having fun in the Virgin Islands?"

"Having tons of fun apparently. I'm a bit jealous."

Astrid came over and sipped at her coffee. She had an odd smile. As she took another sip Sarah noticed a ring glinting.

"Are you engaged?" Sarah asked. She rushed over to inspect the ring.

"I was going to tell you, but you are very perceptive."

"Not to be rude, but how is that going to work? You being immortal and all."

"Doyle has been approved to be initiated into the Everbloods."

"Wow, that's amazing. When are you going to do that?"

"We're going to go to England this weekend to start the process. I would love for you to come with us."

"You should go, I can show you around," Ben joined in as he came out of the kitchenette.

"I would have to check with Brian." "Of course," Astrid assured.

"You came back," Ben said.

"I said I would."

"Shall we?" he said pointing to the supply closet.

"We all should go back to work," Astrid said shooting Ben a glaring look.

"Astrid, I will let you know what Brian says," Sarah said.

"Okay, we'll talk later."

Sarah followed Ben into the archives and she set her purse down in the front office. "I want to show you something," he announced.

"First, before anything, I want to say yesterday was a one-time thing."

"I understand," he said, smiling.

"I'm being serious."

"I want to show you something."

He led her to his living quarters, "What are you trying to pull?"

"Get your mind out of the gutter."

She walked in and noticed an orange tabby cat on his bed, "You got a cat?"

"No. Well, yes, not a recent addition. You left before I could introduce you to Richard."

"You named your cat Richard?"

"Richard the Lionhearted to be exact. He does look lion-like does he not? But he's not what I wanted to show you."

He pulled out a box and with a grin, handed a watch to her.

"A man's watch?"

"Look at the inscription."

She flipped it over and it read "To Teddy from Mongoose and Shakespeare."

"This was my dad's watch."

"I think you should have it."

"Thank you," she said and hugged him.

She looked into his eyes and kissed him.

"I thought you said…" he said.

"Shut up," she said and kissing him again.

They moved over to the bed. As they undressed, she was lost in the moment. She felt surges of pleasure ripple through her as they kissed. She had never felt anything like it.

"How are you doing that?" she asked, as he kissed her neck.

"I learned a while ago how to stimulate a woman with my powers alone. Do you not like it?"

"I mean, wow. Don't stop."

As they made love, he never broke eye contact. She only closed her eyes as she climaxed. He kissed her as her body lurched with pleasure. She heard things falling off the shelves and looked over.

"Don't worry about that," he said and kept going.

After she climaxed a second time, he finished. They collapsed back onto the bed, as they had been hovering again. He held her, still looking into her eyes.

"How was that?"

"You're kidding, right? It was better than last time. I mean I've never had two orgasms before."

"Yeah, you tore the place up."

She looked around, many things had fallen off the shelves and the pictures had been knocked askew on the wall. She giggled.

"Let me help you clean up," she started to get up and he stopped her.

"Don't get up, silly. We are powerful creatures, remember?" he floated everything back onto the shelves. "If you want to help, get the pictures," she lifted her hand and moved the pictures back.

She floated her father's watch into her hand and turned it over.

"Ben, how do you have his watch?"

"I was going to tell you about that. I want to say…" the phone rang and he jumped up, "Hold that thought, let me just get this real quick."

He picked up the phone, "Hello?" The color drained from his face, "No, I'm not busy, but…I guess so…no that wouldn't be a problem. Bye."

He hung up then hurriedly put his boxers on, "My mother is here."

"Your mother? Like Danika, like the first Mover ever. She's here?"

"Yeah, and you need to hide."

"What?"

"Yeah, get dressed," he tossed her clothes to her. "No time to explain, you need to trust me."

After they put their clothes on and made the bed, he led her to the closet.

"I'm sorry, but you need to hide in here."

He kissed her and closed the door. The sound of heels came into the room.

"What are you doing here, Mama?"

"Is that any way to greet me?"

"I don't appreciate you just dropping in on me unannounced."

"I have some excellent news for you though."

"What could be so great that you couldn't tell me over the phone?"

"I'll cut to the chase. We found Hugh."

There was a pause. He crossed his arms, "What do you mean?"

"You heard me. He has been transported to the dungeon at the manor."

"You're serious."

"Son, we have waited a long time for our revenge."

"What's going to happen now?"

She walked over to the kitchen and put water in the kettle. She placed her hand under it to boil the water.

After it started to whistle, she pointed the kettle at Ben, "Care for some tea?"

"No," he said.

"Very well," she made herself a cup.

She sat on the couch and he sat in a chair across from her.

"The council will convene for the monthly tribunal Monday. I do wish you would join."

"I need to think about it. I will be there for Doyle, but for the tribunal, I'm not sure I can look into that bastard's eyes."

She clucked her tongue, "I still think it is foolish to be so upset. It's our revenge. Could you still be angry about my other prisoner?"

"I made it clear that I will not help you or forgive you until you release him. He is innocent."

"You need to be careful, my son. After all, you performed the Everblood ceremony without permission. Without meeting with the counsel. We have rules for a reason. It is out of my kindness that you're not in the dungeon, too. Keep that in mind when you make demands."

"What will happen to Hugh?"

"I told you, he will be going before the tribunal next week."

"I know you too well, Mama. There is something up your sleeve."

She smiled a cunning smile, "He will go before the tribunal alive, but I can't guarantee all in one piece."

"You're sadistic, you know that right?" I only take pleasure in justice. This man is not only guilty of betraying us, but our people. He let loose the daffodils plague, if you forgot."

"I didn't forget what he did. Or what you did to Jocelyn."

"You are lying to yourself if you believe you didn't feel any justice. She betrayed you deeply. A true monster. Don't go soft on me. You are an Alessar after all. You will want to come to the tribunal. I will even allow you into the dungeon for a visit with prisoner number thirty-three. Hopefully you will come. The choice is yours. I must be off, Charles is waiting for me at the jet. Ta for now," she said as she stood and kissed his cheek.

He walked her out and watched her leave in the town car. He went back and opened the door to the closet.

"I assume you could hear all of that. Let me explain," he said.

Sarah kissed him, "You should go. It will at least be closure. Besides, I'm going to be there for Doyle's Everblood ceremony."

"I thought you were going to check with Brian first."

"Don't talk about him."

She started to walk away but he grabbed her hand, "I'm sorry, but I'm not stupid. You're not leaving the good Catholic boy. What I'm saying is, you don't have to leave him. I'm okay with this arrangement."

"You won't be jealous?"

He pushed her hair behind her ear, "You are a not a belonging for me to own. Now, let's get some actual work done, shall we?"

She smiled, "Sure." He led her to a flight of stairs to the second floor, "What's up there?"

He looked back with a grin, "Everything."

Later, Ben rifled through his pantry and picked up a box marked COFFEE SUPPLIES. He set it on the table and opened it. It was not coffee supplies, but a box of folders. He picked out the folder marked ROSE, SARAH. He took a sip of tea and started flipping through Dr. Delving's notes about her as a five-year-old girl. He looked at the TV and noticed a news report about the still missing wife of P.G.I. leader

Alexander Bram. Mrs. Bram was now considered a person of interest in the murders of her husband and teenage son. As a picture flashed on screen, his tea cup crashed to the floor. He could not believe it, but his eyes were not mistaken. He knew that face to be Jocelyn's. He had a feeling he knew where to find her. He picked up the phone and quickly dialed.

"Mama," he said, trying to keep his anger out of his voice.

"Ben, are you coming to the tribunal?" she asked.

"I wouldn't miss it for the world." As he hung up and he heard the archive doors open. He opened his flat door with his mind. Astrid walked in with a half-smile that disturbed him.

"What?" he said crossing his arms.

She shoved him with her powers and he tumbled back onto the bed. She sat on a chair facing the bed and crossed her legs.

"Did you sleep with her?"

"I don't see how that is any of your business."

"Be straight with me, Ben."

He lightly rubbed the back of his neck, "I think I'm in love with her."

"After one lay?"

"Don't talk about Sarah like that."

"I don't want anyone getting hurt," Astrid said with concern.

"I don't mean to cause her any hurt."

"It's not you hurting her I'm worried about. She is going to stomp your heart like a baby kitten when she finds out some of the skeletons in your big-ass closet."

He stood and paced, "Do you think I should tell her the big secret?"

Astrid chuckled and walked towards him, "Just think about the consequences of that line of thought. Now, don't you have actual work to do? Besides dicking around," she said before leaving the room.

Chapter 33

Doesn't Everyone Have a Medieval Dungeon?

Amaira Manor
Oxfordshire, UK
June 24th
2000

Dani, Charles, and two guards descended the stairs into the dungeon area under the posh estate. It was built in the 1500's, making it dark and sinister. They walked down the row of cells until they came to the last. She flicked on the fluorescent lights and a guard opened the cell. A badly beaten man lay naked on the floor, in the fetal position. He looked up and moaned.

"Dani," he softly moaned.

"How dare you say my name, you scoundrel. Guards, pick him up." He could barely stand on his own. "Listen to me. You are no man in my eyes. You not only shag that whore, but then run away like a coward. But your effort to save her recently was in vain. She's right here in this very dungeon. Somewhat poetic, don't you think. So close, yet you can't be with her."

She looked down at his genitals. With her powers, she ripped his scrotum from his body. He screamed out in pain and watched in horror as she floated the bloody scrotum into

278

a vintage avocado green Tupperware container. The guards held him down as he cried out in agony.

"Guards, let me know when he grows some real ones. Until then, these are mine," she said, cackling as she snapped on the Tupperware lid.

"A lot of commotion today, it's disturbing my beauty rest," a voice said from a few cells away.

"I want to have a word with prisoner number thirty-three, go on up to supper, I'll be along shortly," she said.

"Yes darling. Just make it quick, the chef made roast beef, you don't want to miss that," Charles reminded.

"Make sure he doesn't over cook it this time. He always makes it medium and you know I like mine rare. Oh, and would you be a dear and put away my prize," she said, handing him the Tupperware.

"Yes darling," he said as he climbed the stairs.

She walked down the row and stopped at cell 33. She tapped on the cell bars and a man in the shadows turned. She snapped her fingers and the lights turned on.

"Ah, Mr. Rose, how are you today? Cleverness and quips, as always. You have yet to lose your spirit, even in this hell hole. You know, the deal remains the same. I will release you if you tell me what I want know."

"Even if I knew something, I wouldn't ever trust you."

"I know Ben has a soft spot for you. Maybe that's why he risked it all to perform an unauthorized Everblood ceremony on you. Immortality is a pitiful waste behind these bars. Such a shame. I'm a patient woman, I can keep you here as long as I want. All I have is time. One thing you should know about me, Jon, is that I am trustworthy. Brutal, yes I am that too, but only to those who break my trust."

"Please tell me one thing. My family, are they okay?"

Dani looked at him and tapped her fingernails on the bars.

"Your mother, sadly, was assassinated not too long ago. She refused, on several occasions, the Everblood ceremony.

279

Barking mad woman your mother was. Sarah is alive and well...for now. How about being forthright with me and tell me about where Doctor Delving's misplaced research might be."

"Why don't you ask your son?"

"Ben is loyal; he would never cross me like that."

"If that's what you need to believe."

"No matter, the truth will out. In a matter of minutes you will have the pleasure of a few more flat mates, including your daughter."

"Wait, what are you planning? You better not hurt her."

"I'd rather not spoil the fun of the surprise. Let's just say, I have an inside man. Till next time, Mr. Rose," she said as she walked away. The lights went out and all he could hear was the clicking of her heels going down the hallway and Hugh's sobs of agony.

Sarah walked into one of the guest bedrooms upstairs at Amaira Manor with her smaller luggage bag and set it down at the foot of the bed. The bed appeared to be centuries old. She looked around the room and noticed, on the vanity, a brush similar to her mother's with the ivory handle. In fact, it seemed identical. As the light of the setting sun cascaded through the window, she looked out over the acres of English garden and felt like she was in *The Secret Garden*.

"You look tired." She turned and saw Brian carrying a tray with cups of tea. "Have some English tea, I had them make it for us to help settle in."

Sarah took a sip. It was strong tea with a slight bitter aftertaste. She sat on the end of the bed and smiled. Brian set the tray down and sat in a chair in the corner. As she sipped her tea she noticed he kept looking at his watch.

"Do you have somewhere to be?" Sarah scoffed.

"Why yes, he does," she heard Dani say as she came into the room.

Brian stood and Dani caressed his cheek.

"What are you doing?" Sarah said.

Sarah went to stand up but felt a weakness come over her body. She dropped the tea cup on the carpet and her knees buckled.

"Right on schedule," Dani said and gave Brian a long deep kiss.

Brian stooped down and picked up the teacup. He looked at her with a smirk.

"I'm sure this is a shock, but listen to me now. You have been poisoned, but not enough to kill you so don't worry. Stop fighting."

"How could I not know?" she said to herself.

He held up his St. Margaret's medal, "This dampens your soul reading. You never noticed you couldn't read me? You aren't that bright when it comes to me."

"Is this about Ben? I'm sorry," Sarah choked out while feeling woozy. She leaned against the bed and felt the room spinning.

"I couldn't care less about the golden boy. No, you are just too dangerous to our savior. Our real savior, Danika Alessar."

Dani smiled with approval.

"But…" Sarah fainted as she tried to speak and slumped to the floor.

Dani snapped her fingers. A man came in and picked Sarah up.

"Take her to the dungeon with the others."

After they carried Sarah away, Dani turned to Brian, "I am so relieved. On Monday, she takes the axe with Hugh."

"Wait, you never said you were going to kill her."

Dani raised an eyebrow and crossed her arms, "Will that be an issue?"

Brian shifted his weight then caressed her hair, "Of course not."

"Good boy. Now, close that door."

To Be Continued in Book 2 of The Movers Series

* 9 7 8 0 5 7 8 8 9 7 9 7 4 *